A COLD NIGHT FOR ALLIGATORS

Viggy Parr Hampton

First edition, 2024
ISBN Paperback: 979-8-9898755-0-4
ISBN Ebook: 979-8-9898755-1-1
Book Design by Nuno Moreira, NMDESIGN

A COLD NIGHT FOR ALLIGATORS

Viggy Parr Hampton

For my Mom,

who reads everything I write and always tells me the truth.

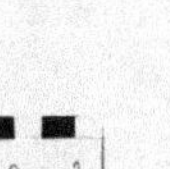

Gullywasher's of Georgia
DOLPHIN SHOW
ADULT POOL
BABY POOL
FOOD COURT
AQUARIUM
GRAVITRON
SAVANNAH RIVER
FIRST AID
GULLYWASHER JUNIOR
ALLIGATOR PIT
TICKETS
BUMPER CARS
LAZY RIVER
THE GULLYWASHER
PARKING
P
CAROUSEL
WELCOME
MIDWAY
GUARDHOUSE
GULLYWASHER'S THIS WAY

CHAPTER ONE

Patrick Fenwick, the last employee of the dying theme park Gullywasher's of Georgia, ambled between the brightly striped tents of the midway. The light was beginning to wane from the early autumn sky, and Patrick gripped the flashlight dangling from his belt just to reassure himself it was still there. Even after years as a security guard at the park, he'd never felt comfortable there after the sun went down.

In Patrick's cozy suburb just outside Savannah, there used to be a popular mall anchored by a few big box stores and full of thriving shops. He almost didn't notice its decline at first, as a few stores drew their rumbling metal gates down permanently. When the JC Penney closed, Patrick took a good hard look around him the next time he was at the mall, shopping for Christmas presents with his youngest daughter. The mall was like a mouthful of broken teeth—some stores were in better shape than others, but everything was suffering.

So, when he started to see those same phenomena popping up around Gullywasher's—neglect, laziness, encroaching decrepitude, not to mention the lawsuits after that kid died on the roller coaster—he knew the writing was on the wall. He'd be able to find another security position elsewhere, he had no doubt about that, but he'd miss the perks of being able to bring all four of his children to the park for free during the summer, catching the delight on their faces and smiling to himself. Gullywasher's decline had started slowly, but finished rapidly, the flow of guests narrowing from a river to a stream, then finally to a trickle. Employees were laid off. One by one, attractions were shut down, "Closed for Maintenance" signs cropping up on the closed doors or padlocked gates.

He exited the Midway, walked past the dolphin show amphitheater with its newly drained pool, and reached the doors of the aquarium. A special team from the Georgia Aquarium in Atlanta would be coming tomorrow to remove the rest of the animals. In the meantime, Patrick wanted to make sure he carried out his last duties: locking up all of the buildings on the premises. Besides the ticket booth at the entrance and the aquarium in front of him, everything else was secured.

He pulled a padlock from a pouch attached to his belt and clicked it open. He was just about to thread it through and be done with this place when a thin cry from inside the building snagged his attention.

He replaced the padlock in the pouch and yanked open one of the aquarium's double doors.

"Hello?" he called. "Anybody in here?"

There was no answer but the steady dripping of water somewhere at the back of the building.

"The park is closed," he said, a nervous shake sending his words jitterbugging through the growing darkness. "If anybody's in here, you're trespassing."

Cupping his ear, he listened intently for any response. When none came, he started to close the door.

Then it came again—a high-pitched tittering that set Patrick's teeth on edge. He hadn't imagined that sound, he was sure.

With a dread he didn't completely understand, he stepped across the threshold and into the dank aquarium. "Hello?" he called again.

Distracted by his growing anxiety, he nearly slammed into the large cylindrical tank in the middle of the cavernous room. Until a few days ago, the tank had held a group of jellyfish as thin and pale as toilet paper. Now, the tank was dark, the black water waiting to be drained.

The tittering, which now seemed to be mocking him, echoed through the room once more.

"Whoever you are, I'm calling the police," Patrick said. "You'll be locked in if you don't come forward."

Patrick was just turning to retreat when a flash of something caught his eye. He whipped his head around, his eyes drawn to the cylindrical tank like a magnet.

As he watched, pale, unnatural figures materialized within the tank's depths.

CHAPTER TWO

Two hundred and fifty miles away and fifteen years later, Independence Day of 2019 found Leona Franks slouched over a gutter in a bad part of Atlanta, a cliché come to life. Between the Johnnie Walker slowly burning a hole in her guts, the cocaine that smelled suspiciously of baby powder quickly burning a hole in her sinuses, and her virulent urinary tract infection burning a hole in her cooch, she was having a bad fucking day.

Her head was doing somersaults in unison with her stomach, and she leaned over the gutter for a sour vomit. She hadn't eaten much in days, and thick strings of mucus and saliva dripped from her cracked lips. She wiped her mouth with the back of a sore-pocked hand, and the smell of her own stinking skin started her retching again. This time, she leaned too far forward and ended up with her ass in the air and her face in a pile of wet garbage bordering the gutter. She was so surprised at the sudden shift in position she coughed, hard, instead of retching. She pushed herself up on one arm, bringing her fist to rest under her chin. Had there been any onlookers, they would have thought Leona looked like a white-trash version of Rodin's Thinker.

Leona was, in fact, thinking. As the gritty muck dried on her face along with flecks of vomit and a dribble of blood pooling in her cigarette-yellowed Cupid's bow, she considered her next move. The puking had sobered her up a little, and the face-first fall into garbage had all but finished the job. She was also coming down from her high, and her head was beginning to pound like someone knocking on a heavy oak door.

"Enough already!" she slurred, throwing her head back and letting out a high-pitched giggle.

A cold feeling creeping across her forehead stopped her from going into what would have been an uncontrollable frenzy. She reached up with the hand not currently supporting her greasy chin and her fingers alighted on a damp piece of paper. One quick tug and a folded sheet separated from her skin with a moist sucking sound, like a sated leech. She sat up a little straighter to free her Thinker fist and unfolded the paper with something like reverence.

It was a flyer.

The paper had once been white with a bright blue border resembling ocean waves, but now it was crinkled and streaked with filth. It reminded Leona of dirty toilet paper, and she giggled again. Within the border, huge circus-style letters beckoned: "Come to Gullywasher's of Georgia!" Below that, pictures of roller coasters, dolphins, starfish, cotton candy, and alligators were jumbled together. At the very bottom was an address.

Leona's hands began to shake, although not from withdrawal or exposure. She threw her head back to gaze at the slowly darkening sky, its color blooming from soft peach to angry strawberry. An almost religious fervor had gripped her, and she felt both powerless and unwilling to stand in its way. The very name 'Gullywasher's' had hit her harder and sweeter than her very first bump of cocaine. She needed more.

She whistled, a tinny, wretched sound. A pigeon roosting nearby flew away in a huff, making Leona giggle again. "I'm coming, I said I'm a-coming home!" She screeched this last part, the sound of her own jubilant voice music to her ears.

After all, who was she to argue with what fate had quite literally thrown in her face?

*   *   *

Finding a ride all the way from Atlanta to the outskirts of Savannah was no easy feat for a homeless dealer-cum-drug user with dried vomit on her shirt and blood under her fingernails. She didn't want to tempt her urinary tract infection into a full-blown kidney issue by offering her services in exchange for a ride—not after the last bastard she'd worked, who'd beat her on the head with two heavy fists until she passed out. She'd woken up with tears and blood adhering her face to the cheap motel sheets, her thoughts fuzzy and disjointed. It had taken weeks for the bruises to fade.

Needless to say, hitching wasn't much of an option either, nor was she the type of person who could rent a car. For one, she had a suspended license, and if that wasn't enough of a non-starter, she also had no insurance. No car rental agency would touch her with a long-handled broom. That was also just fine with Leona—she'd always hated driving; plus, with her head still swimming from the beating, she wasn't sure she'd be able to get herself to her destination in one piece, anyway.

Finding herself high on enthusiasm and low on cash, she made the respectable choice. She camped near a haughty area of Atlanta, wrote a pleading note on a piece of cardboard she found in a dumpster, and placed a greasy paper coffee cup in front of her. The wretched state she was in wasn't feigned—by the time she started begging for bus fare, she hadn't had a drink in nearly sixteen hours. The self-loathing she constantly tried to push away was bubbling up like acid reflux, and she was desperately trying to hold it down so it wouldn't burn her. On top of that, she had the shakes for real—but she knew rich people would toss some coins her way to avoid having to look for too long. *Fucking pigs*, Leona thought, trying to replace pain with hatred. *With their blonde wives and their fancy cars and their shiny shoes. Just fuck all that right to the moon.*

After a hard day's work, Leona had enough for a one-way bus ticket to Savannah, plus a fifth of whiskey to boot. She scrubbed her face with water and the chemical-smelling soap in the liquor store's bathroom and did her best to pick the crust of vomit from her clothes. She wasn't presentable, per se, but she wouldn't be denied passage on the Greyhound, which had surely seen worse than Leona Franks.

*　*　*

Five hours passed in a haze of whiskey-scented belches. Leona had the back row of the bus all to herself, which she relished. She passed out with the empty bottle balanced between her side and the bus seat about three hours into the trip, which mercifully put an end to the dark thoughts swirling through her brain. She woke up only when the shriek of the brakes signaled she'd reached her destination.

The bus depot was gray and ominous, flanked by live oaks dripping with Spanish moss. A bell sounded somewhere, and Leona counted the chimes on her fingers: one, two, three, four, five, six, seven, eight, nine, ten, eleven. It was eleven o'clock.

Leona sighed and walked down Oglethorpe Avenue, hunting for a place to bed for the night. There'd be no more traveling at this hour.

After a few blocks, she found herself between a shining silver river and a chicken and waffles restaurant. The alley behind the restaurant had the double benefit of being secluded while also smelling of waffles, which Leona didn't mind at all. She sat down unsteadily in the shadow of a dumpster, displacing a squealing rat that scurried off into the night. Pulling her filthy garments tighter around her, Leona laid her head on a plush pile of garbage and fell peacefully asleep.

*　*　*

The floating giggle of calliope music woke Leona at first light. Before she was fully conscious, she found herself slipping her scabbed hand into her pocket, checking to make sure the flyer was still there. Once she had closed her fingers around it, the calliope stopped so abruptly Leona sat up, twisting her head this way and that, trying to home in on the source of the music. To the left was the dead-end of her dirty alley, to the right was the empty sidewalk and the street beyond. She crept out from behind the dumpster and brought herself shakily to her feet. She wiped her mouth with her palm, leaving a trail of sticky brown slime on her chin.

The Spanish moss beckoned like lovers' fingers across the street from the alley, and Leona was enveloped yet again by the smell of waffles and fried chicken. She inhaled deeply, shrugging her shoulders and trying hard to think.

I'm in Savannah. I came here yesterday on a bus. I need to get to this Gullywasher's place, what's on the flyer in my pocket, she thought. *Something's leading me there, where I'm needed. Something's leading me home.*

Tears started to prick the backs of Leona's eyes. She couldn't see any simple options ahead of her; she had neared her destination, but she didn't think she could just walk the rest of the way. Was she going to be stuck here? Just when she was getting close to the first place that had wanted her in God knew how many years?

Without thinking too much about what she was doing, she started ambling along the quaint Savannah sidewalk toward the river. She pulled the flyer out of her pocket again, hoping for some stroke of inspiration or luck. Scribbled in fading pencil on the back of the paper, she found both.

Boats arrive every half hour departing from Savannah.

When Leona looked up, a live-wire spark of glee in her eyes, she realized with a start that she had come to the cobblestone-paved street running parallel to the bank of the river. A small wooden dock jutted out like a baby's first tooth into the gently moving water. Tied at the end was a green-painted rowboat. Two dull red oars rested in the oarlocks, making soft knocking noises whenever they struck the boat. Leona stepped off the cobblestones and onto the wooden planks. As she neared the boat, she could just make out faint white lettering on the stern that read "Gullywasher's of Georgia!" She shivered, not with cold, but with a kind of mad delight.

Without any further thought, she climbed into the rowboat and untied its moorings. Her hands fit the smooth wood of the paddles as though years of her own rowing had molded them to her grip. For the first time in a long time, she felt right.

The water was calm, and no other boats were in sight, nor were any other living beings, given the early hour. She used one oar to push the boat away from the dock and started paddling with the current. The going was easy, and Leona felt the boat knew where it was headed. It didn't need her help—which was just fine, just fine indeed.

*   *   *

The sound of the boat whispering onto a muddy bank startled Leona out of her trance. She wasn't sure how long she'd been rowing, but the sun was now high in the sky and the back of her neck was wet with foul-smelling sweat. Her boat had marooned itself in the red clay next to a collapsing dock, its old wood honeycombed with termite tunnels. Leona shook her head and wiped the back of her neck.

The bank was shaded by large trees overhead and crowded so thickly with overgrown shrubbery that at first, Leona couldn't see the narrow path trailing up and up. When she finally did locate it, she giggled.

Using a paddle planted in the soft mud to steady herself, she pushed up and out of the boat. Her peeling shoes squelched into the muck, and as she started walking up the path, both shoes sank deep and stayed there. She wriggled out of them and continued onward barefoot, taking a moment to turn and blow a kiss to the boat.

The boat was gone. There was only the black water, softly lapping in the breeze.

*   *   *

Picking her way through the underbrush, Leona had a few moments to consider her situation. Needle-sharp branches clawed at her skin, opening old sores and sending blood and pus running down her face. Combined with the garbage juice from this morning, she looked only slightly better than a George Romero zombie.

This is where I'm supposed to be, she thought. *That's clear as day, and it don't need more thinking than that.*

Not too long after leaving the bank of the river behind, Leona cleared the jungle of bushes and came face to face with what looked like a moat. The trench was brown with muck and dead leaves, and a decaying rat stared up at her with black holes where its eyes had been. Leona looked left and right and saw the moat wended its way in both directions.

"Let the drawbridge down! The queen's a-coming home!" Leona screamed to the sky, beating her scrawny chest with her clenched fists.

She shrieked with glee, and in one bounding leap cleared the moat and landed with a thump on the other side.

Directly in front of her, a leaning sign warned: 'Alligator Pit. Danger.'

CHAPTER THREE

The July heat sizzled on Leona's skin as she crept toward the alligator pit, ignoring the 'Danger' sign. A rusty iron railing that had once held strong netting ringed the pit, but years of neglect had degraded the barriers, leaving only crumbling skeletons. Leona reached the edge of the steep drop. She looked down.

Layers of mud so dark they were almost black stared back up at her. A few clumps of weeds had forced their way through the muck, clinging defiantly to life as they reached toward the sun. The pit was, if Leona had to guess, about twenty feet across.

"Must not've been many big gators here," Leona blurted, and giggled.

She grabbed hold of one of the rusting spikes of railing sticking from the ground and leaned over to get a better look at a large lump in the center of the pit. Her crusty fingers wrapped around brittle metal, flakes of rust rubbing off in such great quantities it seemed there was nothing solid left in the railing. Leona's fuzzy brain barely had time to contemplate the trustworthiness of her grip before the railing disintegrated in her hand, and she pitched forward into the slimy darkness.

The fall clocked in around ten feet; the mud was spongy enough to absorb her impact and prevent any serious injury. Leona landed with a squelch on her right wrist and tweaked it a bit, but when she sat up and jiggled it side to side, the pain was minimal.

Still sitting, she turned to examine her latest predicament. Her brain worked slowly, the lazy throb of her wrist pounding like a dying heartbeat. Before she could stop to consider her options, curiosity pushed her toward the lump in the pit's center.

She crawled on all fours toward the oblong shape. When she reached one edge of the lump, she started to dig through the muck. Her wrist hurt more than she'd anticipated, and she heavily favored her left hand as she scratched, shoving dirt far under her fingernails. Before long, the tips of her left fingers touched something too metallic to be leather, but too leathery to be metal. It was cold, despite the sun beating down directly into the unsheltered pit.

She scraped harder, ignoring the zings of pain now shooting through both forearms. Seconds ticked by, but to Leona they felt like hours. She was assaulted by the growing feeling that whatever was buried under here would help her. This time, she would be struck by good luck instead of a closed fist, and the thought alone was enough to send small tears drifting down her cheeks.

When she felt as though she could dig no more, she swiped away one last layer of mud, and stared into a cold, reptilian eye.

*   *   *

Leona yelped and crab-walked backwards, dragging herself through the mud. She shut her eyes tight, curled into a ball, and waited for oblivion.

Oblivion didn't come.

Instead, after a few seconds of anticlimactic calm, she opened one crusty eyelid and surveyed her discovery with more precision. The eye in the slime-covered lump stared at her coldly, but it didn't move. It made no sound. A deep breath rattled through Leona's lungs.

She looked around for a stick, piece of pipe, or anything else she could use to defend herself against the creature. Seeing nothing in the muddy pit, she gave up looking and tentatively crawled back toward that unblinking eye, because what else was there to do? She'd rather approach the thing on her own terms, rather than wait for it to lunge for her when she least expected it. She jerked sharply to the left, then to the right, studying the creature for signs of awareness. She found none, so she continued forward on a straight path.

When she was close enough, she reached out a shaking hand and poked the creature, right above its eye. She cringed, steeling herself to be ripped to shreds, but nothing happened. She poked again. Same result.

She grew brave. If this thing were going to tear her apart, it would have done so by now, surely. With both hands, she started swiping at the muck again. After a few moments, she uncovered a long snout, another watchful eye, and a spade-shaped head.

"Well, well, well," she said, no longer afraid. "Fuck me if that isn't a dead fucking gator."

That wasn't quite right. The creature glaring up at her looked like a lifeless alligator, but it was… too fresh, somehow. She poked it again, pressing her finger into the strange metallic-rubber skin. She'd never touched an alligator before, but she knew unnatural when she felt it.

What is this? Some sort of… fake alligator?

Instead of thinking too hard on this source of confusion, Leona worked to uncover the rest of the creature. This time, the work felt brisk and easy, and joy blossomed within her with each handful of muck she scraped aside. When she stopped, breathing heavily, and sat on her haunches to survey the entire animal, the sun had moved farther across the sky, and the heat had dissipated from furious to just irritated. She felt lit from within by a cozy warmth, a sense of rightness—a sense of belonging she'd never had before.

The creature was a sight to behold. Green-black skin rose up in peaks and valleys over armor-like plates. The tail was meaty and thick, curving in an S-shape toward the opposite side of the pit. Needle-toothed jaws reached forward, both a beckoning and a warning.

Leona was delighted. The creature reminded her of the last time she felt truly happy. She was in her second foster home, around eight years old.

One of her foster brothers, the one who didn't slip into her bed at night, was sitting with her in the dusty backyard. The sun was hot, and he suggested they go 'spider hunting.' She wasn't sure what that was, but she agreed anyway. He went inside and came back out with an old coffee can filled with water. She followed him to a back corner of the yard, where he knelt and swept away chunks of dead grass to reveal the mouth of a small tunnel. "Tarantula hole," he said, and Leona nodded as though she understood. "Gonna get him out," he said, raising the can. He started pouring water down the hole, first a trickle and then, when nothing happened, a deluge. A few seconds after the last drop splashed into the hole, Leona heard a tiny scrabbling sound, and a tarantula emerged from the hole, shaking and angry. It looked into Leona's eyes with its eight beady ones, appraising her. Far from repulsed, she felt calm, peaceful, grateful for this creature that saw her. Then her foster brother crushed it with the bottom of the coffee can.

She decided to name the gator Tarantula, which felt like both a kind of resurrection and an apology to the furry spider who was sacrificed for a lonely child's entertainment.

Leona continued to inspect the fake animal. Tarantula was supported by a thick metal pillar jutting through the pit slime. She tried to shake it, but the metal was rusted, and Tarantula was damn heavy.

Putting her filthy fingers to her chin in thought, Leona stood up and glided through the mud, walking in a circle around the pit's perimeter. Her fingertips left dark, wet splotches on her chin.

On the wall of the pit directly behind Tarantula's tail, she found a flat metal cabinet she hadn't noticed before. It was maroon with rust, and the hinges squeaked like banshees when she pulled the door open. Inside, spiderwebs decorated a white plastic control panel, full of switches and buttons. She hovered a broken fingernail over the large red button in the center. She could barely make out the black letters that read "On."

"It's about time I got a little turned on, am I right? Oh, we're all gonna get turned on here tonight!" Leona screeched in Tarantula's direction. "I got you, baby!" Her fingernail stabbed the button.

Nothing happened.

Leona stood still with her finger glued to the button. She pressed it again. Still nothing.

Her face curled into a snarl, and she pounded both fists on the cement on either side of the control box in frustration. Mud squished between her toes as she brought her feet down hard on the slime, punishing the ground. Her vision swam with tears, her head started to pound, and—

A deep groan ripped through the charged atmosphere.

Leona whipped around. Her tears dried quickly on her cheeks, revealing tracks of pale skin and strips of paler scars.

A deep indent trailed behind Tarantula's tail like a racing stripe. Before her enraptured gaze, Tarantula crunched his obliques from side to side, swinging his entire bottom half in a laborious arc. With each swipe of his tail, the animatronic alligator created one half of a mud-angel.

Leona yelped when Tarantula's jaws yawned opened and then snapped shut. *Legato* open, then a sharp *staccato* shut. The music of it brought fresh tears to Leona's eyes; for once, she'd been able to save *something*. For once, she'd been the protector, instead of the one needing protection. For once, the nasty voice of self-loathing was quiet, and her tears were happy ones. When they spilled over her lips, she licked them eagerly. They tasted sweet.

*　*　*

Leona stood in the pit a long time, staring at her new pet with glazed eyes. She whispered, over and over, "I'll protect you." When she resurfaced from her trance, the sun was even lower, nearly tickling the treetops, and throwing dappled light onto her face.

Thirst scratched at her throat with sharp fingernails. Her right wrist ached. She pressed the red button to still Tarantula's thrashing, which had grown more and more frenzied as he kicked off years of rust and decay.

She gazed around the pit again, this time looking for a way out. As much as she loved the pit, she couldn't stay here forever. The walls were solid cement, smooth and slippery. The muck of the pit's bottom pooled ten feet below ground level.

She froze, spying something that shouldn't be there, *couldn't* be there. A thin rope ladder with wooden slats for steps hung below the fractured railing. A moist breeze blew through the pit and sent the rungs rattling against the concrete like old bones.

The ladder had not been there before. She'd walked around the pit several times since falling in, her hand trailing against the walls, feeling nothing but slimy cement. Surely, she would have noticed a ladder.

For the first time since she arrived, Leona was uneasy. She was also sweating and nauseated as her body rebelled against the sobriety she'd frantically avoided for years.

She clambered over to the ladder, her feet sinking into the muck with each step. When she reached the ladder, she gave it a tentative tug to test its strength. Satisfied, she gripped the prickly rope, the frayed fibers needling into her hands. She lifted her right foot and pushed up onto the first wooden step.

Suspended in the air, Leona turned back to look once more at Tarantula. She thought the huge animatronic swung his head to look at her, but her mind swam with waves of detox-induced hallucinations, and she couldn't be sure. She gagged, hot bile filling her throat and spilling into the back of her mouth. She swallowed it back down and climbed the rest of the ladder hastily, nearly slipping on the last step. She didn't want to defile Tarantula's home with her vomit.

The ladder was anchored to the bottom of the metal railing, and she grabbed at a treacherous pole to pull herself over the edge. When she stood up and looked down at her hands, she wasn't sure if they were red from rust or blood.

Wiping her hands on her filthy clothes, she started walking, figuring wherever she ended up was where she needed to be. That philosophy had worked, after all—it had gotten her here. It had gotten her *home*.

To her left, a large concrete building loomed out of the weeds. It may have once been painted blue. The glass in almost every window, except the highest ones on the third floor, had been smashed. As Leona stared, an enormous crow alighted on a first-floor windowsill and cawed loudly. The sound pierced the fetid air.

As if pulled by a magnet, her bare feet crossed the weed-strangled pavement, heading toward the faded blue building and the lone, terrible crow.

*　　*　　*

Leona again tasted wretched bile at the back of her throat. She turned to her left, fell to her knees, and dry heaved onto the asphalt. She heaved again, and this time, ropy strings of mucus dribbled from her lips.

She sat back on her thin haunches and watched with revulsion as the crow hopped greedily from the windowsill to her sick puddle and began pecking. Suppressing another gag, she lifted herself up on shaky legs and stumbled toward the double doors, noticing the faded outlines of tall block letters that had once read 'Aquarium.' A thick, tarnished chain looped through the door handles; at first, Leona was dismayed, until she noticed the padlock that should have kept intruders out was dangling uselessly at the end of the chain, nearly grazing the ground.

In one effortless motion, Leona pulled the chain to the ground. She had to leap back to avoid being hit by the doors, which swung open as the last of the chain-link slid away.

Inside, all was darkness. Leona's eyes struggled to adjust; she blinked and shielded her face, trying to get a better look. After a few moments, vague shapes came into view. Along the far back wall, weak rays of light filtered through films of grime and structural cracks in the concrete. In the very center of what Leona could now recognize as a cavernous room was a massive glass cylinder that rose from the base of the hard floor all the way to the roof. The cylinder's glass was unbroken. Leona shuddered, realizing the cylinder had once been a spectacular tank filled with sea creatures. Now, the tank remained undrained, but the thin rays of anemic light trickling into the aquarium's interior failed to penetrate the glass even a little.

She took a tentative step inside. Behind her, the crow cawed once, twice, a horrible racket piercing the quiet of the park.

Her nose was running. She sniffled, and a caged animal smell burrowed into her nostrils. The stench was so thick she could almost taste it, and it brought her to her knees once again, gagging.

"I gotta get well," she said aloud. She didn't expect a response, but the crow, which had hopped inside behind her, cawed anyway. She wiped her mouth on her mud-crusty shirt and stood up.

Her eyes continued to adjust as she walked closer to the dark cylindrical tank. The aquarium was arranged as a multi-tiered gallery; the entire center was open, with second- and third-story catwalks hugging the walls above. Rickety metal staircases connected the floors, where visitors would have rubbernecked at the small glass tanks embedded in the concrete walls. Unlike the cylinder, most of the wall-mounted tanks were broken, with light green patinas coating jagged shards.

To her right, next to one of the staircases, sat two gray tanks different from all the rest. The dim lighting made them look like TV screens pumping static through the airwaves. When she tiptoed closer, the crow hopped along, acting as a macabre shadow.

As she neared, the fuzzy tanks began to sharpen and gain clarity. Leona could see their glass had been carefully removed, with no jagged edges remaining to cut a wrist open. Piles of small white bags like powdery bricks lined the inside of each tank, from top to bottom.

Excitement quickened in Leona's crippled heart.

She reached a hand into the tank on the right, still expecting her fingers to smash against thick glass. To her surprise, her hand slipped smoothly inside and alighted on a stack of the bags, which were covered in an inch of dust. Whoever had left the massive stash was obviously either long dead or incarcerated.

She squeezed. The bag in her fist was small and yielded gently to her touch, like a stress ball. She pulled the bag out of the tank, tendrils of dust falling to the floor, and held it in her palms like manna from Heaven. Her fingers shook as they pulled the bag open. Her heart rate skyrocketed in anticipation.

She took a heavy sniff. Beneath the permeating pet store stench was the slightest, most delicate hint of vinegar.

"I'm gonna have me a party!" Leona shrieked into the dark cavern, a sloppy grin cracking across her face. The crow cawed, mirroring her excitement.

Leona reached one scabbed hand into her pocket and pulled out the Gullywasher's flyer that had brought her to this strange and wonderful place. She rolled it into a tight tube and pressed one end into her right nostril, and the other into the bag. Her hands contorted in odd shapes as she managed to hold the bag, tube, and her left nostril simultaneously. With one deep, ragged inhale, she snorted the heroin deep into her sinuses.

*   *   *

Leona awoke sometime later slumped against the base of the dark cylinder. The cavern was pitch-black; Leona couldn't even see her hands in front of her face. Nearby, she heard the *hop-skip, hop-skip* of her crow. The rhythm lulled her back to sleep.

The next time she opened her eyes, sunlight streamed through the windows, making even the dark cylinder glow a diseased forest green. It took her awhile to take stock of her body and remember where she was. Her nausea had disappeared. The tacky sweat that had wallpapered her skin had evaporated away. Her head was not pounding.

She took a deep breath and began to rise gingerly to her feet. For weeks, maybe even months (she wasn't quite sure), she'd been avoiding putting too much pressure on her right foot. The space between her big and second toes had been home to a large black abscess that simply would not heal, oozing pus and black fluid any time Leona moved too quickly. She had gotten used to standing up slowly, balancing mostly on her left foot, bracing for the pain that would shoot through her right foot, all the way to her knee.

It did not come.

As she stood up, she realized she was bracing herself for… nothing. There was no pain. At first, she was terrified the lack of discomfort meant her foot had finally rotted away, taking the pain with it. She fell back to the ground with a thump and drew her right foot toward her face. The foot was still there, and when she pulled her toes apart to study her wound, it was gone. Smooth, pale skin covered what had once been an angry black hole.

"Woah," she said, breathlessly. "Somebody's really takin' care of me today!" The feeling was so strange she nearly laughed.

Leona rose again, this time with more confidence. As she pushed herself off the ground, she also noticed the pain in her right wrist from yesterday's fall into the alligator pit had disappeared. Even more astonishing, the track marks and open sores along the insides of her arms had faded, leaving no evidence she had ever had anything but perfect, pink skin.

She brought her hands to her face to feel the old scars, relics of too many scratches while on too many drugs. This time, she wasn't as astonished to find them gone, as well.

Leona took a deep breath, her head clear for the first time in years. Her mind found it easier to put two and two together. She had been sick; she had found Gullywasher's; she had fallen into the pit; she had been covered in mud; she had found Tarantula; she had found the stash of heroin; she had snorted some; she had collapsed… and when she had woken up, she was well. More than well—she was healed. Every blemish, every wound, every scar the mud of the pit had touched was gone.

To Leona, this series of events meant three things. One: the mud in the pit was slimy magic. Two: that was some goddamn good heroin. Three:

maybe the mud and the drugs would be even better mixed together, like Johnnie Walker and weed, or tequila and cocaine.

She smiled. Her crow cawed.

One more thought occurred to her, something so uncharacteristically altruistic she shuddered. Why should she keep this wonderful secret all to herself?

CHAPTER FOUR

After a few weeks spent doctoring her heroin with the magic muck from the alligator pit, Leona felt transformed. Her skin glowed, her hair grew lustrous and thick, her skin became smooth and creamy, and her eyes turned clear and bright. Everything life had taken from her in the past had been returned to her in a rush, mainlined into her system with the modified heroin. As she felt herself become better, more golden, almost Messianic, the others started to come.

At the beginning, it was only a dribble of human refuse that showed up at her door; her crow cawed in lieu of a doorbell. Raggedy men, shifty with paranoia, asked her for help in shaky voices. She led them to the pit, asked them to wait at the edge, and returned with a white brick. She portioned some out, climbed down, and mixed the brown with the white lovingly, as though she were a grandmother baking a chocolate cake for her grandchildren.

As they watched, their arms stopped twisting with anxiety and fell to their sides. Their eyes grew large with wonder, as though entranced. Leona smiled as she worked; she was lovely in a way the troubled people who came to her had never seen before.

After sealing the healing paste into a small scrap of baggie, she climbed out and approached her new friends. Invariably, they asked, "How much?"

"It's a gift," she always said, smiling as she pushed the warm lump into their filthy, wounded hands.

The good thing about junkies, she supposed, was they didn't stand around and barter out of politeness. They took her offer at face value and hustled away. Later, on her nightly park rounds, she'd find scraps of rubber tube and broken syringes. They never made it out of the park before getting their fix.

On July 21ˢᵗ, Leona was sitting in a metal folding chair in her aquarium, pulling apart large plastic bags to fashion smaller ones for packaging the good stuff. She grinned as she worked; she couldn't remember a time when she'd felt this wholesome. She was doing good, honest work, bringing the healing power of this magic place to society's outcasts, the people tossed aside like blistered garbage, those who grasped so desperately at help that would never come. Until it did—in the form of Leona Franks.

A shadow passed across Leona's mind, darkening the lightness of her mood. If only she'd been able to get this well before she'd lost the baby. Things could have been so different.

Leona had enjoyed the company of many different men in her teens and twenties, and it was hard for her, usually drunk or high or both, to be careful every time. She'd been so high taking the pregnancy test in the pharmacy bathroom she could barely see the double blue lines that signified the tiny life growing inside her.

When the fog cleared enough for her to not only read the result but also comprehend it, she wasn't sure how to feel. She didn't normally stop to carefully examine her life, mostly because that act would be unbearably painful, but the possibility of a child forced her into it. What did she have to say for herself? What did she have to show for her two and a half decades of life?

Two bouts of gonorrhea. A grimy mattress in a collapsing flophouse. A pair of dead parents. An abusive former foster family. Chronic depression, undiagnosed. Alcoholism and drug addiction, diagnosed. A shitbag boyfriend with a hard punch.

What could she possibly give to a baby?

The shitbag boyfriend shoved her down a flight of stairs when he found out, yelling that he'd be damned if he was gonna pay child support. Crumpled at the bottom of the stairs, she'd started to bleed.

The blood was a trickle at first, but turned into a gush. She could feel the tiny bud of life slipping away on a river of scarlet, and all of her hopes for redemption, for unconditional love, disappeared with the baby. After that, what was there to live for? Leona lost the boyfriend, lost the mattress, lost any sense of responsibility or self-preservation she might have had.

Years later, when she thought death was finally going to call her home right there in the gutter, and on Independence Day, no less, she felt the call and found the flyer. Or did it find her? Grateful didn't even begin to cover the depth of her feeling for this private park, for the path of transformation it had sent her down. For once, she could be someone whom that baby, that little budding life lost forever, could have respected.

Her crow cawed. She shook herself out of her reverie and stood up to answer the call. In the Georgia sun stood a man and a woman, both young, with hopeful, wide-eyed faces. They didn't look like the typical creatures who showed up on her doorstep, but when they reached out their hands in supplication, Leona could see bright red marks trailing along the tender flesh of their inner arms. Perhaps she could heal them before they had to look destruction in the eye.

They exchanged few words as she led Patricia and Marty Dalco to the pit.

* * *

Leona did not think of herself as a drug dealer, nor was she an addict, not anymore. She had stopped using after a few initial doses—the cravings had left her along with the scars, aches, and sores.

Above all, she was a healer. What she dispensed was not an addictive high, but a painless and holy cure she'd used herself. People did not need to be cured twice, therefore it was no surprise she had no repeat customers. The broken people who showed up shaking at her doorstep left reconciled and whole.

Some of these thoughts were her own, but the bulk of them seeped into her mind from the park. The voices slipped through the atmosphere, emanating from the aquarium's dark cylindrical tank.

When she laid down in a pile of old blankets in the aquarium each night, the voices would flow toward her, then through her. They were sweet but sharp, with enough of an edge to keep her from dropping away into sleep. The voices whispered about the vital necessity of her healing work, about how much good she was doing, about how there were so many ruptured souls in the world, how could she ever stop?

After the voices had their way with her, she would float into a shallow sleep, shimmering with dreams. On this night, she lay awake listening to the voices for what felt like hours, dropping off only when they were finished with her. In her dream, she was in the aquarium, wandering around the perimeter, staring into dark tanks. A stinging sound fizzled in her ears, and she turned toward the black cylinder. As she watched, her eyes adjusted enough to see a cloudy shape suspended in the tank. The form shivered, and pale fingertips pressed against the glass. As the figure shifted, Leona saw white hands, wasted biceps, bony shoulders. Feet, knees, and thighs, all sharp angles, became visible, followed by a sunken abdomen and emaciated torso. Last to come into focus was the head, which loomed shiny and bald out of the darkness like a slow-moving ship. Her own face stared back at her. There, in the inky infinity of the glass cylinder, she wavered, naked, pale, dead. Other figures soon joined the first, beginning to writhe orgiastically. She turned violently away to run from the melee; in the process, she slammed into a metal chair and fell, knocking her forehead against the cement floor with a hollow ring.

When she awoke, she wasn't nestled in her blankets; she was sprawled on the floor. Her eyes took a while to focus, and when they did, she saw a rusty stain near her chair. Her forehead was sticky.

Her crow cawed.

CHAPTER FIVE

The majority of the Epidemic Intelligence Service team returned to their offices at CDC's Roybal campus in Atlanta on Monday, August 12. From what Dr. Archibald Gruber read in the CDC's *Morbidity and Mortality Weekly Report*, they'd been investigating an outbreak in Savannah which was highly unusual, in that they had so far failed to discover the outbreak's origination.

The Epidemic Intelligence Service, or EIS, as those in the know called it, was a collection of highly skilled epidemiologists and scientists who were dispatched in teams to handle outbreaks across the world. Gruber had been an EIS officer himself, back in the beginning of his CDC career, and he had loved it. He had lived for the thrill of leaving his stuffy cube, hunting down the microscopic culprits, and solving the puzzle. If he'd been permitted, he would have stayed an EIS officer forever—but the usual term of service was a scant two years. Dr. Archibald Gruber lived his dream for two years…and then returned to the stuffy cube he still hadn't managed to escape, even eleven years on.

For this particular mission in the hot summer of 2019, an EIS team led by Dr. Kurt Finney had been dispatched to Savannah to investigate an outbreak of a fatal gastrointestinal illness. The *Morbidity and Mortality Weekly Report* indicated nine Savannahians had died, and two were in critical condition at the hospital. Gruber overheard a few of the returned EIS officers talking in the break room, which gave him much more actionable information. Apparently, there wasn't much the team could learn from the dead victims concerning potential exposures—not one of them had visited a doctor before their demise, there didn't appear to be any evidence of secondary transmission, and even rooting out friends and family who may have heard complaints of symptoms proved virtually fruitless. This was mostly because all of the stricken were longtime drug users, several with possession charges on their records, many of them transient or homeless. Even if the team could have tracked down friends and acquaintances, they were unlikely to find a helpful lead.

The two in critical care were a slightly different story—which Gruber had had to pry from an EIS officer who owed him a favor. Their names were Marty and Patricia Dalco—siblings, not spouses. They were both in their mid-twenties, college educated. They'd presented to the ER with respiratory distress, severe vomiting, abdominal cramping, and neck stiffness. The officers hadn't gotten much out of them—they'd been barely audible and drifted in and out of consciousness. The team knew little more than their symptoms.

After a week, Patricia went into respiratory arrest and was placed on a breathing machine. Patricia's condition had not changed, and neither had Marty's, when the majority of the EIS team were called back to CDC headquarters a month later. The Savannah County coroners, desperately backlogged, needed to do their jobs with the nine bodies cooling in the morgue refrigerators. In the meantime, the EIS officers had work to do back in Atlanta.

Gruber was fascinated by this story, especially since he had spent much of his childhood in Savannah. Not once in his eleven years at CDC had he heard of a team pulling out after only a month with the case still unsolved. Sure, there were a few officers still assigned to the Savannah outbreak in the event of another confirmed case, but they couldn't do much good being four hours away from the outbreak's epicenter.

The facts are so highly unusual, Gruber thought. He fiddled with the large

black face of his watch, something he did often while he was ruminating .
What could possibly fit?

As Gruber contemplated the particulars of the outbreak in his
claustrophobic cube, he heard his boss, Commander Samantha Clements,
and her supervisor, Dr. Theodore Lucas, Director of the Division of
Foodborne, Waterborne, and Environmental Diseases. They were speaking
in very low voices, but Gruber could still make out their words as they
conversed in the small break room next to his cube.

"Considering Dr. Gruber for that position?" Clements asked. "I think he
would be a good fit."

"Nah," Lucas said. "Gruber's a great epidemiologist, there's no doubt
about that, but…I don't know. Hanson seems like a better fit. Gruber's too
much of a loner. Thinks he can do everything all on his own. I can't imagine
why he doesn't try to collaborate more, especially with someone like you."

Gruber inhaled sharply, his brain swirling with winds made of angry
thoughts. He *could* do it all on his own; most other people were completely
incompetent. Of course Lucas was talking about the Branch Director
position Gruber had assumed was his. But *Hanson?* She was barely four
years out of her postdoc and already getting too big for her britches, not
unlike Commander Clements herself—who had, many years ago, surpassed
Gruber at a blistering pace. Even as his student, she'd been uppity. Now all
this? He wouldn't let it happen again.

*If Lucas thinks he's going to promote Hanson instead of me, then that's the last
straw,* he thought. *How much humiliation am I expected to suffer? If I let this junior
epidemiologist jump the line for promotion, there's no stopping it. I'll be no better than a
New York City subway turnstile—everybody hopping over me, paying me no mind.*

Gruber sighed. Commander Samantha Clements had joined his division
at the CDC at the same time he had, right after they both finished their terms
as EIS officers. He hadn't been surprised when she'd followed him to the
same department; she was clearly walking in his footsteps for some annoying
reason. Now she was a Commander, and, unfortunately, his boss. The irony

was not lost on him; he spent many sleepless nights twisting his pillowcase into knots, trying to open the release valve on his anger. He already knew what people said about him—he was unsociable, a little gruff—and he didn't want to add fuel to the fire. Slightly unsociable people could get promoted; angry ones couldn't. Gruber didn't think Clements was smarter than him, but he could tell from the minute she'd walked into his classroom over a decade ago that she was charismatic and savvy in a way he would never be. She was always kind to him, he had to admit, but he thought he caught a whiff of pity underlying her every word. He hated it, and he preferred to keep her at arm's length as much as possible, which wasn't easy.

Gruber scowled as he heard Clements ease into the chair in her office opposite his cube. She didn't bother poking her head in and saying hi, as she used to do up until last month, when Gruber had put a stop to her intrusions with a snarled "I'm *working* here, and I need to *concentrate!*" He had regretted his tone, which was ruder than he'd intended and revealed the anger boiling inside him, but he didn't regret the result: she no longer bothered him with niceties. He did, however, try to apologize in his nearly invisible way by watering her desk plants when she was away at a conference. He didn't know if she knew he'd been the one keeping her plants alive, but he didn't really care. His actions had atoned for his previous rudeness in his own mind, and that was what really mattered.

He sat there, one ear cocked for the *ping* of incoming emails, still smarting from the conversation he'd overheard between Clements and that bastard Lucas. That Branch Director position was his, goddammit. He'd earned it.

Needless to say, his current relationship with Clements was strained, which would be even more of a problem if he needed her to push for his promotion. Would she ever recommend him for a promotion, beyond just indicating offhandedly he might be a good fit for something? Not if things continued this way, that was for sure.

Maybe everything doesn't have to stay this way? he thought. *I'm forty-one years old and I still work out of a cube. What if…?*

A new thought popped into his head, overshadowing the anger: *Go to Savannah. Find the source. Solve the puzzle. Grab that promotion.*

Despite this brewing storm of thought-winds sounding like the plot of a Southern-fried Bond movie, Gruber was immediately enchanted. If he could be the superstar here, the solver of puzzles, the great and wondrous Dr. Archibald Gruber who had earned EIS superstar status all those years ago, maybe he could kill two birds with one germy stone: *Get the recognition I deserve and the promotion I deserve even more.* He would be so good, so goddamned intelligent, they would have no choice but to give him the job.

Win win.

CHAPTER SIX

At 7:43am on Tuesday, August 13, Commander Samantha Clements received a troubling email from her subordinate, Dr. Archibald Gruber. In typical Gruber style, the message was short but overly formal, and indicated he wasn't feeling well and would have to take a sick day.

The content of the email itself didn't bother Sam. There was nothing unusual about an employee taking a sick day. What was unusual was Gruber taking a sick day. In the eleven years he'd worked at the Centers for Disease Control and Prevention, Gruber hadn't taken so much as an afternoon off of work. The man was practically bionic.

He was also one of the best damned epidemiologists Sam had ever worked with; together, they studied the sources and patterns of disease outbreaks. She had first met Gruber when he was a PhD student teaching her graduate course on epidemiological modeling for her MD/PhD program. The next time she encountered him was as a fellow officer in the Epidemic Intelligence Service, after she'd already received her own double doctorate. In addition to being an EIS officer, Sam had been working her way up in the U.S. Public Health Service, within spitting distance of the Commander level. Gruber had been a newly minted epidemiology PhD, ready and raring to go. Sam wouldn't say they were really friends, but she loved working with Gruber— the man was methodical, logical, and resourceful almost to a fault. On their first assignment together, Gruber had singlehandedly found the source of a *Legionella* outbreak in Fargo. A contaminated grocery store mister was the culprit. Lazy employees hadn't cleaned the misters for weeks (although to Sam, it had looked more like months, or even years), so they ended up spraying the broccoli, the carrots, the tight balls of lettuce with millions of disease-causing bacteria. This was a brilliant find, but Gruber never grew cocksure—he just kept his head down on the numbers and his boots on the ground, seeking new epidemiological puzzles to solve.

Looking back, Sam realized it was probably Gruber's disdain for others that had slowed his career advancement. Where Sam was politely affable, Gruber was gruff; where Sam was social, Gruber was reticent; where Sam was creative, Gruber was rigid. When Sam was promoted time after time over the years until she reached Commander, Gruber progressed at half-speed, respected, but not really liked. Now, she found herself in the strange position of being her former teacher's direct supervisor, a role which she suspected grated on him. She couldn't be sure, because he rarely showed any human emotion, only a quasi-robotic focus.

Suffice it to say Sam was unsettled by Gruber's email, but not so unsettled that she made a fuss. Her reply was simple—"No worries. Feel better soon."

CHAPTER SEVEN

After pressing Send on the email to Clements about his sick day, Gruber began to hyperventilate. He never took days off. Clements would surely think something was suspicious. He couldn't shake the dreams he'd had last night…seeing himself swooping in to save the day, ready for glory, already gathering up the few personal items in his cube to transfer to his new office… then Lucas walking in, announcing Hanson's promotion…feeling victory slip away, and hearing everybody's laughter…

Still in bed and wreathed in the smelly sweat of anxiety, he'd typed up the email to Clements before he could really stop to think. Now he was thinking, and his internal monologue was driving him to the edge of madness. *What if Clements suspects something? What if I can't solve the puzzle? What if I get caught? What if I get fired?*

Then Lucas' voice came back to him, *"He thinks he can do everything all on his own."* Gruber gritted his teeth, forced his breathing to a halt. *I can do it on my own,* he thought, *and I will. I can't spend one more second inside that crappy cube while everybody else laughs and moves past me.* Surely it couldn't hurt just to look around Savannah. If he failed, nobody would have to know.

Armed with a shaky but persistent resolve, Gruber decided to take the Amtrak from Atlanta to Savannah. He'd downloaded copies of the Savannah outbreak case report, the epidemiological assessment, and various internal memos to review during the trip. Even though he'd read through most of the material already, he wanted to go over everything again and take more comprehensive notes. He didn't want to be going in ignorant. He wanted a plan.

Before leaving his apartment, which was so spare it resembled an Ikea catalogue, he packed a few clean shirts, a pair of chinos, a pair of jeans he never wore, a hat, some socks, pajamas, underwear, and his toothbrush into a small suitcase. The luggage was cheap, bought in haste when he was unexpectedly deployed to Sierra Leone during the Ebola crisis. There was a rip in the black canvas, and he struggled to pull the zipper closed. As he hefted the suitcase up and off the bed, memories of the last time he'd used it flooded back, unbidden. The faces of the people he couldn't help, the pleas for medicine, for treatment, for anything, the Ebola wards full to bursting, sick people lying on the floor in puddles of blood and vomit. He gulped, trying to swallow the disturbing memories.

Glancing at his watch, its impassive black face confirming he was right on schedule, he carried the suitcase and his briefcase out of the apartment and locked the door behind him. Patting his front pocket to assure himself his printed train ticket confirmation was still there, he took the stairs to the lobby, walked out of the automatic glass doors with a whoosh, and set out on foot to the station.

Four blocks and only a thimbleful of sweat—which Gruber considered a victory in the oppressive Atlanta heat—later, the epidemiologist sighed gratefully upon entering the aggressively air-conditioned train station lobby. The place was empty at 9 a.m. on a Tuesday, and Gruber gave thanks for small mercies. In case things went poorly, he didn't want to leave behind any trace of this unorthodox mission that could compromise his career. He'd even booked his ticket using his mother's credit card, to befuddle any would-be investigators.

He was half an hour early, according to his watch, so he ambled into the small news shop to buy a bottle of water. The refrigerated case was sweating despite the air conditioning. After purchasing the water and a packet of salted pistachios, Gruber pressed the cool bottle to his forehead.

Ambling into the lobby, he sat in a cracked leather seat, crossing his legs. Sweat was beginning to run down his face, and thirsty gulps of the cold water failed to interrupt the trickle. His face itched where the sweat had left salty trails. The skin under his leather watchband embossed with his initials—ANG—started to tingle with discomfort.

He was scrolling through a few memos on his phone, trying to latch on to something. The text wove in and out of focus; Gruber couldn't seem to concentrate. His mind was elsewhere—many elsewheres, actually. Part of him was still turning over the epidemiological puzzle awaiting him in Savannah. Another part was picturing the kudos and much-deserved promotion that would come his way once he'd succeeded where an entire team of EIS officers had failed. The last part was still in Sierra Leone, staring into the face of a sick woman as she cried tears of blood.

His watch confirmed the train's arrival at the station with perfect punctuality, and he boarded as soon as the doors opened. The compartment was cooler than the station, and Gruber smiled for the first time that day as he eased into his seat by the window. Thoughts continued to jockey for attention in his head, none of them gaining much traction. Gruber often experienced these mental tornadoes, as he called them, mostly when he was faced with a difficult scientific problem. They also came when he was faced with unwelcome memories that continued to haunt him, even though it had been years since he'd come back from Africa, shaky and traumatized.

When the thought-winds started pitching and he could feel a tornado coming on, Gruber resorted to his favorite childhood activity: watching movies. His tastes ranged from well-researched documentaries to foreign romances, but his sweet spot was horror movies—the older, the better. To Gruber, horror movies aged like fine wines, their quality improving with the years.

He pulled out his laptop and set it on the small tray table. An extremely risky road lay ahead of him, so he selected his all-time favorite—*Frankenstein*. Boris Karloff at his finest.

Gruber opened a folder of downloaded movies on his desktop. As he gazed at the icon photo for the film file, he became sharply aware, as though he had reached the eye of the mental tornado. Everything slowed down, and his vision grew to a pinprick that was filled with Karloff's face—the eyelids heavy and hanging down, the cheeks slack and expressionless, the mouth slightly ajar as though the monster were pleading with his creator.

The drooping eyelids. The paralyzed facial muscles.

Could it be?

With an eerie calmness that belied the frenzy in his mind, Gruber pulled out the photographs of the outbreak survivors, Marty and Patricia Dalco, that had been taken when they were admitted to the hospital. He'd only given them cursory glances before, but now he brought the photos so close to his face his nose left a circle of grease on Patricia's hospital gown-clad torso. He gasped with delight when he saw both Marty and Patricia's eyes were half-closed. To everybody else, this probably just looked like fatigue. Not to Gruber. He fired off an email to the EIS officer that had slipped him information about the Dalcos. In the email, Gruber posed two simple questions:

Have the Dalcos been given neurological examinations?

Are the Dalcos black tar heroin users?

With that task completed, Gruber settled back to wait for the reply. He felt poised once again, the tornado of painful memories calmed, and he spent the first hour or so of his journey with Dr. Frankenstein and his monster.

*   *   *

When the final credits started rolling across his laptop screen, he exited the movie, checked his watch (still a ways to go until arrival), then opened his email.

One new message. It was from his EIS contact:

Last I heard, the ER doc did neuro exams when the Dalcos were first admitted, but the exams were inconclusive and haven't been repeated.

They had track marks at their elbows and wounds in between their toes. Not sure if it was black tar heroin, but heroin of some sort is likely. We're still waiting on the toxicology results. Is this helpful?

Gruber smiled. He knew the email's final sentence was just another way of trying to pump Gruber for his expert opinion, which he would not be sharing. His throbbing need to be the superhero of this particular outbreak story took precedence over collegial collaboration, which he despised anyway. No one else would be taking advantage of him anymore or stealing the credit he was due. He closed his laptop without replying and spent the rest of the journey looking out the window, a ghost of a smile dancing on his lips.

*   *   *

Everyone knew Savannah was the most haunted city in America, crowned with a plaque to make it official. If one believed the guidebooks and tourist websites, the entire downtown was crawling with ghosts, a spiritual mishmash of slaves, soldiers, children, wives, and husbands. When Gruber stepped out of the train and onto the station platform, he was hit not with apparitions, but with a humidity so thick it was almost alive.

His hotel, the DeSoto, was over three miles away. Normally, he would have been content to walk the distance, happy to stretch his legs after hours in a cramped train car, but three miles was over the limit in the August heat. He hailed a taxi, waving away the driver who offered to put his bags in the trunk. *That's how they get you,* Gruber thought. *Make it seem like they're just being polite to help you with your baggage, then tack on a few dollars extra for their trouble.*

"Where you headed, friend?" the grizzled driver asked.

Gruber clipped in his seatbelt. "The DeSoto," he said. "On Liberty."

"Oh, I know where the DeSoto is," the driver, whose name tag hanging from the rearview mirror said 'Eugene Frasier.' "Some wild stuff happened there a few years back."

Gruber looked down at his watch, pointedly uninterested in asking any follow-up questions. Eugene was undeterred by his silence and continued anyway. "You hear about the soldier boy?"

"No," Gruber said, with finality.

"My Lord, that was a sad story," Eugene said, too cheerily for Gruber's taste. Without waiting for any prompting, Eugene told him the 'sad story' with relish, the tragedy sucked away in the theatricality of the telling. "Well, see, this soldier boy—really no more than a boy, a college kid—was on leave from the Army. He'd just come back from Iraq. He was stationed over at Fort Stewart, and he'd come into town to have some drinks with his buddies, you know, let loose kind of thing. Anyway, he has his fun, and the next day, he's gone. Just gone. Nobody can find him, and his parents start to get real worried. Weeks go by, and his family's just going wild with worry—I would too, if it were my kid—they're putting up posters, search teams are looking in every nook and cranny downtown, and still nothing. Finally, after nearly two weeks, a hotel maintenance guy at the DeSoto finds this poor kid's body in the *industrial air conditioner*." Eugene paused for dramatic effect. He didn't seem to care that Gruber was patently not listening, staring out the window at the mossy oak trees passing by. "The industrial air conditioner. Can you believe it? Apparently, the hotel guests had been complaining of a bad smell in their bedrooms. Some say they could even hear eerie moaning sounds coming from their air vents. Can you imagine? You're sleeping there, and you're smelling these terrible smells and hearing moaning, and the whole time a poor kid is getting ripped to shreds in there by the air conditioner's giant blower wheel."

Even the hotel has a ridiculous ghost story, Gruber thought.

As though divining Gruber's skepticism, Eugene said, "I bet you're thinking 'No way, that's not true, I would have heard of something like that on the news,' but you bet your britches it's true, mister. You can look it up."

To shut this idiot up more than anything else, Gruber replied, "Sure, maybe I'll do that."

Before Eugene could open his mouth again, the taxi glided into the front driveway of the DeSoto. Gruber shoved a twenty, which was overpaying even with a 75% tip, at Eugene, and launched himself out of the car. He grabbed his bags from the trunk and smiled hollowly as the bellhop opened the door into an oasis of air conditioning—which, Gruber noted, smelled neither foul nor ghostly.

* * *

After struggling through check-in with a clerk whose accent was thicker than molasses, Gruber took the elevator to the fourth floor and found his room. He swung his suitcase onto the bed and started unpacking. He was fastidious—shirts in the top drawer of the dresser, pants in the second drawer, and pajamas, underwear, and everything else in the bottom. He placed his toiletries on the bathroom counter. He was desperately thirsty, the heat and humidity robbing his body of moisture with every second, and he leaned over to guzzle water straight from the tap. When his thirst was quenched, he splashed his face with the cool water and washed and dried his hands. Feeling fortified, he gripped the countertop on either side of the sink and stared at himself in the mirror.

A pale, sunken face stared back at him. His cornsilk hair was thinning at the crown, bristly patches of stubble dotted his jaw, and deep bags underlined his watery, almost colorless eyes. A painful moment of clarity crept up on him, and he saw himself as his colleagues must see him. Gutted. Old. Pitiful. *A joke.*

The slap was so quick he was unaware it issued from his own open palm. His right cheek burned where he'd hit himself, needles prickling under the red skin. There was a small but angry red welt growing on the side of his face where the clasp of his watchband had snagged his skin. He shook his head and narrowed his eyes at his reflection. *I'm no joke*, he thought to himself. Then, to emphasize the point, he said it aloud: "I am no joke!" He wagged a finger at his reflection. "I can do this." He took a deep breath, completely inflating his lungs, and then exhaled slowly.

When he was ready, he exited the bathroom and opened his briefcase. He checked that he had his laptop, a slim file folder of documents relating to the outbreak, a legal pad, and a pen and zipped the case closed. Before leaving the room, he inhaled once again, deeply, as though readying himself for battle.

*　*　*

Carrying the briefcase, he walked out of the hotel, taking a right on Drayton Street. At the corner, he took another right onto Harris and walked until he came to a small park. A sign proclaimed this cube of trees 'Madison Square.' Gruber found an empty bench and set his briefcase beside him. He found nature calming, and he did his best thinking while walking along the winding paths through CDC's campus or meandering along Atlanta's BeltLine toward Piedmont Park. Spanish moss spilled from the branches of enormous live oaks and tickled the humid air. Gruber pulled out his file folder and read through the information yet again. When he'd read all there was to read, he sat back and closed his eyes.

If the Dalcos were black tar heroin users, then maybe the other patients were as well. He decided to follow this thought train, couching everything in hypotheticals until he came to an answer pulsing with so much probability it must be close to the truth.

Okay. Let's say Marty and Patricia Dalco are indicative of a pattern. For argument's sake, all of the victims were black tar heroin users. Although their symptoms would generally point toward some sort of gastrointestinal pathogen—E. coli, or maybe Salmonella—*that clearly isn't the issue, and besides, even the EIS team would have figured that out. If those half-closed eyes aren't plain tiredness but actually drooping caused by paralyzed facial muscles, then this isn't a simple bacterium at all. This isn't a virus, either. It's a…what? What can paralyze muscles like that? Think, Archibald.*

He squinted his eyes shut even harder and racked his brain, trying to recall case reports and textbook pages from memory. He was meditating on the symptomatology of a fungus versus a mold when a lightning flash of inspiration came to him, so bright it was almost painful.

It's a toxin. Botulinum toxin.

He opened his eyes. *Botulism?* The probability of a botulism outbreak was so small Gruber was probably a fool to think of it. There were maybe ninety or so cases per year in the entire country. The illness was so rare that any more than just one case was considered a full-fledged outbreak, call the CDC, send the antitoxin, do not pass go, do not collect two hundred dollars. If patients ingested a large quantity of toxin and didn't get treatment quickly, then they would absolutely drop like flies. The pattern fit.

Gruber was so excited he started to feel faint in the August heat.

Wait. If this is botulism, then the Dalcos need antitoxin.

But, the part of his mind that wanted glory and recognition whispered, *if it's not, then you can't get involved and blow your chance at getting everything you want. If you're wrong, you'll look stupid. Everybody will laugh at you, even more than they already do. You have to wait. You have to be sure. Plus, it's been weeks since they were afflicted. The damage has been done.*

He wasn't sure if that was really true, but he looked at the sky and grinned anyway, his face dappled with the sunlight rippling through the canopy of trees. He was happier than he'd been in months, maybe even years. He had a plan. He had a strong working hypothesis. Plus, CDC's resident botulism expert was none other than Commander Samantha Clements who, when she'd first started (and long before she'd become his boss), had asked Gruber out for coffee as a way to get to know her new colleagues. Gruber had wanted to decline but had ended up accepting at the last minute. At a time like this, he was so glad he'd gone through with that particular conversation.

He closed his eyes, thinking hard back to that memory, reliving it in real time.

Clements stood up just as his watch announced the exact time of their coffee meeting, peeking her head over the wall between them. "Dr. Gruber? Are you ready?"

He mirrored her position, bringing himself up to his full height. "Yes."

She smiled. "Great. Shall we head downstairs?"

"Sure," he said, shrugging.

He'd followed her through the maze of cubes to the on-campus café. Clements asked for some ridiculous drink that was more sugar than caffeine, and Gruber ordered a plain black coffee. When they received their drinks, he followed her to a small round table nearby.

"I invited you to coffee because I wanted to get to know you a bit better, outside of the classroom, since we're cube mates and all." She smiled, but Gruber wasn't particularly charmed. He hadn't liked her much as a student, and he wasn't inclined to like her now.

Well, too bad, he'd wanted to say, distaste curling the corners of his mouth. Instead, he asked, "What are you working on?" That always seemed to be a safe topic of conversation; it was his go-to. It didn't make him popular at parties, but at least it kept him from standing silently in the corner, awkward and self-conscious.

"I'm the new botulism subject matter expert," she said. "Right now, I'm working on surveillance and—"

Gruber cut her off, his eyes alight and hungry. Of course she was the bot expert, she had the snobbish air one would expect from a rare disease doctor, always thinking their particular area of interest was somehow more fascinating than the more common pathogens like E. coli *or* Salmonella. *Well, at least he could benefit from what knowledge she did have, even if it was narrow. He didn't love working with colleagues as a rule, but getting information from her this way now would be faster and more convenient than trying to look it up later. "I'm working on a model for a rare enteric disease, and I'm having trouble with a few pieces of the equation. As the subject matter expert, I hope to receive your professional opinion on some of the variables I'm using."*

She smiled, surprised at the abrupt switch in the conversation. "Sure, but you should know bot doesn't really act like many other diseases, rare or not."

"Sure, sure, but I think your expertise could help confirm my own hypotheses."

"Okay, then. How much background do you need on bot?" Samantha asked.

Gruber gulped, sending his Adam's apple bobbing furiously. "Let's start with the basics. I know enough, but it never hurts to refresh my memory."

She smiled and took a sip from her drink, and Gruber imagined the sickly-sweet sugar concoction dripping down her throat. "Sure. Well—and please stop me if I'm telling you things you already know—botulism is a very rare disease, with fewer than one hundred cases per year. It's caused by the botulinum toxin. I should mention that lots of people willingly inject a medically produced and diluted version of the toxin into their bodies for cosmetic enhancement in the form of Botox, which will paralyze the targeted muscles but does not cause systemic botulism. In nature, the toxin is produced by spores, which are present all over, especially in the dirt. Normally the spores are dormant, but when exposed to an anaerobic environment, they germinate and produce the toxin."

Gruber nodded along, sipping his coffee, trying not to look too impatient. "Okay, sure, I knew most of that already," he said.

She looked slightly taken aback but recovered quickly. "What next? Okay, symptomatology. People with botulism tend to have gastrointestinal upset—vomiting, diarrhea, cramping, you know—difficulty swallowing, droopy eyelids, and blurry vision. The severity of the symptoms is really dose-dependent, although even a tiny amount of toxin can kill. Ultimately, without treatment, a person will die of suffocation as the toxin attacks their neurons and paralyzes their muscles. Antitoxin can help slow the progression enough for people to regrow neural connections and recover, but it's not a cure."

She paused, considering again. "What am I leaving out? Oh, right—how do most people get botulism. Well, you've probably heard people say home-canning food can be dangerous, or not to store baked potatoes in aluminum foil, or not to give kids under the age of two honey—that's all because of the risk of botulism. More and more, though, we're seeing cases pop up in black tar heroin users."

Gruber looked up, puzzled. Finally, she was giving him some new information. "Black tar heroin users? Why?"

Her lips curled up in a delighted grin. "It's pretty fascinating, actually. Most heroin— the white kind—comes from China. Black tar heroin, on the other hand, comes from Mexico. The heroin there is processed with dirt, and that's what makes it black. The botulism spores are in the dirt mixed with the heroin, but that's not enough to cause botulism on its own. You still need an oxygen-free anaerobic environment—which heroin users create when they skin-pop."

Gruber wasn't familiar with that term, which irked him. He was about to inquire further, but she preemptively explained, "They inject themselves under the skin instead of in the vein, which causes the heroin to be released more slowly and give a longer high. It also creates the perfect environment for the spores to release toxin, and boom. Botulism."

"Wow," he said, mostly to himself. "That's very interesting."

"Isn't it? There's a whole lot more to the story, obviously, but we're still learning. I'm actually starting a new project right now—I'm leading the charge to create the national clinical guidelines for botulism. Because botulinum toxin is a Class A bioterrorism agent that can kill a ton of people with just a tiny quantity, we've been tasked with creating the guidelines so the country as a whole is prepared. There are already guidelines for anthrax and smallpox, and now we'll have some for bot."

Gruber smirked. "You think somebody would actually try to attack the US with botulism?"

She shrugged. "I don't get paid to think about likelihood. Just the response."

"Well—" he started to say something else when Clements looked at her watch and stood up abruptly. "I'm so sorry, Dr. Gruber—I've got another meeting in five minutes and I really need to be going. We didn't even get to discussing your model variables!"

He stood up as well, nearly catching his knee on the underside of the table. He should have been the one to rush off somewhere, not this upstart with her patronizing tone. "It's alright," he said through gritted teeth. "You've been helpful."

"Glad to hear it. Shall we?"

He followed her back toward their department, up the elevator, and through the cube maze to his own cubicle, working out equations in his head all the way.

Now, sitting here in this Savannah square, Gruber found himself hoping desperately the elusive source of the outbreak was botulism. He knew this was a bit of a shitty thing to hope for, considering nine people had died and the Dalcos were likely to follow. If that many people happened onto a bad batch of heroin, there would be more victims on the way.

If and when that happened, he would be ready.

CHAPTER EIGHT

Gruber pushed open the main doors of Savannah's Candler Hospital and tried to head straight for the critical care wing, figuring he could pass through the halls by acting confident, like he belonged, until he found Patricia's room. After all, he'd been in plenty of hospital wings throughout the course of his career—observing patients, interviewing families, meeting with doctors. It should be easy.

Not so. A small woman in pink scrubs, evidently a nurse—her name tag said *Ramona*—stopped him before he'd gone five steps down the main floor hallway. "Sir?" she asked from behind the front desk. "Excuse me, sir, are you looking for a patient?"

He turned around, uncomfortable and increasingly sweaty. He plastered a grin on his face that he thought was natural, but must have looked ghoulish in hindsight, because the nurse's eyes hardened. "Oh, yes, I'm sorry," Gruber said, trying to sound non-threatening as he sidled up to the desk. "I'm here to visit my friend." The lie slipped through his lips before he had a chance to consider the ramifications.

A mirthless smile touched the corners of Nurse Ramona's lips. "And what is your friend's name, sir?"

Gruber paused, his eyes shifting, trying to think of the best way to answer. In the end, there was nothing he could say but the truth. "Patricia," he said. "Patricia Dalco."

"One moment please," Nurse Ramona said, then began clicking through her computer, her fingers typing in short bursts. Sweat trickled down Gruber's back.

Before long, Nurse Ramona's eyes flicked back up to him, now alight with suspicion. *Shit*, Gruber thought. He tried to hold it together as she folded her delicate hands on top of her keyboard. "I'm sorry, sir. Patricia Dalco is not seeing visitors at this time."

Gruber decided to switch tactics. "I'm sorry," he said, summoning up as much sincerity as possible. "There seems to be a miscommunication." He reached into his pocket and pulled out a slim, cracked leather wallet. *Here goes nothing*, he thought. He flipped the wallet open and flashed his CDC badge at her as briefly as possible, hoping she would see the credentials and wave him along. "I'm here with the CDC. I'm sure you're aware of the investigation?" he asked, his palms sweating.

Nurse Ramona nodded gravely, and Gruber thought he saw the ice in her eyes beginning to melt at the edges. "Yes," she said slowly. "I am aware."

Gruber nodded. "Good. Then you understand how careful we have to be," he said, trying subtly to make the entire situation feel above her pay grade, which it surely was. Maybe that would make her back off. "I'm an epidemiologist, and I need to see Patricia Dalco. We're trying to keep things quiet—we don't want to cause a panic. I'm sure you understand?"

The suspicion didn't leave her eyes, and Gruber held his breath. In his pocket, his phone vibrated with an incoming email. He'd logged today as another sick day, but he hadn't emailed Commander Clements. She'd been pinging him all morning, trying to check in. He'd ignored every message, hoping she would stop and think he was sleeping off a fever or otherwise engaged in the business of healing.

"May I see your badge again, sir?" Nurse Ramona asked.

Gruber sighed and handed over his wallet. She examined the badge carefully, no doubt taking in his name. He'd already caused enough of a scene here—he would surely be remembered. *Goddamnit.*

Finally, after what felt like ages, she handed his wallet back, along with a clipboard trailing a pen. "Please sign in," she said. As Gruber wrote his name on the check-in sheet—no way he could lie about his identity now—she continued, "Patricia Dalco is in room 313. Up the elevators to the third floor, then turn right."

Gruber was shaky and anxious, but he tried not to show it. He clipped the yellow "Visitor" pass Nurse Ramona handed him onto his shirt pocket, swiveled on his heel, and headed for the elevators. He didn't exhale until the doors shut firmly behind him.

*   *   *

Patricia Dalco was so thin Gruber could see the ridges of her hipbones jutting from beneath her faded hospital gown. The gown was a bilious green color, which, to Gruber's horror, almost perfectly matched Patricia's skin. A flexible plastic breathing tube snaked out of her taped lips and off to the side, where it fastened to the only machine keeping Patricia alive. His throat ached in sympathy.

Gruber clasped and unclasped his hands in front of him. Now that he was here, staring down at Patricia Dalco, he wasn't quite sure what to do. His EIS contact had given him all the pertinent clinical information, and clearly Patricia's status hadn't changed much in the last week. Her chest rose and fell, pathetically artificial, reminding him of his father's last days in hospice.

Sweat tickled Gruber's armpits. He felt more alone than usual, and powerless, and, for once, stupid. This entire hero narrative he'd constructed around himself was painfully childish. Forty-one was too old to go running around hunting bad guys. Even if the bad guy was a bacterium. Or a virus. Or a toxin.

Gruber sighed, loudly. The idea that the outbreak could be botulism was still stuck in his mind, playing on repeat like an ear worm. He couldn't let it go, but he was also becoming increasingly aware he had reached a dead end.

59

These two thoughts were playing an agonizing tug-of-war in his mind, which manifested physically in the clasping and unclasping of his sweaty palms.

Not wanting to despair, because that seemed such a pitiful action, but doing just that nonetheless, Gruber plopped down into a hard plastic chair at Patricia's bedside. He glanced at his watch (it had barely been three minutes), then over at the jumble of Patricia's personal items piled on the room's only table: a ragged pocketbook, the fake leather peeling; a scuffed tube of lipstick; a folded pile of filthy clothes; a single high-heeled shoe. He rested his chin in his hands and immediately regretted it, pulling his face up quickly with disgust, his jaw moist. Mid-recoil, he paused abruptly.

His eyes narrowed. He wasn't sure how he'd missed it before, or how the legion of nurses, doctors, and his own CDC colleagues had failed to see it… unless it hadn't been there before, and someone else had deliberately placed the crumpled wad in Patricia Dalco's cramped fist?

Gruber's shoes squeaked on the linoleum as he tiptoed to Patricia's side. He pried her fingers apart and pulled out the treasure clutched within. Her skin was dry and papery, and he suppressed a shudder.

The wad was a piece of thin paper, folded many times over, so worn that the edges had grown furry. With trembling fingers, Gruber pulled it apart.

"Come to Gullywasher's of Georgia" screamed up at him in circus-block letters from a white background. Denim-blue waves lapped around the edges of the flyer. Alligators and starfish, dolphins and roller coasters, cotton candy and blue-and-white striped boxes of popcorn danced below the invitation.

A memory slapped at the back of Gruber's eyeballs; he closed his eyes, and he was transported back to 1986. He was eight years old, having just moved to Savannah from the blight of Detroit. His hair was still thick on his head, his skin glowing with the health of childhood. His father took him to Gullywasher's to cheer him up after having uprooted him from the painful but familiar Michigan snowscape. Gruber Senior wanted to show his son the dolphin show, ride with him on the roller coasters, and maybe, if he was good, share some cotton candy. After the dolphin show, with his fingers sticky from the cotton candy, he and his father walked toward the alligator pit.

He did not like that pit, not one bit. Around the pit, spectators were screaming with fear or shock or delight, he wasn't sure. To him, it all just sounded like pain. Below the screaming, he could hear booming thwaps and angry splashes. The mingled smells of blood and sulfur burned his nostrils.

He started to cry. His father pulled him roughly away by the elbow, muttering under his breath about how *It's just a show,* and *Jesus Christ, stop crying* and *You're almost ten years old, get a fucking grip, you little coward.* He shoved a sticky thumb into his mouth and sucked the last grains of sweetness from his skin, stumbling in his father's wake…

Gruber snapped his neck left, then right, blinking hard. His mouth tasted foul; he realized he'd been sucking on his thumb. The rotten, cheesy smell of his own body odor coated his taste buds, and he fought the urge to gag.

He yanked his thumb out of his mouth and wiped it on his shirt. He was still holding the flyer in his other hand. Now that the painful flash of memory had dissipated, he tried to approach this piece of evidence more clinically. *I can do this.* He repeated the mantra again and again in his head until he believed it.

He turned the paper over, and found three words:

Leona. Good shit.

CHAPTER NINE

The call came in as Commander Samantha Clements was sitting at her desk, checking and re-checking her email for something from Gruber. She'd seen the second sick day request come through early that morning, but he hadn't emailed her directly, and she was getting worried. If it wasn't like him to be sick, it certainly wasn't like him to ignore her messages.

Sam answered her phone greedily, expecting Gruber to be on the other end.

"Hello, this is Commander Samantha Clements," she said into the receiver.

"Hello, Commander, this is Nancy Trello from the CDC hotline center. I have a Ramona Carson on the line who says she has information about one of your subordinates, a Dr. Archibald Gruber. Would you like to be connected to Nurse Carson?"

Sam was taken aback—why would a nurse be calling her? Was Gruber so sick he was in the hospital? "Yes, please, connect me," Sam said eagerly.

The line beeped, and Sam heard a woman's voice say, "Hello?"

"Hello, Nurse Carson. This is Commander Samantha Clements with the CDC. I hear you have information about Dr. Archibald Gruber?"

The woman on the other end sounded relieved. "Yes, Commander. My name is Ramona Carson, and I'm a nurse at Candler Hospital in Savannah, Georgia."

When she paused to gather her thoughts into a coherent sentence, Sam prodded, "And what are you calling about today, Nurse Carson?"

"Well, this may sound silly, but this morning an epidemiologist claiming to be from the CDC showed up to see a patient, specifically a patient involved in a recent outbreak that some of your people investigated. Which wouldn't have been strange, except he tried to get past me at first by telling me he was this patient's friend, which was clearly untrue."

"That's highly unusual," Sam said, a frown creasing her forehead as she tried to keep the shock out of her voice. "This man's name was Archibald Gruber?"

"Yes, that's what his badge said. He also had this pretty distinctive watch with a big black face he kept fiddling with. I'm not sure if that helps, but I think it's worth mentioning."

Sam inhaled sharply. That was definitely Gruber, and he was clearly up to something—but what? "I see. Which patient was he visiting?"

The nurse paused before saying, "Patricia Dalco."

Sam froze. Just what exactly did Gruber think he was doing visiting a patient like Patricia Dalco without authorization? This was not the sort of thing the Gruber she knew would ever do—violate protocol so flagrantly, lie to his superiors, act impulsively and foolishly. For God's sake, the man was putting his entire career in jeopardy to—what? Insert himself into the Savannah investigation, and in secrecy no less? As his superior, Sam was furious, but as his former student and longtime colleague, she was concerned—for his livelihood, for his safety, for his mental health.

For now, though, Sam needed to keep things quiet while she figured out what Gruber was doing—and that meant placating a rightfully suspicious nurse.

"Oh, yes, of course," Sam said, clearing her throat. "Just to set your mind at ease, Dr. Archibald Gruber is indeed an epidemiologist with the CDC, working on an investigation. I very much appreciate your call, and I'll be in contact with Dr. Gruber. He likely didn't want to call attention to his CDC connection in this sensitive matter." Not a lie, but not the whole truth, either.

"Okay, thank you," the nurse said. "As far as I know, Dr. Gruber is still in the ICU room with the patient. Should I be worried?"

Sam answered too quickly, "No, of course not. Thank you again for your help."

"You're welcome," the nurse said, her tone wary.

"You have a nice day now, Nurse Carson," Sam said, hanging up the phone and praying for a good plan to come to mind.

*   *   *

Sam sighed, trying to decide on the right course of action as she replayed the conversation in her head. She was flabbergasted. Not only had Gruber lied about feeling unwell the day before, but he had also skipped on over to Savannah and paid an unofficial and unauthorized visit to a patient in critical condition, in flagrant disregard of CDC protocol and the EIS team's ongoing outbreak investigation.

What the hell?

Sam's first thought had been whoever the nurse at Candler had spoken to wasn't actually Dr. Gruber, but an impostor with a decent fake CDC badge. Why a stranger with no connection to the CDC investigation would go to so much trouble to watch a person on a breathing machine was beyond her. Sam had to consider the alternate possibility: the real Gruber was at Candler. Given the nurse's description of that watch Sam was convinced Gruber loved more than any living human being and the fact that Gruber wasn't at his cubicle, where he should be, she started to grow uncomfortably confident Gruber had actually forced his way into Patricia Dalco's room under false pretenses. Why?

Sam stood up and began to pace around the perimeter of her office. Gruber had always been a closed-off guy, not the sort of person you'd want to bring along to a barbecue. When he attended staff picnics or events, he always looked out of place; he stood awkwardly at the periphery of groups lost in conversation, holding his paper plate of food high up to his face, his shoulders hunched. When he did speak, it was all shop talk. People knew his name, but they definitely didn't know *him*. Sam knew that even she didn't really know Gruber, despite working closely with the man for over a decade and, in the distant past, being his student. For some reason, the thought made Sam shiver.

Maybe Gruber just had an innocent scientific interest in the case? If that were so, Gruber would have gone through the proper channels to learn more. He wouldn't have just taken off like he did. *Maybe he felt the EIS team was working too slowly, and he could work faster?* That didn't feel quite right either, but Sam thought she was getting closer to the truth.

A memory floated to the forefront of her mind as she continued to pace. Four years ago, she and Gruber had both attended a debriefing session held by an EIS officer returning from a particularly nasty hepatitis outbreak in North Dakota. As the EIS officer spoke, Sam watched Gruber out of the corner of her eye. The man was furiously scribbling in his notebook, a scowl on his face. Sam tilted her head and managed to read the words *Clearly a point-source outbreak* and *Drug diversion* and, in smaller, cramped script, *I could have done better*. That last sentence chilled Sam then, and it completely iced her now.

Maybe Gruber thought he could solve this on his own? Sam stopped pacing. If Gruber had gone this far, misrepresenting himself and the CDC and lying to his supervisor, what else would he do to be the hero? Maybe Lucas had been right about Gruber after all—he was too much of a loner.

Sam may not have loved Gruber the man, but she respected Gruber the epidemiologist. If Sam could corral Gruber before he did too much damage to his reputation, or, God forbid, broke any laws, maybe she could save his career.

When Sam picked up the phone again a few minutes later, it was to inform her superior, Dr. Theodore Lucas, Director of the Division of Foodborne, Waterborne, and Environmental Diseases, that she was headed to Savannah to support Dr. Gruber, who had been dispatched as a consultant the day before. She didn't really want to get Lucas involved—he didn't like Gruber, didn't understand him, and on top of that, Lucas was a bit of a creep. On the other hand, without Lucas, she might be putting her own career on the line, and she didn't think that was something Gruber would do for her. Plus, she would need extra help locating Gruber and bringing him back quickly and quietly, with her other colleagues none the wiser. So, when Lucas decided to accompany her, and, even worse, to drive her, Sam dreaded the ordeal to come, hoping she could keep him in the dark.

*   *   *

Sam's history with Lucas was short but troubling. One afternoon several months prior, not long after Lucas became her supervisor, Sam was reading through her student researcher's latest analysis when an urgent message from Lucas popped up with a ping in the corner of her screen.

THEODORE LUCAS: Hi, how's it going? :)

At the time, Sam hadn't known much about Lucas other than his name and his title. She definitely wasn't sure why he was contacting her, much less through instant message and using such a casual tone. What the hell was with the smiley face? She typed out her response warily.

SAMANTHA CLEMENTS: Hello, Dr. Lucas. It's going well. How are you?

His reply was lightning-quick.

THEODORE LUCAS: I'm very well, thank you. So, you're the botulism subject matter expert?

She relaxed—talking about bot was her happy place.

SAMANTHA CLEMENTS: That I am, at your service. Is there something I can help with?

THEODORE LUCAS: Yes, actually. Could I possibly get your cell number?

Sam's eyes widened and she frowned involuntarily. Why would Lucas need her number? He was already messaging her, he had her email, and, for goodness' sake, he could just walk over to her cube if he had an urgent question. What could he be after, really? She wasn't sure what to say to that, so she leaned again on her professionalism.

SAMANTHA CLEMENTS: If there's something urgent, I can always come to your office. Would that be better?

THEODORE LUCAS: It's not urgent, exactly…

Sam squinted at the screen as Lucas continued to type.

THEODORE LUCAS: We might discuss this over dinner.

Sam's entire body went cold. She had heard enough in her career to know this 'dinner' was code for something she wasn't going to like, and anger boiled deep in her belly. She'd never wanted to do anything more at CDC than excel at her job. She wasn't looking for a man in a position of power to step down and acknowledge her, much less bring her with him to the top. She knew of others who had thought the short-term benefit was worth the years of whispers, but it wasn't. Who was this man to turn the CDC, the pinnacle of her career accomplishments, into a pickup bar? She typed out a reply.

SAMANTHA CLEMENTS: I'm sorry, Dr. Lucas. I'm afraid I'm not available.

She didn't hit Send yet. Something stilled her furious fingers. After all, she was single. In her experience, most men were intimidated by an intelligent, competitive, career-driven woman. She hadn't had much luck in love lately, and her schnauzer could only alleviate her loneliness so much. If she really considered the possibility, Lucas was distinguished, maybe even fairly handsome for someone a dozen or more years her senior.

So… why the hell not?

She deleted her first response and retyped, but still didn't hit Send. He was her boss, for God's sake.

Suppose she followed through with this 'dinner,' and things went poorly? She loved her job at CDC, and she didn't want to open the door to any awkward personal interactions, whispered gossip, or anything else that might tarnish her reputation. Her finger lingered over the Enter key… and then traveled to Delete. She typed something that struck a balance between cordial and professional.

SAMANTHA CLEMENTS: I'm a bit uncomfortable with that. I hope you can understand.

There was a long pause, and Sam's palms started to sweat. Had she just made a huge mistake?

THEODORE LUCAS: Of course. I understand completely. My apologies for putting you on the spot like that. I just thought it might be more convenient.

Sam heaved a sigh of relief and typed quickly.

SAMANTHA CLEMENTS: No worries.

Lucas hadn't responded after that, and Sam knew she'd made the right choice. Rising in the ranks through dalliances with superiors was not her style.

Since then, she'd been scrupulous to maintain the normal boss-employee relationship—regular check-ins, one-on-ones, that sort of thing—but Lucas didn't make things easy, despite his 'apology.' Glances that lasted a moment too long, his fingers grazing hers as he handed her a report, stopping by her cube randomly and complimenting her appearance. His behavior was just enough to irritate her, but not enough to go to HR or complain to Lucas' own superiors. What would she say? That he was nice to her? That he held eye contact for too long? His reputation at CDC was pristine. The folks in HR would label her 'difficult,' and it would follow her around for the rest of her career.

She was glad she hadn't indulged her momentary weakness all those months ago and agreed to that 'dinner.' That would have been disastrous, given how creepy he'd become. Sam was nervous about being alone with Lucas for an extended period of time, but she was more nervous about Gruber's rogue actions and about compromising her own career. She'd just have to handle Lucas as best she could.

CHAPTER TEN

As Gruber walked past the hospital reception desk, the flyer stuffed deep into his pocket, he noticed the nurse looking at him with a mixture of curiosity and suspicion. He tried on a smile that was more of a sneer, and the nurse's gaze shot down to her hands.

He checked his watch, then turned right out of the hospital and started down Reynolds Street. He had no desire to walk the three and a half miles back to his hotel, but he desperately needed some air, and he did his best thinking when he was moving.

A sharp panic barreled through him, and he stuffed his hand into his pocket to ensure the flyer was still there, that he hadn't imagined it. He felt instant relief when his fingers brushed the frayed creases of the paper, and he pulled it out. As he remembered, the back was adorned with three cryptic words: *Leona. Good shit.*

Now, what could that possibly mean? Leona was obviously a name. He had a location—Gullywasher's. That place must have been out of commission for over a decade; he remembered seeing farewell commercials on TV. Why would anybody go there, much less have a flyer for a defunct theme park clutched in one paralyzed fist?

He refocused on the last two words. *Good shit.* If this outbreak really was due to botulism, specifically heroin-related botulism (as he was starting to believe even more based on Patricia Dalco's injection sites), then what else could *Good shit* mean? Gruber frowned in contemplation, testing the idea, weighing its probability. In the narrative he was concocting for Patricia Dalco, it seemed very plausible that she and her brother had gone to Gullywasher's to find this drug dealer named Leona to get a fix of her *Good shit* heroin. Then, of course, the botulism set in. After all, wouldn't an abandoned theme park be a great place for a drug dealer to hide, and to ply her trade without attracting unwanted attention?

His fists clenched in anticipation. Sweat dripped from the tip of his nose, splattering on his shirt as he walked. Car engines revved around him, drivers mired in stop-and-go traffic, but the cacophony felt distant. All he could see were the words on the flyer, beating a tattoo in his brain.

There was no more time to waste; he needed to get to Gullywasher's and find the evidence he needed before Commander Clements got too antsy about his absence. He was already pushing it, being out of the office for two days.

If he could get a sample of this *Good shit*, then he could have it analyzed for the toxin. He could solve the puzzle of the outbreak, something a whole team of EIS officers failed to do, and he could do it without even seeing the official toxicology reports, which still weren't ready.

He'd be a hero again. After all, he knew he was right.

*　*　*

The next time he looked up from the weirdly hypnotic flyer, Gruber found himself at the corner of Reynolds and Park Lane. He'd walked over two and a half miles. Sucking in a breath, he checked his watch; an hour had passed. Sweat poured from his armpits, soaking his shirt nearly to the waist.

Behind him was a seedy-looking church, a one-story depressing affair that, if anything, made him want to turn away from whatever God would force his people to worship in such a place. He looked to his left and saw a sign for "Hearse Ghost Tours." *Jesus Christ*, he thought. *This town loves its ghosts way too much.*

Now that he was aware of his surroundings once again, he recommitted to the idea that he would not be walking all the way back to his hotel. What he needed was a cold shower, a change of clothes, maybe a quick lunch. Then, when he was refreshed, he'd find a cab that would take him to an abandoned amusement park in the middle of the woods.

He waited on the corner for a few minutes before spotting a taxi. Seeing the wave of his arm, the taxi driver pulled over and he climbed in.

"The DeSoto, please," he said.

The cabbie turned around, appraising him. "Hey! I remember you! You're the guy who hadn't heard of what happened down at the DeSoto!"

Gruber tried to make his rude groan sound more like an appreciative sigh. He didn't think he succeeded, but he also didn't think the cabbie cared. His 'Eugene Frasier' name tag swung on the rearview mirror.

"Yes, that's me," he said.

"How you doing, mister?" Eugene asked.

"Um, fine," he said.

"Good, good," Eugene said cordially. He glanced back at Gruber. "You look mighty weary, my friend."

"This heat'll do that," Gruber mumbled.

Eugene chuckled. "Amen, brother."

Gruber was relieved when a silence fell, but Eugene quickly jumped to fill it. "So, what you got planned for the rest of your stay here? Maybe looking into one of those ghost tours?"

"Surely not," Gruber said. "I don't believe in ghosts." He coughed lightly into his fist. "I have some personal plans to keep me busy."

Eugene would not be put off so easily. "Personal plans? Well, let me tell you, man—if you're looking for some personal time, I know a gal who helps arrange such things." The cabbie glanced back again and winked at Gruber. "You just let me know, I'll take care of ya."

Gruber grimaced. "I most certainly will not be needing that kind of help.

And I'm insulted you would ask such a thing."

"Woah, man—I didn't mean that. It's just—and I'm already in the shithouse with you, so why not push a little further—you look a bit like the kind of guy who might need a pick me up. All I was saying was I know a chick who helps with that. She's a bit of a hike to get to, but everybody says she's got some good shit."

Gruber's head jerked up, the frown evaporating from his face. "What did you say?"

"I said I know a girl who has some good shit."

"I heard that, I'm not deaf," Gruber snapped, impatient. "What exactly does good shit mean to you? And who is this girl?" Gruber paused. "And where is she?"

For the first time, Eugene looked a bit flustered. "Say, you're not a cop or anything, are you?"

Gruber huffed, closing his eyes in frustration. "No, I'm not a cop or anything. Please, just answer my questions. It's important."

Perhaps it was the animal gleam in Gruber's eyes, or the way he was sweating so profusely, or maybe the deathly pallor of his skin. Whatever it was, Eugene's easy demeanor returned, and he gave Gruber another wink. "Tell you what. Let me drive you there. I get a small commission fee for letting you in on this, and in return you get there and back again safely. Sound good?"

"Fine, fine! But you need to tell me her name and where we're going!" Gruber nearly shouted.

"Woah. Okay. So—this is the good shit. Black tar H. I don't ride that horse myself, I just help those who do get back up in the saddle. Gal's name is Leona. She's really something…works out of an old place used to be a theme park. Maybe you've heard of it. Called Gullywasher's…"

Eugene continued talking until they'd pulled up in front of the DeSoto, but Gruber didn't hear anything after Eugene said 'Gullywasher's.' Everything clicked into place, and with a harried, "Wait here," he jumped out of the cab and went to change clothes. Forget the lunch—he was on his way to the land of cotton candy and caramel apples, no matter the degree of decay.

*　　*　　*

Gruber's grooming was perfunctory; he swabbed his sweaty armpits with a wet washcloth, its surface nubby from overuse. He gargled Listerine to avoid the time-consuming task of brushing his teeth, which he hated anyway. The feel of bristle on bone always set him on edge, and he was already vibrating with a mixture of excitement and anxiety. He pulled on a fresh button-down shirt and stepped into a new pair of boxer-briefs, grateful for the airy scent of clean laundry. After sliding into the same pair of pants from that morning, he stuffed a few plastic baggies and a pair of tweezers into his pocket. He didn't want to make the idiotic mistake of finding a sample without the tools to actually capture it properly.

He took one last look in the bathroom mirror, his skin sallow in the yellow light. A new cold sore was bubbling to life at the corner of his lip. He made a mental note to buy some ointment for it on his way back to the hotel, after he'd finished this little errand.

He plunged back into the cool of Eugene's cab. The man gave him a smug glance Gruber really didn't care for, and then they were off, gliding through the tree-lined streets and weaving in between the bucolic squares.

"Oh," Eugene said, breaking the blessed silence. "I forget to mention something."

When he didn't continue, Gruber responded wearily, "And what was that?"

"I handle all the payment for Leona," he said. "She doesn't like to touch the money, so you can just give it to me—plus my commission of course—and I'll square it with her."

"Um," Gruber said, unsure both of what to say and if such an arrangement was normal. "Okay, I guess."

Eugene considered for a moment, his chin upturned. "How much you think you'll want?"

Gruber frowned in confusion. "Uh…a gram?"

A choking, chortling sound ripped out of Eugene's throat, making Gruber jump against the cracked leather of the seat. "Jesus, man," he said. "That's a shit ton of horsepower." Eugene looked to the rearview mirror, studying Gruber. His expression was thoughtful. "Didn't take you for that kind of guy, but hey, we can make it happen."

Gruber brought a hand to his collar and tugged at it, desperate for air. Perhaps this entire mission was foolhardy…what kind of respectable PhD gets into a cab with some disreputable crook who promises to bring him to an abandoned theme park in search of illegal drugs?

The kind with something to prove.

A vision came to Gruber at that moment, as he struggled on the verge of a panic attack in the back of the grubby taxi. He saw himself as an Indiana Jones-type hero, bravely charging forth to face unknown dangers head-on, tackling each challenge with strength, intelligence, and fortitude. He saw Lucas shaking his hand after informing him of his promotion, saw himself walking into his new office and plopping his nameplate on the blond wood desk as Clements and all the others watched in envy…

He snapped back into the present, his panic evaporating as it was replaced by his own fantasy. He may have nothing to lose, but he absolutely had something to prove and everything to gain.

Eugene was talking again as the Georgia pine forest rolled by outside. "Hey, I got another ghost story for ya. You know the land that old park's on used to be a special meeting place for some demon cult?"

Gruber didn't respond, but Eugene was undeterred, as usual. "Yep, some crazy folks would meet in those woods before the park was built and dance around naked. I heard they drank goat blood and did a bunch of other freakish stuff. Rumor has it they also did some sacrificing back there."

Eugene paused for effect even though he didn't need to—Gruber was already terrified. "Human sacrifice. They only stopped because some reporter was down here when this little girl was taken and wrote a story about it. It was in all the papers, and some folks even got arrested."

Gruber finally spoke. "I never heard of that."

Eugene sized him up in the rearview mirror. "Of course not, you were probably too young." He lowered his voice to a growl. "I heard they pulled off all of her fingernails before they killed her."

Nausea rose in Gruber's throat, and his fingers grasped for the door handle. What was he doing? He could still turn around, check out of the hotel, return to Atlanta, get back to his cubicle…but no. If he had to spend another day in that gray box, he'd suffocate. As gruesome and dangerous as this mission was becoming, it was still preferable to the unbearable stagnation that had become his life in Atlanta.

Eugene's voice returned to its normal cheerful timbre. "How you think those Gullywasher folks got all that land so cheap? Nobody else wanted it. In fact, the good people of this city *wanted* better memories there. Newer ones. Happens all the time here in Savannah. But something stays behind, ya know, no matter how much you build on top or how deep you bury it."

He exited the highway, and Gruber caught a glimpse of a faded sign. Gullywasher's of Georgia.

"We're here," Eugene said, pulling to a stop near an old guardhouse with an arched entrance. The cabbie shifted, turning to face Gruber. "Now," he said, "about that money."

CHAPTER ELEVEN

Eugene didn't lie about the cult, but the evil didn't *start* with the cult. That land was *hungry* before the naked dancers, their hearts burning with rage, drank blood and dug the pit to store people before they hurt them. The land acquired a taste for panic, for pain, for human flesh, for *terror*—the most filling food it had ever found. It tricked and cajoled and promised the fulfillment of those deepest desires to whomever it wanted most, whomever would provide the most delicious bite of fear, or whomever would do its bidding.

The weak fed it with sharp terror; the strong with enduring flesh; the wicked with piquant loathing. The land grew powerful, it grew *hungrier*, and it developed clever ways to draw its meals to it. The land lured the people with their demonic god into its depths, where it feasted on their evil as the people brought it more and more fear through their sacrifices. The land developed a particular taste for eyes, helping it see inside the fearful humans, where the sweat-salty globs of terror clustered like exquisite caviar.

The land changed as the times changed, switching one tactic for another when the demon worshippers stopped coming. There were lean years before the theme park people arrived, hooked on an idea and as ravenous for money as the land was for sustenance.

There were decades of good times, of screams sucked away as children rode the rollercoasters, of fear gobbled like popcorn from the alligator audience, and rare gems of hatred speckled throughout. The darkness in the park grew fat and got too greedy; it picked a little boy off the roller coaster and made a sacrifice of him.

The land had overstepped. The park declined, and the food supply distanced itself.

When the park eventually closed, the land, for the first time in its long, long life, was afraid.

It was afraid of starving.

…But not for long. The land simply changed course again, reaching out to the people it needed, the food it *wanted*.

And it grew fat yet again.

CHAPTER TWELVE

In Atlanta, Sam's phone jingled with a text just as she was zipping up her bulging overnight bag, stuffed with jeans, walking shoes, toiletries, makeup, a suit (just in case—always err on the side of professionalism), and a pair of heels.

THEODORE LUCAS: I'll swing by to pick you up in about half an hour. Does that give you enough time to prepare?

SAMANTHA CLEMENTS: Yes. Just finishing packing up now.

Her palms itched with anxiety. How was she going to maintain the facade of 'assisting' Gruber?

She let her mind consider that problem in the background as she changed out of her work clothes from that morning and into something more comfortable—a pair of leggings, a loose, short-sleeved top, and a pair of running shoes. She wasn't at all sure what she was walking into in Savannah, but she thought she should be prepared to run.

She brought her overnight bag to the door and finished her last few preparation rituals. She scooped up her worn but serviceable backpack and stuffed in her laptop, charging cords, wallet, trail mix, and a couple of bananas. She filled her reusable water bottle, taking a minute to chug half of it, and then refilled it to the brim before adding that to the backpack's mesh side pocket. She briefly considered tucking her keychain-sized pepper spray into her pocket—just in case—but decided against it. Surely Lucas wouldn't jeopardize his career by being aggressive with her. If he did get too rowdy, she'd just excuse herself and catch a train or even a short flight back to Atlanta alone. She was perfectly capable of handling Theodore Lucas.

She took a seat on a barstool at her kitchen counter. Shmoo, her miniature schnauzer, let out a whine—he knew what packed bags meant. His favorite person was leaving him, and who knew when she would be back?

"It's okay, Shmoozy," Sam cooed, beckoning the dog toward her. "Annie's going to come over and stay with you while I'm gone. You love Annie!" She gave Shmoo a pet on the head. In response, he rolled over onto his back and presented his belly to rub, as though it were his gift to her.

"Oh, I see how it is," Sam said, rolling her eyes.

Mid-belly rub, she noticed a thin white string hanging from Shmoo's mouth. She sighed, exasperated but amused.

"Shmoo! Have you been rooting around in the trash again? I know you like to have minty fresh breath too, but come on, seriously. This isn't for doggies." She pulled the used wad of dental floss out of Shmoo's mouth without much protest. As she stood up to drop it in the trashcan, she remembered she hadn't yet packed her toothbrush. She ran to get it.

Her sojourn to the bathroom and back, toothbrush in hand, took less than fifteen seconds. Somehow, during that time, she had both gotten a text and failed to hear the corresponding alert jingle from her phone. When she picked up the phone, Shmoo let out a whimper that didn't sound anything like his usual repertoire of noises. Sam absentmindedly patted his head, reassuring him, while she read the text.

UNKNOWN: This weekend only! 75% off admission price to Gullywasher's of Georgia!

The name thrummed a chord in her memory, the sound flat and discordant. She moved to delete the text, but the name Gullywasher's reverberated back and forth, back and forth in her mind. She was just about to Google it when Shmoo let out that queer, unsettling whimper again. Her mouth scrunched into a frown. Why would some random number bother to text her with a discount offer to an amusement park she'd never been to before? Maybe—

Shmoo barked, alerting her to Lucas's arrival.

* * *

"You all ready to go?" Lucas asked when she opened the door.

"Yep!" she said, trying to mask the dread she felt.

"Let's move!" he said, shouting to be heard over the indignant schnauzer.

"Okay, let me just leave a note for the dog-sitter," Sam said, shutting the door and scrambling for a pen and paper. After jotting down a few quick notes about Shmoo's new diet, she lured the schnauzer into the laundry room with a treat.

"I'll be back in just a few days, Shmoozy," she said, tossing the treat onto his bed. "Don't worry! Annie will be here soon to take you on a walk." She knew they were in a hurry to leave, but she couldn't stop herself from walking over to the sweet schnauzer curled up in the dog bed, crunching through the treat. She knelt and gave him a kiss on the head and a hug. He swallowed and looked up at her with his puppy-dog eyes.

"I'll be back before you know it!" she said.

Shmoo whined.

* * *

Five minutes later, she was tucking herself into the passenger seat of Lucas' Jeep Grand Cherokee, her backpack in her lap.

"Finally ready?" he said, raising an eyebrow in a way he might have thought was flirty, but just came off as lewd.

"Finally ready," she said, grimacing.

"And we're off!" He revved the engine and pulled them smoothly away from Sam's house.

She swallowed, hoping he would keep his hands to himself and not ask too many questions about Gruber's mission. The next three and a half hours were bound to be awkward.

Lucas broke the silence, much to her relief. "Well," he said, "what exactly are we heading off to do in Savannah? I've heard about the outbreak, obviously, and I know we're assisting Gruber or something, but more background would be helpful."

So much for dodging questions about Gruber. "Right," she said, growing serious. "About that." She wasn't sure where to start, how to couch things in a way that would make Gruber seem like a rational actor worthy of his position at CDC.

When she didn't continue, he prodded, "Yes. About that."

She sighed. "First off, I want to be clear our superiors know we're heading to Savannah to work on the outbreak."

Another pause. "I know that…" he said, irritation creeping into his voice

"They don't exactly know the circumstances."

"And neither do I, clearly," he said. "So can you let me in on the secret?"

Sam exhaled deeply. He wasn't going to let this go—she might as well come clean. She wasn't sure she could trust Lucas, but she didn't have much of a choice. If she didn't make it clear to him Gruber was not acting under her command, then she might be out of a job herself. Maybe she could use Lucas' interest in her to her advantage, if she could just get him to understand her motivations. First, she had to start with the truth. "So, Dr. Gruber…kind of went rogue."

Lucas frowned. "'Went rogue'? What does that mean?"

"It means Gruber told me he was sick when he was actually on his way to Savannah to investigate the outbreak on his own. I got a call this morning from a nurse at Candler Hospital in Savannah, where Patricia Dalco is being treated. The nurse called because Gruber tried to get in to see Dalco by saying he was her friend. He eventually told her he was with CDC, there to investigate the outbreak. He obviously raised her hackles because she called as soon as he left her desk."

"What?" was all Lucas seemed able to manage, his mouth dropping open into an *O*. Sam understood his feelings—awkward, logical, risk-averse Dr. Gruber going rogue? That made absolutely zero sense.

"Yeah," Sam said, shaking her head. "What indeed."

"I mean—" Lucas paused, collecting his thoughts. "Nice to be let in on the full picture," he said wryly. "What do you think he's doing down there?"

"Like I said, I think he's trying to find all the answers on his own. Why this one, why now, I don't know."

Lucas leaned his head back against the seat, shell-shocked. "Well, this trip just got a whole lot more interesting." He gave her a sideways glance she really didn't care for. "Which is saying something, because it was already interesting."

Sam wasn't sure how to respond to the sudden shift in his tone—she had hoped she'd put all that flirtation nonsense to rest a long time ago. She opened her mouth to say something, but then closed it again.

Lucas shifted back to boss mode. "As I'm sure you know, Gruber's actions make this situation much more complicated. Just what he's done so far could be a terminable offense…"

Sam rushed in to stop his train of thought. "I know that, but obviously Dr. Gruber's onto something. He wouldn't risk his career otherwise. He's an excellent epidemiologist, you know that." Sam paused, chewing a fingernail. "Quite frankly, I don't want to lose him. That's why I decided to go to Savannah personally to try and keep this low-level. That's also why I'm telling you." Sam swallowed down bile that itched at the back of her throat. "I was hoping we could keep this between us, as much as possible."

Lucas took the bait. "I sure don't mind having a secret to share with you." He winked, and Sam resisted the urge to cringe. Shifting back to boss mode again, he said, "Look, Gruber's not my best friend, but I agree with you he's a damn good epidemiologist, and he's saved my ass a few times, too. I'd hate to lose him just because he decided to finally grow a pair for once in his life."

"Wow," Sam said, pulling a bag of trail mix out of her backpack. "That's a bit harsh, but I'm glad we're on the same page." She opened the bag and offered it to Lucas. "Want some?"

"No thanks," he said. "We'll have time to go out to dinner when we get there."

Sam squirmed, feeling whipsawed by his unpredictably shifting demeanor and unsure what a dinner date with her boss while on a clandestine work trip might mean. "Only if we can split the bill."

"Sure, sure. By the way, I went ahead and booked us rooms at one of the hotels in Savannah." When she didn't say anything, he hastily added, "Separate rooms."

Sam squirmed in her seat, her lips puckered with discomfort. "Great, thanks," she mumbled.

Lucas continued unperturbed. "It's a nice hotel close to everything downtown. I know this is a working vacation, but why not try to enjoy Savannah while we can? Actually, can you put the address into my GPS? I've kind of been on autopilot—I know how to get to Savannah itself, but I'm hopeless inside the actual city."

"Sure," she said, pulling up Google Maps on her phone, happy to have a task to distract her from the awkwardness she felt. "What's the name of the hotel?"

"The DeSoto."

*   *   *

"What do you think Gruber is doing right now?" Lucas asked as they reached the outskirts of downtown Savannah, breaking the silence that had lapsed between them off-and-on throughout the hours of driving.

"I don't know," Sam said, wishing the silence would return. Having to constantly think about his double entendres, all while wondering if she'd put herself in a terrible position over Gruber's mess, was exhausting.

"Hm," Lucas mused. "My guess is he's probably holed up in his hotel somewhere, scouring his notebooks and flipping through his charts like he does at his desk."

"Yeah," Sam said. "You're probably right. Although who knows, clearly he can surprise us."

Lucas sighed. "You know he was up for promotion last year?"

"Was he? I didn't know that."

"Yep. I meant to mention it when we were speaking a couple of days ago about the open position. The possibility of his promotion didn't get very far, so we didn't notify you. The medical officer brought him in for a pseudo-interview, just to see how things would go. From what I hear, everybody up above thought he was a shoo-in for the role."

"What happened?"

"The man totally fell apart. He was sweating like a stuck pig and going off on semi-incoherent rants about epidemic curves and point-source outbreaks. The medical officer finally got Gruber out of his office. I think there was even a question of whether Gruber was drunk on the job. For the record, I don't think he was—he's not that kind of guy, that much I know. They didn't end up pursuing that thread, anyway. They just passed him over for promotion and kind of called it even. As you know, he's up again this year, for the Branch Director position. But I still think he's too much of a loner, and a stunt like this doesn't exactly change my mind."

"Jeez. Poor guy." It wasn't fair—he worked so hard, yet he just didn't have the social or leadership skills needed to advance the way he wanted to.

Lucas cleared his throat, his eyes flicking to the dashboard clock. "Well, I'm starving. How about we check in and then head out and see what we can find. I have a hankering for some chicken and waffles."

Sam's stomach rumbled. Maybe he'd back away from the double talk. She dared to hope this trip might actually be bearable. "That sounds pretty good to me, too."

CHAPTER THIRTEEN

The Savannah Tribune, April 3, 2006

EYEBALL FOUND IN OLD THEME PARK MAY BELONG
TO MISSING UNIVERSITY OF GEORGIA SOPHOMORE

Katrina Ryen, 19, was reported missing on Saturday by her boyfriend, Henry Barker, who last saw her at Gullywasher's of Georgia, a theme park that shut its doors last year. Ryen and Barker had planned a long weekend vacation in Savannah, and left the UGA Athens campus in Barker's car on the morning of Friday, March 31. Ryen informed her parents she and Barker would be staying at a friend's place in downtown Savannah.

According to Barker, he and Ryen had almost reached Savannah when she spotted the Gullywasher's of Georgia sign and asked him to take the exit. He said he warned Ryen the park was closed, but she insisted on visiting the property in spite of his protests. During questioning, Barker broke down after admitting he had dared Ryen to look inside the tunnel slide located in the waterpark area of Gullywasher's. He said Ryen climbed to the top of the slide and then simply disappeared.

A police search of the area Saturday afternoon uncovered the remains of a human eyeball, which is currently undergoing DNA testing. No other clues were found to indicate Ryen's whereabouts, but investigators are holding out hope Ryen is still alive. No arrests have yet been made, and Ryen's family has asked anyone with information to please come forward.

CHAPTER FOURTEEN

Leona's first customers from just a month earlier would not have recognized the figure sprawled in the alligator pit muck on this muggy August morning. Gone was the thick lustrous hair. Leona's wandering fingers had pulled out nearly every strand at the root. No more was the smooth golden skin; hours spent inside the aquarium had cast a pall on her complexion. The curves that had, however briefly, distracted shivering drug users from their habit had deflated. Feeling purified rather than grotesque, she had lost interest in food. As a result, she lay withered, like a pallid worm, writhing in the dirt, rooting around for anything good.

When her crow cawed sharply, shattering the stillness, she looked up. Mud coated her left cheek and the side of her nose and forehead, making her look like a black and white cookie.

"Just what the fuck do you want?" she wailed, grime dribbling from the corners of her mouth. She wasn't feeling well, but with her cravings gone, she didn't know how to fix the sickness.

The crow alighted on the side of the pit and stared down at her. It cawed again.

She laid her face back in the slime, which was mercifully cool against her skin. It was still early; the sun hadn't yet removed the dark shadows standing guard over Tarantula. Leona wriggled until she could feel the scaly press of the alligator against her right side.

"Who's my good boy?" she said in a lilting voice as she stroked the mechanical animal.

Tarantula's tail twitched.

Leona wasn't alarmed; he'd been doing this more and more lately. The first time it happened, she'd been sliding around in the muck, gathering what she needed for her customers. She'd heard the crow caw, she'd felt a single raindrop on the tip of her nose, and then she'd seen a slight swish as the great animatronic alligator moved its tail. Sure, she'd been a bit unsettled at the idea of what was essentially an alligator-shaped robot moving on its own, without the power even switched on—but she hadn't been that upset, because the entire situation had been…correct, somehow. In the pit, with the alligator that was a little too alive, she felt safe. She felt home.

Since then, she had come to expect Tarantula's occasional unprompted movements, which were usually accompanied by a caw from her ever-present crow. Often, she laughed in delight at the strange little family that had grown around her.

Today was no different. When she felt Tarantula twitch, she threw back her head and guffawed, completely unselfconscious, her feelings of sickness dissipating. The crow cawed with her, a screeching duet, dissonant notes flung at the hot summer sky as the sun gradually dissolved the protective shadows of the pit.

CHAPTER FIFTEEN

Gruber was wary, then dismayed, then slightly frantic in quick succession after Eugene turned to face him, his hand out and waiting for cash. Gone was the loquacious cabbie; in his place was a grizzled thug.

"Um," Gruber stammered. "How much is it?"

Eugene considered for a moment. "You still think you want a gram?"

"Maybe a half gram?"

"Nah, man—don't start getting cold feet on me. If you want a gram, a gram is what you shall have."

"Alright." Gruber said, checking his watch. There were still plenty of hours of daylight left—he wouldn't be caught here in the dark.

"So…a gram would have to be about $200. Plus, my commission and driver's fee, of course, which would be another $150. All told, we're looking at $350 dollars, my friend." Eugene smiled. Gruber was surprised he hadn't noticed before how sharp the man's teeth were.

Gruber blanched, patting his pocket to check for his wallet. He pulled it out slowly, noting with strong displeasure the hungry look in Eugene's eyes as they followed Gruber's movements. Gruber had no idea if, or how badly, he was being cheated.

"I'm afraid I don't have that much in cash," Gruber said weakly. "How about I just buy whatever…" Gruber paused to count the wrinkled bills. "Whatever $67 can get me?"

Eugene's smile didn't fade. "Afraid not," he said. "Unfortunately, that won't even cover my commission." Eugene tapped a dirty finger to his chin, making a show of being magnanimous. "How about I take that watch of yours there as an insurance policy?"

"Insurance policy?" Gruber echoed, feeling faint.

"Yeah. You give me the watch to hold on to, plus that $67. You go get what you need from in there, you come back out, I drive you back to the DeSoto, you bring me the rest of the cash, and then you get your watch back. Easy as pie, and everybody's happy."

It did indeed sound easy, and what other choice did he really have? The man wasn't taking no for an answer, and Gruber was quickly growing terrified of what could happen if he didn't agree to Eugene's plan. He sighed in acquiescence and lifted his wrist, but his fingers slipped around the clasp. When he finally held the beautiful black-faced watch in his hand, he felt another fiery spark of fear in the center of his chest. This wasn't right.

Despite his misgivings, he pulled the $67 out of his wallet and forked it over to Eugene. The watch remained in his hand.

"And the watch, my friend?" Eugene said, his patience starting to wear thin.

With another sigh, Gruber thrust it toward the driver.

"All set," Eugene said, his smile softening. "Go on, then. I'll wait for you here, but I don't plan to wait around all day. This place gives me the creeps."

Gruber opened the car door with shaky hands and started up the path toward the park.

*　*　*

His wrist felt naked and vulnerable without the comfort of the watch. He moved his arm to examine it more closely, and found he had a pale strip that looked scarred into his flesh where the leather strap had shielded him. He risked another glance back toward the idling taxi at Eugene, who was leaning out the open driver's side window and cleaning his nails with a pocketknife.

Gruber stumbled over broken asphalt and potholes as he traversed the parking lot toward the park. When he reached the edge, he paused to survey what lay ahead.

At the corner of the lot was another sign signaling the entrance. The paint looked less weathered here than it did on the archway over by the guardhouse; if this were a quieter moment, Gruber would have paused to consider what kind of environmental conditions would be necessary to preserve one sign while ravaging the other one just a few dozen feet away. This was not a quieter moment, though; Gruber's restless hands were shaking so hard he swore he could hear his bones rattling.

The sign adorned a leaf-littered walkway. The path was so choked with dark green foliage Gruber couldn't see where it led. Normally, being a cautious man, Gruber would have stopped and considered a map or some other form of orientation. Gruber could no longer stand to be a cautious man, and this was not a normal situation. He plunged onward.

Eugene honked the taxi's horn in either encouragement or impatience; given the man's distasteful character, Gruber hypothesized it was the latter.

He had to sidestep obtrusive trees and lift untidy branches out of the way; one prickly stick scratched his naked wrist. He let out a soft cry, and then felt immediately ashamed. Indiana Jones wouldn't cry from a simple scratch. He wouldn't cry at all—unless there were snakes, of course.

After what felt like an hour, Gruber finally emerged from the claustrophobic path, coming face-to-face with the ticket booths. Beyond the dirty windows and tattered awnings, Gruber could see the Gullywasher roller coaster rising ominously out of the decay. Even decrepit, it was still magnificent.

He stepped closer to the ticket building and paused, considering. Until this moment, he hadn't given much thought to how he would actually find this Leona woman once he was inside the park, and Eugene hadn't given him any guidance. There were no signs; why would there be? Drug dealers didn't tend to announce their presence.

I guess I'll just go in then? Gruber thought. *Even if I can't find her, I'm sure she'll find me. It's not like there's a crowd.*

He was about to move around the ticket building when he caught sight of a scrawled message. He turned to face the soaped-over window and found 'BTH' inscribed from the inside.

Black tar heroin. He'd read enough botulism clinical papers over the past few days to recognize the acronym. If there was any doubt he was in the right place, the crudely drawn letters put that to rest.

He bent his head to check his watch, remembering too late that instead of being safe on his wrist where it belonged, it was hugging the greasy skin of a criminal cab driver.

Unnerved, he moved around the building and was confronted by an ugly concrete channel and a wooden bridge that looked like it was made of toothpicks, and just as strong. *Lazy river,* he thought. A memory sparked behind his eyelids, and when he slid them shut, he saw the Gullywasher's lazy river projected in the darkness, as it was when he'd visited it as a child of eight. The water had been clear, an unnatural yet beautiful aquamarine blue, and the slow current had carried a motley crew of humanity along in fat rubber inner tubes: mothers with wriggling toddlers, teenagers holding hands, newlyweds quarreling, fathers asleep, their hands loosely clasped around sweating Coca-Cola cans. He'd wanted desperately to join the throng, but his father had tugged him away, promising him more interesting things than a 'damned dribble of urine-filled pool water.'

A crow cawed somewhere up ahead, and he snapped his eyes open, feeling dazed by the force of his recollection. Oddly, the air still held the smell of chlorine and popcorn. Gruber breathed deeply and stepped toward the bridge. Surely, whatever he needed lay on the other side.

Nearly at the bridge, his foot came down on a lumpy object and he almost went sprawling, clasping the handrail of the bridge for balance. The bridge groaned at his touch, and Gruber detected a worrying wobble. He gave the railing a stronger push to test its strength; when it didn't collapse, he figured it would do well enough for crossing the measly six feet over the channel.

Looking down, he searched for whatever had upset his stride. Pressed into the ground by his weight was a lone high-heeled shoe, concealed in a clump of weeds.

He shrugged, and with one hand on the railing, he stepped up onto the bridge.

It wobbled again. Gruber took a step, cautious, and then another one. One more step brought him to the bridge's apex.

That step also brought a screeching crack, a deep structural shudder, and, finally, a splintering and violent descent into the trash-lined channel below.

*   *   *

A loud caw assaulted Gruber's ears, and he pried his eyes open. The sun was shining down on him malevolently. He dimly registered his right leg, twisted up underneath him at an improbable marionette angle. He brought his wrist up to his face to check the time, his arm moving in jerks and spasms.

When he once again found a pale strip of flesh where his watch should be, the pain that had been a tickle became a roar. The transition was so sharp Gruber screamed, clenching his eyelids tight against the glare of the sun.

The glare didn't last long—without warning, a shadow blotted out the light. His eyes flew open, but all he could make out was a blurry oval shape, backlit by the sun. He squinted and moved his hand to shield his face, hoping to get a better look.

He wished he hadn't.

The figure staring down at him was bald and ragged and only vaguely feminine. Through the swaths of torn clothes and drying muck, swatches of deathly pale skin glowed. The figure grinned at Gruber, bloodless lips stretching across a jumble of stained teeth. The smile grew wider, reaching from ear to ear, sunken coal-dark eye sockets taunting him with their emptiness.

Gruber slipped into merciful unconsciousness.

CHAPTER SIXTEEN

Puffs of dry dirt exploded under Gruber's heels. Occasionally, an errant chunk of gravel would pass under his limp body and send one or both of his feet popping into the air, before coming back hard onto the arid ground. Gruber was dimly aware he was being dragged. His backside was starting to chafe through the fabric of his pants, and he felt a tense tug on his upper body, under his armpits. He pulled one dangling hand from his lap and touched his chest; a thick strap was threaded underneath his arms. Behind him, in the gathering darkness, he could hear animalistic grunts as whatever had found him took him back to its lair.

*　*　*

Gruber didn't realize he'd lost consciousness again until he was falling. His arms trailed above his head in a brief moment of weightlessness, and then his body slapped with a squelch into what felt like a swamp. When he wrenched open his stubborn eyelids, he could see only inky darkness. He brought his hand within a foot of his face and couldn't make out his own fingers. Had he gone blind? Blinking rapidly, he started to hyperventilate. His leg was a mass of searing pain, collateral damage from the damned bridge's collapse.

Just as he was about to give himself over completely to the panic rising up his parched throat, he saw a glow far up above. He wasn't blind, after all, thank God. The ball of light grew brighter and larger, until he could make out a long torch. He followed the torch from the tip of the flame down, down…

His stomach flipped in dread when he saw the ghostly white hand clasping the wood. The hand moved lower and thrust the torch into the ground. Gruber's eyes traveled from the tips of the pallid fingers, up a thin wrist, a darkly clad arm, a sunken chest, to the mud-covered skull with the bloodless lips that had greeted him hours before. He opened his mouth wide and began to scream.

To his horror, the creature opened its mouth and spoke to him. "Hello, Dr. Gruber," it said. "I've been expecting you."

CHAPTER SEVENTEEN

Leona smiled beatifically down at the broken man lying in the pit below, the light from the torch encircling her bald skull in a halo. She reached one hand up to caress the top of her head and smiled; each day, she was becoming a better version of herself, becoming the queen the park needed, a pure being. She yielded to the park and the park lifted her up, in turn—just like a family.

Poor Dr. Gruber had broken his right leg, that much became clear as she transported him here; jagged edges of broken bone crested above the shredded edges of his pant leg with each divot or bump in the path. A lesser woman might have been squeamish; hell, even Leona might have been squeamish just a few weeks ago. Now, she was changing, and she was used to healing the lowest of the low. Gruber didn't pose much of a challenge.

The man cowering in the mud looked terrified and exhausted. She wanted to offer him whatever comfort she could—in this case, the knowledge he was among friends. Maybe that would at least stop his screaming, which pierced her eardrums like needles.

Leona stood still as Gruber screeched himself hoarse. She wished he could see the park as she did—a saving grace, a vehicle to ultimate transformation—but not everybody could.

When he finally grew quiet, pulling in breaths in great wracking heaves, his eyes rolling in his head, she spoke again. "You're going to be just fine, Dr. Gruber."

Without looking at her, Gruber puled, "No, I won't!"

"Yes, you will. I'm sure of it."

Gruber sat up with difficulty and studied her. "Who are you?" he moaned.

"My name is Leona," she said simply.

Gruber snorted, the force of it sending his head snapping back on his neck. "You're Leona?"

She shrugged. "Yes."

Gruber stared down at his mangled leg. "Jesus Christ."

"I can help you," she offered, but Gruber didn't seem to be listening anymore.

"I'm going to die here," he said flatly.

"No, you're not."

"I'm going to die, and nobody will ever find my body," Gruber said, his voice becoming more and more hysterical as the words tumbled out of his trembling lips. "Nobody will ever know what happened to me, because I was stupid enough to let a criminal take me to this hellhole to meet with a frigging drug dealer. I will die here, and everybody will think I just disappeared, and what will my mother think? She'll never know!" Gruber ended with a squeal; his voice was so high Leona thought only the crow could hear it with any clarity.

At the mention of his mother, a warm gush of sympathy flowed through Leona. She wanted to make him feel better, but his cries were beginning to drown out her thoughts, making her impatient. "Enough!" she yelled. "Enough," she said, more softly. "Dr. Gruber. You will not die here. I can cure you."

Gruber stared up at her, fat tears drawing clean stripes through the grime now coating his face. "I don't think frigging heroin can cure my broken leg." He forced the word 'heroin' out with such hateful force Leona could see globs of spit flying from his blubbering lips.

"I'm not offering heroin," she said.

He squinted warily. "Then what do you want?"

"I want," she said, enunciating each word, "to heal you."

Gruber fell back into the mud, sending a wet splat echoing throughout the pit. Leona knew the look of exhausted resignation gracing Gruber's features well; he was tired of fighting. He would give in now.

"Because you're a scientist, Dr. Gruber," she said loudly, trying to elicit a positive reaction from the broken man below her. "I would like to explain the ritual to you."

Gruber's eyebrows knitted together, so close they were almost kissing. "The ritual?" he said in a small voice.

"It won't hurt," Leona said, even though she knew it would.

* * *

Before Leona could explain, Dr. Gruber slipped back into unconsciousness. Hopefully, he'd be more pliable when he woke up. Plus, this gave her time to prepare everything she needed to satisfy both her and the pale figures in the cylinder, with their insistent, sinuous voices.

Leaving the burning torch thrust into the dirt at the edge of the pit, Leona walked back to the aquarium. The cavernous building was dark except for a blue-black light glowing from the cylindrical tank in the middle of the room. Leona walked forward and placed a hand on the cool glass; she felt a thin but persistent vibration rising through her palm.

The figures had told her the only way to save the good doctor was to use the ritual. Normally, desperate drug users performed it willingly—she would mix up the medicine in the pit, and they would shoot up without hesitation. Leona could tell that for Dr. Gruber, force might be necessary.

Her bare feet slapped against the cement as she walked toward the empty tanks on the wall that held one ingredient of the medicine. She secreted one bag of white powder amidst her rags. A twig snapped somewhere outside; she paused, curled protectively around the bag in her clothes, snarling like a cornered animal. At the doorway, her crow cawed.

"Shut up, stupid bird," she mumbled.

The crow did not respond, only perched on the leaf-littered ground, peering in at her impassively.

She stumbled out of the doorway, ignoring the crow, and walked back to the pit. Her skull bobbed through the humid night air like flotsam adrift in a roiling sea.

When she reached the pit, she peered down and saw Dr. Gruber was still unconscious, sprawled in the slime like a slug. As quietly as she could, she tiptoed to the ladder and descended. When her grasping toes found the cool mud, she slipped down with a sigh of pleasure. What a gift it was to be in the pit. Soon, Dr. Gruber would think so, too.

She slid through the mud like an eel. Dr. Gruber didn't move, even when she leaned over him. That was good. She slipped a hand into her clothes and brought out the bag of white powder, pulling it open in silence. She licked her finger and dipped it into the bag. When she pulled it out again, her fingertip was coated in tiny white crystals; they looked like sugar.

With relish, she thrust her finger into her mouth and sucked. Her tongue undulated as she swished the powder around, using her saliva to turn it into a slurry. When she'd gotten the right consistency, she leaned over Dr. Gruber and spat, the fat white glob landing on the bridge of his nose and dripping down the sides to pool in what would have been smile lines on a different man, but were frown lines on his. He finally stirred.

His hands went to his face and he started feeling around. He sat up, blinking at his fingers.

Finally, he asked, "What did you do to me?"

Leona shrugged. "We're starting the ritual."

He was still calm as he said, "What was that? What's on my face?"

"Medicine," she replied with another shrug.

Despite the gravity of his situation, he managed to roll his eyes. Leona almost laughed, but restrained herself before the sound escaped her lips. The moon was heavy in the sky; they needed to get started before it was too late.

"Dr. Gruber," she said, shuffling back so he could look at her without having to twist. "This is part of the medicine," she said, lifting up the powdery bag for him to see. "It helps a little, but I have to mix it up just right for it to work all the way." As she said the words, she felt more like a ventriloquist's dummy than a full-fledged human being; sentences flowed through her from the lips of an unseen presence. She was grateful; so often, especially after the worst beating she'd gotten from her shitbag boyfriend, words didn't come out the way they should. She was coming to realize she didn't need to worry about that ever again.

Gruber didn't say anything; he just kept blinking, his mouth frozen in a frown.

"This pit," she said, "has special... properties." He was a scientist; she—or, more accurately, the hidden ventriloquist—wanted to sound as scholarly as possible, out of respect. "When I mix the essence of the pit with this powder, it can cure just about anything." She gestured toward the ruin of his right leg. "Even that."

He remained silent.

"First," she said, a smile stretching across her thin face, "I want you to meet Tarantula."

CHAPTER EIGHTEEN

The Savannah Tribune, June 15, 2007

17-YEAR-OLD RUNAWAY POSSIBLY HEADED FOR DEFUNCT THEME PARK

George Bigby, of Charleston, was reported missing by his foster family on June 10. His foster father, Sam Anderson, said, "George is troubled, sure. He's run away a few times, but he's a good kid." The Anderson family did not contact the police until a week after George left their home. "He always comes back. We keep thinking he'll walk back through the door any minute now," Anderson said.

Police traced George's most recent movements through his cell phone. They believe he hitchhiked from Charleston to Savannah, where he was last seen in a coffee shop on Broughton Street. One shop employee, Leticia Grange, told police George had been agitated when she saw him. "The kid ripped something off of our community bulletin board, then posted up in a corner where he started talking on his cell phone. I don't know what he said, but eventually I had to ask him to leave because he was blocking the bathrooms," Grange said.

When investigators examined George's phone records, they found this last call was to the defunct Gullywasher's of Georgia theme park. Further investigation indicated the Gullywasher's phone number has been disconnected for nearly two years.

Based on his cell phone data, George's last known location was on the exit ramp toward Gullywasher's. A search of the area yielded no further evidence.

Police are encouraging the public to come forward with any information they might have that could help locate George.

CHAPTER NINETEEN

Sam lifted her fork to chuck the last bite of syrup-soaked waffle into her mouth. The restaurant Lucas had chosen, Rhett, was every bit as good as the online reviews suggested, and the food was putting her at ease. Maybe this time with Lucas wouldn't be as bad as she'd expected, after all.

"That was so good," Sam said, swallowing.

Lucas smiled. "Fun fact about me: picking out restaurants is one of my many talents."

Sam raised an eyebrow, hoping this conversation wouldn't go down a sleazy path. "Oh, really?"

He swept a hand around the restaurant. "Isn't it obvious?"

Sam chuckled. If he was being genuine, then maybe they could actually be work-friends—professional but cordial.

When the check came, as promised, Lucas split it with her. She was pleased with his respect of her boundaries, but at the same time she was on edge, wondering if he was just biding his time.

* * *

Outside, the evening was warm, with stars just beginning to blink on in the sky. A breeze caressed their faces as Sam and Lucas walked back to the DeSoto.

"So," Sam said. "We haven't discussed what to do about Gruber."

"What a mess," Lucas said sleepily. "If he lied to you about being here, then it's safe to say he doesn't want to be found."

"You're probably right, but that doesn't mean we shouldn't try to clean this up before anybody else finds out. We need a plan." As much as she loathed the situation, they were in it together.

"Maybe you could send him an email," said Lucas. "Let him know you're in Savannah because there's been a new development in the outbreak investigation, and you'd like his help if he's available."

Sam nodded slowly. "That could work, but he hasn't answered any of my other emails. Plus, do I want him to realize I know he's already here?"

Lucas considered, his steps veering a bit too close to hers. "I'm sure he's looking at your emails, even if he's not responding. A guy like that can't just cut himself off from work, trust me. And I don't think you need to tip him off that you know he's here. Make it seem sympathetic, like you know he's not feeling well but you could really use his expertise on site."

"Hm. Yeah. I could try that."

Lucas' hand brushed hers, and she pulled her fingers away quickly. "Why not, right? We don't have anything to lose, but he certainly does."

Sam was quiet a moment, then said, "I wonder if he sees it that way."

They turned right onto Whitaker Street and continued walking. To their left, Chippewa Square rose leafy and wild; to their right, Orleans Square brooded, its trees drooping with the weight of Spanish moss. The air smelled simultaneously of decaying magnolias and cigarette smoke.

"The guy's smart, but he's clearly gone off the rails," Lucas said, his shoulder touching Sam's, the heat from his body oozing onto hers.

"I don't know," Sam responded after moving far enough away from Lucas so he couldn't touch her—accidentally or not. "I mean, I've never given Dr. Gruber much thought beyond his work—and I think that's what he's always wanted. Maybe that's why I never saw this coming." Sam rubbed her face with one hand.

"Nobody could have seen this coming. It's not like Gruber is much of a sharer. Except when he thinks he's right."

"I don't take it personally. He tends to keep pretty much everybody at arm's length."

"I wonder why that is? I mean, sometimes it's nice to be close to another person," Lucas purred.

Alarm bells went off in Sam's head, and she quickened her pace as her stomach churned. "Well, I think somewhere, under all that gruffness, Dr. Gruber's a good guy. He was my TA in grad school, you know."

"Ah! No wonder you've got a soft spot for him." Lucas' tone was light, but Sam saw the way he clenched his fists at his sides as he hurried to catch up to her.

"I just prefer to see the good in people whenever possible."

"Well, I hope that applies to your boss, too," Lucas said, his voice loaded with expectation. Good God, the guy wouldn't let up.

Talk about an HR nightmare, she thought. *If he's doing this to me, what would he do—or has he already done—to a more junior person? Or, God forbid, an intern or student researcher?*

They arrived at the DeSoto and slipped inside, the sudden blast of air conditioning raising goosebumps along their arms and distracting Lucas enough that Sam didn't have to respond. When they reached their rooms, side by side on the third floor, Lucas paused.

"Well," he said. "Have a good night."

"You, too," she said, racing to slot her key card into the lock.

Her door finally clicked and she pushed it open, but Lucas put a hand on her arm to stop her. Without looking her in the eye, he said, "I like hanging out with you."

Through gritted teeth, Sam replied, "Yes, it's been enjoyable." She tried not to exhale too loudly as his fingers finally slipped off her flesh. "Now, I really should be getting some sleep."

Lucas nodded and turned away to enter his own room but then

stopped. "Wait!"

Her heart started beating faster, and tears pricked the backs of her eyes. *Please don't do this*, she thought. *Please don't make me have to say no.* Lucas was her boss, after all, and she knew she'd be the one to suffer if she was forced to reject him. Times hadn't changed that much, and he hadn't yet crossed a line she could file a complaint about.

Luckily, Lucas' gaze was serious instead of flirtatious. "Remember to send that email to Gruber."

"Sure," Sam breathed, relief washing over her like a wave. "Thanks for the reminder."

Lucas inched closer to her, clearly intending for her to send the email right then and there. Sam obliged, hoping to end the encounter as quickly as possible. Her fingers crawled over the touchscreen keys on her phone as Lucas loomed over her. When she was finished, she read it aloud.

"How does this sound? Hi Dr. Gruber, I've received word there's been a new break in the Savannah investigation. I've just arrived in Savannah, and it's looking like I could use some backup. I know you're not feeling well, but is there any chance you could come for support? I could really use your expertise on site. Regards, Comm. Samantha Clements."

"Sounds fine to me."

"Excellent. Now, goodnight." She turned and disappeared behind the door before Lucas had a chance to say anything more to keep her near him for any longer. Sam fired the email off to Gruber, willing him to open it. She hoped she could get to him before he did something unforgivable.

*　*　*

That night, as Sam lay curled in her bed, a foul odor crept into her twitching nostrils, pulling her from a thin sleep. As she came fully awake, she sniffed, detecting the smell of vomit, or a dead mouse in the ductwork, or maybe rotting food squirreled away somewhere in the room. The smell continued to grow stronger, assaulting her until she plucked a hand from under her pillow and squeezed her nose shut.

"Ack," she said aloud, shaking her head in disgust. "What—"

A low moan interrupted her. The sound drifted through the vents, rising in an excruciating crescendo until it was almost a roar.

"What the hell is going on?" Sam said, sitting up straight in bed.

She listened, tense and motionless, and clutched her arms to her chest as the sound crested, faded away, and then grew once again. The sheets grew moist under her skin, the nervous sweat trickling from her body in rivulets.

Should I call the front desk? Sam thought, as the second moan died in the air.

She turned to look at the clock on the bedside table: 3:04 a.m. The concierge definitely wouldn't be in.

Sam closed her eyes, weariness overtaking her. *Just ignore it, Samantha.*

She braced herself for another moan, but none came. She waited awhile longer, muscles clenched, but the silence persisted. Eventually, Sam removed her pinched fingers from her nostrils and noticed the odor had retreated, too.

Did I imagine that?

She tried to settle and let sleep reclaim her, but she couldn't keep her fingers from clenching. As she lay there in the dark, she squeezed her fingernails into her palms so tightly she felt the warm trickle of blood.

CHAPTER TWENTY

Gruber had never been afraid of spiders; as a child, he collected bugs, beetles, bits of wasp nest, even shed snakeskins. He'd thought he wanted to be an entomologist when he grew up, so he'd made a point to observe, handle, and catalogue every insect, arthropod, and arachnid he could find. Even though he'd retired his bug collection long ago in favor of microscope slides, Petri dishes, and statistics, he still wasn't afraid of something as fascinating as a tarantula. He had time to think *This might not be so bad* before Leona fiddled with something in the wall of the pit, and what he'd thought was a mound of filth a few feet away came to life in the form of a massive, beastly alligator. An abyss of pure black terror yawned before him, sucking him in.

Gruber cowered, pulling his feet toward his chest in a fetal position despite the sharp pain shooting through his injured leg. For nearly a full minute he huddled in the muck, sheltering himself in a gooey cocoon. He could hear the thrashing of the alligator, rhythmic and menacing.

The sounds carried him, kicking and screaming, to the past. He was eight years old, visiting Gullywasher's as a child. The sweet chemical taste of cotton candy lingered on his tongue. His cheeks were sticky, and he made a game of pressing his fingers against his skin, then seeing how much force it took to peel them away.

He was grabbing for his father's dangling hand, trying to grasp it, to have something solid to hold onto. His father quickened his stride, always keeping just out of reach.

As he stumbled in his father's wake, one set of fingertips stuck to his cheek and the other clutching at the air, he heard it. Slapping, thumping, cheering, shouting, laughing, screaming, tearing—the sounds of madness. The horrible music of the Alligator Pit.

When Gruber returned to reality, he found himself cowering, crying, dirty palms glued to his eyes, just like he'd been as a scared child. If the end was going to come, at least he wouldn't have to see it. For others, this may have been worse; for Gruber, it was the only thing that could make death tolerable.

He waited.

When he didn't feel the penetration of jagged teeth, didn't smell the stench of carrion, didn't taste bile or blood at the back of his throat, and didn't hear the splintering of bone, he carefully fanned out one of his hands and peeked through his fingers.

Five feet away, the massive lump was swinging back and forth. In the flicker of the torchlight, Gruber could see the angular head, the meaty tail, the slick scales. With each swish, the animal flung more of its mud camouflage against the walls of the pit in vomit-like splatters.

Gruber gulped in air, preparing to scream, but the alligator stayed back. A thought drifted toward him from what felt like very far away. *Is it real?*

With a herculean amount of bravery, Gruber jiggled his left foot toward the thrashing animal. The creature took no notice; it didn't lunge forward, it didn't pause, it didn't change its course of movement in any way.

Across from him, his ghastly tormentor was still standing next to what he could now see was some sort of electrical box, her face a study in rapture in the dancing torchlight. If she happened to collapse right there, Gruber thought she would die happy.

He fought around the scream still stuck in his throat and managed to ask her in a choked voice barely audible over the screeching of the creature's movements, "Is it real?"

"His name is Tarantula," was her only reply, her voice dreamy.

What kind of name is that? For a reptile? he thought. "Fine, but is it…is Tarantula…animatronic?"

With visible effort, Leona dragged her eyes from the wriggling robot to Gruber, still wedged in the mud. "Technically," she said.

"What does that mean?" Gruber asked.

"He's not made from life, but he can move into it," she said.

Gruber had no idea what to make of this, but the matter-of-fact declaration chilled him nonetheless.

"Why are you showing me this?"

She shrugged, maddeningly casual. "Because," she said. "That's how the ritual must begin."

"Was it always like this? Fake?" Surely all those cheering crowds from Gullywasher's heyday weren't frothing at the mouth to see robot alligators?

Leona rushed over to him with surprising speed and nearly pounced on him, her pale features scrunched into a snarl. "Fake? There is nothing fake here." As she spoke, clenching her bottom lip to force out the words, gobs of phlegmy saliva spattered against Gruber's cheeks.

Her answer still didn't make sense, but her ferocity quelled his appetite for information. He sank back into the mud, exhausted.

Leona stood up, making a show of brushing herself off, as though the rags she wore could ever possibly be clean.

"Anyway," she said, staring down at Gruber imperiously. "We will move on now."

Gruber moaned in response.

Leona's face shifted into a look of compassion, which on her was grotesque instead of comforting. "Dr. Gruber," she said, cooing. "Everything will be fine."

When he still said nothing, she continued. "You're hurt, but you won't let me help you. What to do with you?" She paused, lifting her head to the sky, as though listening for a message traveling through the hot air like an electric current. "Mm-hmm," she said, whether to herself or to an unseen companion, Gruber wasn't sure. He also wasn't sure which possibility frightened him more.

She looked back down at him, the compassion still gleaming in her otherwise flat eyes. "We must follow the ritual into its darkest, deepest grooves. Those who came to me before you were freely willing, so beautiful in their pain, in their need. The ritual could be light; none of the others even met Tarantula properly. In that way, you can consider yourself lucky—he is sacred."

She paused again, tilting her head up, and nodded once.

"Dr. Gruber," she said, "you will more or less be exposed to what the others went through, from here on out. The level of force is really up to you—either you want to get better easily, or I will make you get better…less easily." She began pacing back and forth around Tarantula, at times having to shout to be heard over the mechanical screeching shooting through the stifling night air. She held up the baggie of white powder. "As I said before, this is part of the medicine. A small part, in my opinion—the larger part comes from here." She pointed to the ground with one scabby finger. "I mix these things together, because I am the healer."

Gruber returned his gaze to Leona, who had stopped pacing and was now crouched down low, just out of the strike range of Tarantula's tail. With one hand, she flicked the baggie, sending a cascade of white powder falling into the muck with a puff. Gingerly, she started to mix the two together with her hands, as though she were kneading bread.

"They others didn't get to meet Tarantula. With them, I just handed them their medicine and they stumbled away. Most of them administered it right here in this sacred place, so eager were they to be healed."

Neurons started firing in Gruber's brain at that moment, sending electrical signals and making far-flung connections. Even though he was broken, bruised, and tormented, his mind worked like the efficient, brilliant piece of machinery that he knew had made him so indispensable to Commander

Clements and the rest of the CDC. As he listened, he began to realize Leona's story paralleled the outbreak—drug users came here to get their fixes, she gave them heroin mixed with nasty pit muck, and they injected themselves. Before long, they were sick, and for most, death followed. He thought back to the flyer he'd found in Patricia Dalco's room as the hollowed-out woman inflated and deflated by way of the breathing tube. She and Marty had probably come here together, looking for that next essential fix.

After all, what was this mud, this necessary ingredient of Leona's 'medicine,' but a special type of microenvironment? Gruber knew, based on his previous research and the hunch he'd nursed since he'd watched droopy-eyed Frankenstein chase villagers during the train ride to Savannah, botulism spores were plentiful in soil-rich environments just like this one. If someone were to mix this muck with heroin, they'd get something thick and… tarry. A kind of homemade black tar heroin.

His mind started racing faster. He was so close to the answer, he could taste it. If someone were to inject that heroin mixture under the skin to prolong the high, that could create just the right anaerobic environment for the botulism spores to germinate. When they germinated, they'd spew botulinum toxin into the user's veins. Without speedy medical attention, the users would probably never realize what had happened as they started losing muscle control, their vision blurring as they sagged into the street, eyes drooping. They'd lose the ability to swallow, sending strings of saliva dripping from their lips. At the end, their breathing would become labored as the toxin killed the nerves in their diaphragm, paralyzing their lungs and leaving them suffocating, unable to move or cry out.

Fortunately, a botulism outbreak couldn't spread beyond that set of drug users who'd injected themselves with the poison. Unfortunately, the rarity of the disease meant it was usually overlooked and difficult to diagnose, and it resulted in an incredibly traumatic death if left untreated.

He knew it—he'd been right about botulism all along.

"…can take your medicine either orally or, if you'd prefer, I can get a needle. I've cleaned it, of course."

Gruber resurfaced from his thoughts to catch the last of what Leona had been saying. He considered her offer, no longer cripplingly afraid. Bravery flickered in him like the torchlight dancing over his face; this could be his chance. He could do something most people would consider suicidal. He wanted to be the hero, to solve the puzzle, to get that goddamned promotion. He wanted it so badly he would put his own life on the line. If he could recreate the circumstances the drug users had had, if he could be brave enough to skin-pop this poison like they had, then he could use himself as experimental proof that the outbreak was caused by botulism originating from black tar heroin sold by a criminal named Leona out of an abandoned theme park. If that wasn't headline-worthy, Gruber didn't know what was.

He looked up at Leona, who was staring at him intently. She looked alien and slippery, and Gruber shuddered despite his new convictions. *What is this woman, and how did she get here? Why isn't she sick? What if*—but his own unexpected words cut off those thoughts. "Okay," he said, with far more confidence than he actually felt. "Bring the needle."

A smile stretched across her face, but it didn't touch her eyes. Gruber fought the urge to shudder again. She scampered off with surprising speed for the ladder, calling out "I'll be right back" as she climbed. She crested the lip of the pit and dipped out of sight.

Gruber laid his head back and continued to think through what he was about to do. Pro: he'd get his proof and save the day in the most dramatic way possible. Con: he could die. Pro: if he got sick, he'd know what ailed him, and he could ask for antitoxin—already conveniently stockpiled at the CDC. Con: if he was wrong about botulism…

He didn't finish that thought. He wasn't wrong. Archibald Gruber was never wrong.

Couldn't I just take a sample and have it tested in the lab? He pictured Leona's face, the naked hunger in her eyes that seemed to come from someplace outside of the woman's wasted body. *No isn't really an option here,* he concluded.

Maybe, if I just go along with it, it will hurt less.

As he lay waiting for Leona to return, he thought of Dr. Barry Marshall. Nearly forty years earlier, Dr. Marshall and his colleague, Dr. Robin Warren, had been studying the bacterium *Helicobacter pylori*. They had researched and researched, culturing Petri dishes of the bacterium and examining it under the microscope. They were convinced it was the causative agent behind acute gastritis and stomach ulcers, but they couldn't seem to convince others. In a feat of what Gruber considered dazzling courage and admirable scientific certainty, Marshall drank a beaker of cultured *H. pylori* bacteria. When he got sick days later with nausea, vomiting, and ulcers, the researchers had their proof, finally. He'd received the Nobel Prize for it, for Christ's sake. Gruber longed for that kind of validation.

Maybe Gruber could be a kind of Barry Marshall for the twenty-first century. *Not that I have much of a choice, anyway*, he thought, and frowned.

He heard the slapping of Leona's footsteps returning, accompanied by the caw of a crow. She appeared over the lip of the pit, syringe in one hand, that hungry gleam in her eye.

Now was his chance. It was his turn to put his life on the line for his convictions.

Clamping the syringe between her pitted teeth, Leona descended the ladder and landed with a squelch in the muck. She slid over to Gruber, who was still lying prone.

"Are you ready?" she asked. He nodded. Then, "You will do this willingly?" Another nod.

Leona passed the syringe over to Gruber. He took it, fondling it between the pads of his dirty fingertips. From within the folds of her rags, Leona pulled a worn piece of rubber tubing. She handed it to him as well before walking over to the small pile near the damned alligator's still-thrashing tail. As he watched, she scooped up some pit muck and waddled back to Gruber on her knees, leaving wormlike trails behind her.

Gruber was shaking as he used his free hand and his teeth to tie the tube around his scrawny bicep. This operation took him a few tries; he was far from the drug user that taxi driver, Eugene, had thought him to be. When he succeeded, he submerged the tip of the needle into the pool in Leona's cupped palms. He drew the stopper with visible effort, his muscles straining against the tightly bound tubing.

He let his left arm fall to his lap, his forearm facing up, the delicate veins in the crook of his elbow exposed. He pushed on the plunger lightly, careful to remove any air bubbles. It would do no good to come all this way, display this much courage, only to die of an idiotic air embolism.

A small bit of brown goo dripped from the tip of the needle. Satisfied, Gruber pressed it to the flesh above his vein. His resolve wavered; he tried to push the needle in, but the conscious, rational, non-hero-obsessed part of his mind objected with all its might.

"What are you waiting for?" she asked.

He didn't reply; he just sat there pressing the needle to his flesh, creating an indent, but no puncture. He tried picturing his new office again, his colleagues crowded around the doorway, congratulating him for his heroic victory. Even with these thoughts echoing back and forth in his head, he couldn't bring himself to break the skin.

"I will help you, if you need me," she said, her voice kind on the surface, but Gruber could detect the threat of violence lurking beneath.

Gruber moaned and hung his head, the hand holding the needle flopping back down into his lap. He couldn't do it. He was a coward, living up to the imprecation his father had leveled at him so often as a child.

In one swift motion, Leona seized the needle, stabbed it through his skin, and rammed the plunger down, forcing the muck into his body.

In response, Gruber yelped, mostly from the barbarity of Leona's pounce. He looked up at her, his face burning. She smiled, then plopped into the mud next to him, her eyes glowing with a fire that looked hot enough to scorch.

CHAPTER TWENTY-ONE

Moisture from the pit muck seeped through Leona's ragged clothes as she sat next to Gruber, satisfaction pulling her skeletal features into something like a smile. The lost man had needed her help, but his cowardice didn't matter much now that the ritual was complete. The night air possessed a cool dankness Leona found refreshing.

She waited, even though she didn't need to; the ritual could and would continue whether she sat sentinel or not. That's what the pale figures in the cylinder had told her.

She'd first noticed the figures speaking to her several weeks before. The cylinder had always been a source of wonderment for her, sending a titillating shiver up her spine that balanced on the knife-edge of being painful. It began with dreams; when she slept, she saw figures dancing in the black water, suspended like pallid fish in the deepest parts of the ocean. They twisted sinuously on the other side of the glass, sending Leona messages through their movements. In her head, their voices explained the magic of the pit and its effects on other people—believers and outsiders alike. Everything in the park was infused with an inky, demoniacal force that came up through the ground, growing fat on the heat and light given off by living things. It was a force borne of hatred and sacrifice that saturated everything it touched and, if you were very good, it would crawl inside you and heal you from within.

Leona had wanted nothing more than to be healed. Scars both visible and invisible crisscrossed her body—abuse, violence, losing a child, falling into drugs with such sick-sour surrender. So, she had listened.

Later, when it was time, she obeyed.

*　　*　　*

The crow cawed, impatient. Leona snapped her eggshell head upward, catching the sound of whispers on the wet breeze. There would be no more waiting by Gruber's side as he succumbed; she was being summoned.

With a grinding creak, Tarantula swept his tail through the muck before stopping abruptly, the scaly tip pointing toward the ladder and the dark cylinder that lay beyond.

She pulled her rags, heavy with moisture, around her pencil-thin frame and rose. Gliding over to the ladder, she stole another glance at the doctor. He was lying very still, his eyes open and glassy, an expression of bliss on his slack features. A thick white runnel of drool stretched from the corner of his mouth. Leona felt some pity for him, but mostly she felt a sense of ambivalent inevitability. The doctor had come here, deliberately seeking her out. He in turn, received what he was looking for.

She gripped the ladder and hoisted herself to the top. The climb was growing harder these days; with every step, the rungs dug into the delicate arches of her feet, sending thudding vibrations snaking through her bones. At night, holed away in her aquarium nest of old blankets, she could feel thick bands of bruises running across her soles. They were always gone by morning, the tender flesh of her feet regaining their pearly hue.

Her hip bones slid beneath her jutting pelvis as she walked across the dirt and gravel to the aquarium. Ice-cold tendrils whispered across her body, pulling her gently but firmly toward the dark cylinder standing impassive in the aquarium's center. Goosebumps broke across her flesh and she shivered hard, as though she were standing naked in the winds of Antarctica rather than the sticky-hot summer of Georgia. The crow cawed, hurrying her along.

She pulled open the heavy metal doors of the aquarium and stepped inside.

In front of her, the cylinder cast a dark glow, an unsettling not-light, on the rest of the cavernous room. Leona's bare face was corpse-mottled where the not-light touched it.

Clutching herself, she stepped closer to the cylinder, waiting for the pale figures within to tell her what she needed to do. Sickly shadows broke through the darkness to press against the glass. They began to move, undulating like seaweed. Leona stared, glassy-eyed, absorbing their messages. Through their movements and the words they pushed into her head, the figures explained more outsiders were coming, two boys and an older couple. They spelled danger, threatening to disrupt the equilibrium of the park, to desecrate its unholy places. This could not be permitted. Leona must keep them away, by any means necessary.

Leona nodded, trancelike.

Except for the boy, the figures told her, shapes swirling in the blackness. *We would like him. Here.*

Leona's head tilted like a confused puppy. How would she know which boy was the right one?

You will know. When it is time.

Sweat broke on Leona's pallid brow. The crow cawed, sending the figures rushing back into the darkness and snapping Leona from her trance with such suddenness she felt something like a migraine flash behind her eyes. The painful spark flickered, then died. The new world Leona inhabited did not know prolonged pain, and neither did Leona, not anymore. She felt her transformation was almost complete, and when it was—no one would be able to hurt her ever again.

*　*　*

Leona needed time to prepare. She brought her hands to her eyes, pressing out the fatigue. When she pulled her fists away, the last of her eyebrow hairs were stuck to her folded fingers.

On the floor next to her nest of blankets was a small stack of stale crackers, individually packaged in thin red plastic that had long since lost its shine. Leona contemplated unwrapping a cracker, popping it in her mouth, chewing, swallowing. She gagged at the thought of something so dry, so bone-dusty in her mouth, and instead turned away, heading back toward the metal doors. She took the loss of her appetite as a good sign. Soon, she would be one of them.

When she emerged into the burgeoning dawn, the crow erupted into a series of frenzied caws. Leona joined him, sending a gush of wild laughter out into the atmosphere, where it settled over the park like a greasy miasma. With renewed vigor, she set off across the broken ground toward the Gullywasher roller coaster.

As she walked, without any insight into what she was doing, one layer of rags finally disintegrated and fell in a frayed heap onto the ground. She didn't stop; there was no need. Conscious thought had been replaced by a kind of dull drumbeat thudding steadily in her ears, increasing in tempo as she drew closer to the towering coaster.

Her tools were laid out neatly in the dry grass struggling for life next to one of the coaster's struts. She laid her ghostly palm onto the wooden surface of the strut, and felt the low thrum emanating from within that synced gloriously with the drumbeat echoing through her own body.

The grass was crispy; it broke off in yellow chunks as her fingers ran through it, searching for the right tool. A rusty hammer lay on one end next to a set of three sharp screwdrivers. A large wrench followed, and finally a ghastly rubber mallet bookended the collection at the other end. Before she let her fingers alight on the right tool, she brought a handful of the grass confetti to her nostrils and inhaled deeply. The scents of ash and death enveloped her. She inhaled again, inviting the smells inside. Peace rolled over her like a warm wave.

She pulled her palms apart, letting the bits of grass rain back down to the ground. She knelt, her fingers skating over the tools. With a will that did not feel at all like her own, her fist closed around the sharpest screwdriver.

Standing up, she once again placed her hand on the wooden strut. The vibration was fainter now. She slid her palm farther up, as though caressing a lover. The vibration grew stronger, and she knew she would have to climb.

She moved with a strange speed, scaling the thick wooden strut like a tree-dwelling animal, with the screwdriver clenched between her teeth. When she stopped, grinding, squeaking groans erupted through the still night as she attacked a spot on the strut where it connected with a latticework of wooden planks. The smell of wood rot wafted through the air as she worked. When she was finished, she scaled back down the strut with such shocking rapidity she felt like she was falling, or maybe flying, before hitting the ground and scrambling off again toward the aquarium, a ghostly shape gliding through the darkness.

CHAPTER TWENTY-TWO

In the initial moments after Leona violently injected his arm with her 'medicine,' Gruber's panic, fear, and shame disappeared, the flame of the high burning away all of his negative emotions like useless candle wax. The euphoria was interrupted briefly by a sudden gush of watery vomit, which he splattered across the muck, nearly hitting Tarantula's open jaws on one side and Leona's spindly legs on the other. He could hear her laughing interspersed with the crow's caws as he lay back down, the warmth rushing through his body, eliminating all pain. He was adrift on a lazy river of pleasure, luxuriating in the sensation of floating, untethered from the anguish and awkwardness he pulled behind him in the real world like a ball and chain.

The darkness around him no longer felt so claustrophobic, so pressing; the air felt like a velvet blanket wrapping him in its embrace. A dreamy smile spread across his face as he relaxed into his body, releasing all tension. He'd never used drugs before, but now he could understand why they were irresistible to so many.

Overhead, the black sky glittered with the stars he normally couldn't see in the light-polluted confines of metro Atlanta. Silently, he counted every star, giving them secret names and forming friendships he would, he told himself, be able to treasure if he ever felt lonely.

He drifted, blissful, occasionally sliding his arms across the surface of the muck just to feel its slippery smoothness. The sensuality of the environment entranced him; he breathed deep, grasping at the earthy smells, the soft textures, the acrid-sweet tastes blanketing his tongue.

Hours passed, drugs coursed, and something germinated in air-starved pockets of skin.

Poison released.

Infection spread.

* * *

Gruber's mind exited the normal plane of consciousness and went into default mode, which for him involved thinking about disease. He felt as though a duplicate version of himself, Gruber Two, was sitting right in front of him, revealing the story of botulism as though it were a Boy Scout campfire tale.

"What most people don't understand about botulism is that it's not the organism, *Clostridium botulinum,* that kills; it's the botulinum toxin it produces that gets the job done," Gruber Two said. "Listen up, Gruber—*Clostridium botulinum* is bountiful in our environment; speckling the earth like stardust. Let a child play in the dirt, and they're picking up hundreds, maybe thousands, of these bacteria. If conditions are poor, think frost, heat, pressure, starvation, then those bacteria will turn themselves into spores with protective coatings that shield them from destruction. Unless they're agitated, they're benign— not unlike most of the world's predatory creatures, huh, Gruber?"

Gruber nodded and watched Gruber Two nod back.

"Nothing agitates *Clostridium botulinum* quite like an environment with little to no oxygen. In this kind of anaerobic environment, the locked-down spore will germinate, releasing botulinum toxin into its immediate surroundings."

Gruber Two was well-dressed, impeccable, the version of himself he always wished he could be. Charisma oozed from his pores, and he didn't stumble over his words or lose his train of thought.

"How much damage can a microscopic bit of toxin cause? One one-millionth of a gram can kill an average-sized man. An entire gram can kill over ten thousand people. The worst part, Gruber, is that botulism doesn't offer a soft, gradual death. Death is often slow, but accompanied by humiliating deterioration, growing helplessness, and, finally, overwhelming, invisible panic. Now I'd say that's a bad way to go."

Gruber Two continued, speaking loudly and with mesmerizing hand gestures. He was impossible to ignore.

"The toxin begins by imprisoning acetylcholine, a necessary neurotransmitter, preventing it from passing along messages between motor neurons and muscle cells. Disrupting this game of cellular telephone leaves muscle cells paralyzed. Victims usually first notice the paralysis in their faces and throats; droopy eyelids, blurred vision, difficulty swallowing. If they don't get help, and if there's enough toxin in their systems, victims will start to feel the paralysis creeping up and down their limbs, settling in their torsos. Are you listening, Gruber? This is important. They will look apathetic, bored, uninterested; inside, they are fully conscious, screaming pleas for help nobody can hear. Finally, the paralysis will spread to the muscles controlling their breathing, and they will suffocate. Quietly."

He blinked and watched Gruber Two blink back.

"Watch yourself, Gruber. Watch for the signs, unless you want to go quietly, too."

As suddenly as he had appeared, Gruber Two was gone.

*　　*　　*

Without Gruber Two to anchor him, he drifted, sailing high above the pit, above the Gullywasher roller coaster rocking in the night breeze, above the entire yawning abyss of the park. Gruber Two's words sprouted like weeds in his mind, growing and blooming into gruesome pictures of limp limbs, drooping eyes, rotting puncture wounds, even an anatomical diagram pulled from a medical textbook, a black line labeling the diaphragm, which flapped to keep the lungs breathing. As quickly as they arrived, the images began to fade, curling and turning black at their edges, withering to dust, before being blown away by the wind.

Hours passed. Gruber's troubling thoughts wouldn't stay away; they kept cropping up and pestering him, drowning out the warmth of the high, until all he could see, all he could feel, was the myriad of ways botulism would take over his body.

Slowly, the nightmare images receded and Gruber began to come back to himself. The inside of his arm where Leona had stabbed the needle throbbed, hot to the touch. When he swallowed, he felt a soft lump, and wondered distantly if the obstruction was dehydration or the toxin at work, paralyzing his throat muscles.

His broken leg throbbed agonizingly once again. No longer sailing above the pit, he was instead weighted down into the muck, saturated with moisture and filth. Powered by an underlying urgency he wasn't yet sober enough to grasp, he dragged himself to a sitting position, head twisting to examine his surroundings.

Corpse-pale light was creeping along the upper edge of the pit, making the shadows Gruber steeped in feel darker. Without his watch, he couldn't be sure, but he figured it must be near six in the morning; the sun would rise soon to start frying him again. In the center of the pit, the damned alligator robot sat, jaws closed, his stillness a threat. A shiver writhed through Gruber, and he struggled to rock onto his feet.

He succeeded in levering himself into a sort of low crouch, one heel sinking into the muck while the other jutted out at an awkward angle. The movement sent piercing pangs of pain shooting through his injured right leg; he thought he heard another ominous crack, something pulling loose, hanging in a place it didn't belong. He fought against the tide of blackness as his consciousness wavered. When he finally succeeded in steadying himself, he glanced around—Leona was nowhere in sight.

Pushing aside the pain, he fixated on Leona. She mystified him. She had the slippery caginess of a lifelong drug user, plus extreme delusions of grandeur, but she also exuded a catlike calmness that baffled Gruber. She spoke like a prophet, acted like a self-appointed saint, ministered like a nurse, all while looking like a walking corpse. Which of those qualities made her dangerous? What exactly was she capable of?

Gruber set these thoughts aside, concentrating instead on summoning the energy and mental fortitude to stand. He heaved his weight forward onto his uninjured leg and hoisted himself up, scrabbling wildly at the cement wall for purchase. His right index finger found a crag in the surface, and he managed to find a tenuous balance, swaying gently. Something behind his right knee pulled and tore, sending fuzzy dots drifting across his field of vision. If he fell back again, there was no way he'd be able to stand, and he was increasingly coming to realize staying in this pit meant certain death.

Gruber pulled several deep, rank-smelling breaths through his nose and open mouth into his lungs, paying close attention to their capacity, the feel of the oxygen hitting the alveoli. Would he be able to notice the signs when his lungs started failing?

The inhalations left a light sour-sweet dusting on his tongue, the taste unpalatable enough to push away the dizziness. He forced himself to swallow, to hold in the rancidity, in case he needed its sensory power to keep him moving later.

Eyeing the wall for more handholds, he gripped the next closest crag and hopped forward on his good leg, the muck emitting a snarling, sucking sound as it surrendered his foot. A small cry escaped his lips, but he kept moving.

Be a man, he heard his father whispering in his ear.

The ladder hung limp against the wall on the other side of the pit. There was no telling when or if Leona would be back.

Beads of sweat burst on his clammy forehead as he half-hopped, half-dragged his body around the pit, breathing and swallowing the fine film of rot that lingered in this place whenever he needed a boost. He could see the neon gold rim of the sun peeking over the edge of the pit by the time he reached the ladder, sweaty and exhausted.

With a gut-wrenching sigh, he assessed the climb. He was reasonably fit for his age, but he enjoyed walking more than weightlifting, which had never seemed like a disadvantage until now. He'd have to rely completely on his skinny biceps to pull himself up while trailing a useless broken leg. On top of that obstacle, he felt sure a fever was lurking in his bones, but whether it was from ordinary infection or the burgeoning effects of a deadly toxin, he couldn't be sure.

Overhead, a crow cawed. Thin fingers of panic crept through Gruber's skull, urging him forward, but he felt rooted to the spot. He was just beginning to move his body upward when a gale of wild laughter in the distance pumped terrified adrenaline through his veins and sent him scrabbling up the ladder with unprecedented agility. The lip of the pit was dry and silty, pebbled with tufts of dehydrated grass and small pieces of gravel. He heaved himself up to a sitting position on the edge, breathing hard, his shoulders and biceps burning, his leg in agony.

Minutes were precious, but he forced himself to think. Leona was probably near; that much was obvious. He needed to get out of here, find help and antitoxin, and maybe an exorcist for this godforsaken place. He needed to have his blood analyzed, and maybe even get his hands on a sample of the 'medicine' to take back to the lab. He had to do all of this while silent sickness overtook him, dehydration drained him, and his leg hung useless behind him, the pain ever-present.

Sample, he thought. With sudden animation, his hand dove into his pocket and pulled out the contents. The tweezers he'd brought were still there. Two of his three baggies had ripped, but he only needed one. He lifted the tweezers in one hand and ran his fingers over his body with the other. When his fingertips sank into a quagmire of mud behind his left ear, he grinned and scraped off a small sample with the tweezers. Working quickly, he transferred the muck to the intact baggie, sealed it, and replaced everything in his pockets, satisfied. *I can still do this all on my own.*

To his right, the sign for the alligator pit faced away, still trying to lure in visitors. To his left, a small, ill-begotten tree sprouted defiantly from the sour earth. Immediately, Gruber began pulling himself through the dirt to reach it, bits of gravel gouging small cuts in his exposed skin. Gradually, excruciatingly, he slithered over to the tree. He pressed his forehead against its rough bark with relief.

"Alright, Gruber," he said, steadying himself with the sound of his own voice. "Let's make a splint."

The next fifteen minutes found Gruber alternately wrestling with the tree, pulling its gnarled branches with a combination of his body weight and the force of gravity, karate chopping thick pieces into the right length, and tearing his shirt to use the fabric strips to bind the makeshift splint to his bad right leg. When he was done, he lay back against the trunk, head and leg throbbing, trickles of blood starting to coagulate where the gravel had buried itself in his skin. His face was red and sweaty, exertion, fever, and sunburn taking their physical toll all at once.

He lay still, the spindly tree offering little relief from the scorching sun or the pains knocking against his bones like angry ghosts. A soupy breeze lapped at his skin, coating his face in a moist film.

Whatever high had enveloped him in its deceptively comforting embrace was now gone, leaving him shivery and nauseated. Directly in front of him, the alligator pit still yawned, a lewd orifice. Dry leaves whispered across the ground, trickling into the pit. Something bad was coming. It was time to leave.

I will not die here.

He tried to assess the situation rationally, which was becoming more difficult every minute as his strength waned, an itchy blanket of fever enveloping him.

His legs were currently straight out in front of him, the bad one splinted inexpertly and visibly swollen. Without the support of the trunk behind him, he would fall back, exhausted. He took a deep breath, sucking in the humid air like a thick rotten milkshake, and pushed his palms into the ground at his sides, lifting his hips into the air. Using the momentum of the thrust, he whipped his left leg around to get his foot underneath him. A bolt of pain electrified his bad right leg. He took another breath, then hefted himself up to a hunched standing position by gripping the branches above him. His heel dragged through the dirt and pain once again exploded through his broken parts, but he finally succeeded in steadying himself vertically, balancing all of his weight on his good leg, sending fat bubbles of sweat running down his spine. With extreme effort, he pushed away the dots of dizziness that had returned to fizzle at the edges of his vision.

From his vantage point, he could see the alligator pit ahead of him, the deathtrap Gullywasher roller coaster to his left, and the shell of the dolphin show amphitheater to his right. There were no people, no animals, no signs of movement at all beyond the swaying of the coaster and the ongoing drift of crispy leaves. The sun was still rising to its zenith; Gruber guessed it was around 8 or 9 o'clock in the morning now.

Instead of bolstering his confidence, the absence of any signs of life set him even more on edge. *Where the hell is Leona?* He'd always preferred the enemies he could see—whether that be through microscope lenses, epidemiological models, or symptomatic patients—to the ones he couldn't. He really didn't know what Leona was capable of, or how far she'd go to 'cure' him.

Another hot breath inflated his lungs, eliciting a small, satisfying crack from his sternum. Time to move.

When Leona had dragged him from where he'd fallen through the bridge to the pit, he'd been mostly unconscious, and it had been dark. He figured any place in the opposite direction of the damned pit was a good choice, so he started hobbling between the Gullywasher and Gullywasher Junior coasters, hoping he was headed toward the exit. The sun continued to scorch the exposed flesh of his neck, adding molten fuel to the fire of his fever. The splint was poorly made, and with each drag-step he could feel the wood shifting, bending. At least the pain was receding; either he was going numb, or…he didn't want to think of the other possibility. The toxin at work, severing his neuronal connections, taking away control.

As he limped, the sun traveled from the base of his neck to the back of his skull, rising higher in the sky. He passed the coasters and wove his way between the dull plastic of some circular ride called the Gravitron and a half-collapsed bumper car ring.

Fever continued to nip at his reason; he could have sworn he saw a small hand dangling from a pink bumper car. He shook his head to clear the hallucination and continued on, realizing with unbridled joy the short white building looming ahead of him featured a painted red cross and the words First Aid.

A rest stop was in order.

*   *   *

The metal door was padlocked, but closer inspection revealed the rusty lock was so brittle with corrosion that it practically crumbled at Gruber's touch. He knocked it loose and pulled the door open, leaving the lock dangling from the door handle.

Inside, shelves lined three of the four brick walls of the single room. Every surface was carpeted with a thick layer of dust, but miraculously, very little appeared to be disturbed. Glass jars of tongue depressors, cotton balls, and Band-Aids filled the shelves, which were sagging dangerously in the middle.

A wave of heat, followed sharply by a chill so cold it was painful, washed over Gruber, sending him reeling. He tried to brace himself by grabbing onto the closest shelf, but it was too late. His weight shifted onto his bad leg, shooting off fireworks of agony that went only so far as mid-shin. As he fell to the ground, pulling most of the shelf contents down with him, he realized he couldn't feel either one of his feet. He hit the ground hard, pain radiating through him. His dazed brain sent the message to wiggle his toes, but the message bounced back, invalid.

Before losing consciousness, he was dimly aware of snow falling in soft, cotton candy heaps all around him. The touch was feather-light on his face, which he took as an excellent sign—he could still feel something.

*   *   *

When he regained consciousness, his mind felt soupy and slow; following the trail of a thought was like dragging a rope through quicksand. Every part of his body he could still feel was heavy, leaden. One molasses-slow thought came to him: *I need to get out of here.* Another one followed, several seconds later: *I'm dying.*

He pulled open his eyelids with difficulty, noting distantly that his eyes were starting to droop. All around him, a display of his own inadequacy stared back at him: a small puddle of blood seeped onto the concrete floor from his bad leg; cotton balls covered every dusty surface; a box of needles lay overturned, spilling out onto the floor.

Needles.

With a surge of joy so strong it felt separate from him, he read the word on the red upturned box. The letters swam before his eyes, first reading 'Needles,' then 'Medicine,' then…could it be? The words solidified, and he began to weep with gratitude.

The words on the needle box read 'Botulinum Antitoxin.'

Hallelujah!

He didn't stop to wonder at the improbability of the situation as his fingers moved slowly, scrabbling along the floor to pull one of the filled syringes from the box. The needle held a payload of clear liquid antitoxin. There was no time to waste; deliverance had come for him, and he needed to take it.

As he uncapped the needle and shoved it into the vein of his bruised forearm, he thought he heard gruff voices outside the building. One sounded deep, sonorous: a man. The other, higher-pitched: a woman. Leona?

With considerable effort and a great deal of fear, he dragged his prone body underneath the fallen shelves, out of sight of the single window at the front of the squat structure. The voices grew loud, louder, loudest, a conversation Gruber could hear but couldn't understand. The words were too bulky to yank through the syrupy slowness of his mind. Before he could push himself to make something of their banter, they faded away into silence, and Gruber couldn't really be sure they'd been there at all.

Doesn't matter. Got antitoxin, leave now.

Somehow, in his fever daze, the bad leg offering less complaint now that it was almost entirely without feeling, Gruber pulled himself to a standing position, fighting the black wave that threatened to roll over him yet again.

He managed to half-walk, half-drag himself out of the First Aid building, grabbing at shelves, walls, the doorframe, anything within reach.

Before he exited, he looked back at the mess he'd made. A series of thoughts tickled his mind, sending confusing ripples through his consciousness—*Doesn't that box just say needles? And isn't bot antitoxin supposed to be refrigerated? And delivered through an IV? Did I even use a needle at all?*—but they were too complex to penetrate deep. He turned his head back toward the gravel path that led him, slowly, agonizingly, to the lazy river, where he found a log placed neatly over the now bridge-less chasm. Was he dreaming? He struggled over the bridge, past the ticket building, through claustrophobic scrub forest to the cracked parking lot, and finally, to the large guardhouse under the splintered archway.

Inside the guardhouse, where his mind sluggishly insisted he would find a radio, he slumped to the floor, on fire with fever. His bad leg was bleeding heavily, soaking his trousers, but when he touched his palm to the broken place, he felt nothing.

Standing up again was not an option; he'd reached the end of his physical rope. With the last of his draining strength, he slapped his hand up toward the counter running along the inner perimeter of the guardhouse, praying his fingers would find the hard plastic of a radio. Instead, his palm collided with the gritty glass. *No radio. No time.*

He lapsed into unconsciousness for the final time, the only evidence of his search for help the red-tinged handprint on the glass.

CHAPTER TWENTY-THREE

Hours after she'd been awoken by the terrible smell and the moaning, Sam sat up in bed so suddenly her head spun. Pale light filtered through the curtains. After a few deep breaths, she swung her legs over the bed and walked to the dresser to check her phone, wishing for an email from Gruber explaining everything.

She unlocked the phone with the pad of her thumb and navigated to her email inbox, hopeful. She had one new message.

It took Sam a moment to realize the new message was not a reply to the email she sent Gruber the previous night. Instead of Archibald Gruber, the sender was a fat, capitalized Unknown, and the subject line read: 'Free Admission Today Only!' Puzzled, Sam scrolled down to read the message.

To: Comm. Samantha Clements

From: UNKNOWN

Subject: Free Admission Today Only!

Time: 3:04 am Thursday August 15

Dear SAMANTHA CLEMENTS,

As a valued patron of RHETT, we're proud to offer you and a guest of your choice FREE ADMISSION TODAY ONLY to Gullywasher's of Georgia, Georgia's premier amusement park! Located near thriving downtown Savannah, Gullywasher's has been a beloved family fun destination for over fifty years.

Attractions include the Gullywasher roller coaster, a three-story aquarium, the famous alligator pit, a lazy river, a midway, and more popcorn and cotton candy than you could ever eat!

Grab your swim trunks and come beat the heat at Gullywasher's today!

Offer is non-transferable, valid TODAY ONLY.

-Your friends at RHETT

Sam read the message a second time, then a third. She didn't think she'd given Rhett her email address, but maybe…

Wait. Gullywasher's of Georgia…she'd heard that name before, and recently—but where?

She thought for a moment before it came to her in a flash: that strange text she'd received the day before had also urged her to come to the park. Curious, she popped open her laptop on the room's small desk and searched for Gullywasher's of Georgia. The first search result took her to the park's website. Pictures of massive roller coasters, enormous clouds of cotton candy, and aquamarine fish tanks spangled with rainbow-colored fish littered the page. Overlaid text boxes proclaimed the park to be, as the email had promised, 'Georgia's premier amusement park' and 'a beloved family fun destination.'

Sam was still exploring the park's website when she heard a harsh rap on her door.

When she tugged it open, Lucas was standing there, freshly showered and dressed, his hair still damp. "I thought you might be awake," he said.

"Oh, I'm sorry, I'll need another minute to get dressed," she said, trying to discreetly hide her pajama-clad body behind the door.

"No problem," he said. "I was just about to have some coffee. Would you like one as well? The rooms have some decent Keurigs."

She hesitated. "Um, sure," she said.

"Great—I'll just slip in and get that started while you finish getting ready."

Before she could stop him, Lucas pushed past her and headed for the Keurig at the back of the room. He sidestepped her suitcase lying open on the floor, her carefully folded underwear in full view.

"I mean, would you mind—"

"Don't even worry about me, I'll be catching up on emails," he said, raising his phone in her direction. "Take all the time you need."

Sam closed her eyes and tried to take a deep breath. Clearly, Lucas wasn't going to give her her space. He wasn't going to play nice, and he wasn't going to keep things appropriate and professional. She would have to work hard to keep things as level and above board as possible—no easy task.

Trying to shove aside her discomfort, Sam barked, "Okay!" She grabbed the first outfit she could find from her suitcase and hustled to the bathroom, where she locked the door and collapsed on the toilet, head in her hands. When her breathing finally evened out, she slipped into her clothes, brushed her teeth, and plastered a fake smile on her face before emerging to face Lucas again.

"Want to know something weird?" Lucas said, acting as though there was absolutely nothing unusual about his presence in her room as she got dressed.

"Sure," she said, wary.

"I just got this email for free admission to Gullywasher's. It's this theme park—"

Sam snorted. "I got an email from them, too."

"Really?"

"Yeah—I actually got a text right before we left offering discounted admission. They must be really hurting for visitors."

Lucas brightened. "Want to play hooky and go float down a river with me?"

"What?" Sam said, eyes narrowing. "We can't just…we can't just do that. We've got a job to do."

Lucas' eyebrows knitted together. "Come on, Sam. What leads do we have? Did Gruber respond to your email?"

"No," Sam admitted. "He didn't."

"Then what else can we really do?"

"I don't know, visit the hospital? Talk to a coroner? Something?"

"That's not anything the EIS team hasn't already done."

"But…" Sam trailed off, trying to grab hold of a decent objection to Lucas' proposal. She really didn't want to spend any more non-professional time with him than she had to. Plus, she didn't want him slowing her down, throwing obstacles in her way. She had come to Savannah to find Gruber, and that's what she was going to do. Bringing Lucas was turning out to be a huge liability. Sam could feel her career smoking from two sides: Gruber's rogue mission and her boss's continued advances. She tried one last appeal. "We're not on vacation. This is a work trip."

Lucas didn't miss a beat. "Yes, and after a short morning of rides and cotton candy, we'll get right back at it, and hopefully by then Gruber will have emailed us back."

Sam fixed him with a hard stare.

Lucas relented, coming to meet her somewhere in the middle. "How about this—we'll work extra hours in the evening to make up for our morning off. I'm sure discussions about outbreak investigations over tacos can count as work time."

Sam's expression was pained, but clearly he wouldn't be taking no for an answer. Best to keep him placated for now. "Fine," she said through gritted teeth.

"Yes!" Lucas said, grinning. "It'll be fun. All that workplace wellness research shows when employees get a chance to take a step back, refresh, and forget about work for a while, they actually end up being better workers later. Who knows, maybe we'll have some sort of epiphany on a roller coaster."

"Right," Sam said, wishing she was back in her office at CDC instead of heading out to a kid's park with an asshole she couldn't seem to shake.

CHAPTER TWENTY-FOUR

The morning light was creeping over the dusty landscape of the park as Leona made her way back to the aquarium. The Gullywasher roller coaster squeaked behind her, as if in pain. She shrugged; she hadn't mortally wounded it, only equipped it to mortally wound another.

She needed more instruction.

The cool darkness of the aquarium fell over her like a balm; she closed her eyes and breathed deeply. The musky scent reminded her of the fancy perfume one of her foster mothers used to wear; she'd put it on before going out on one of her dates. After she'd left, Leona would sneak into her room and spritz herself with the scent, an olfactory proclamation of adulthood, of femininity. It had made her feel important, like somebody worthy of love.

Standing in front of the dark cylindrical tank, she felt a strange sense of duality. This had been happening more and more often. She would be out of view of the cylinder, and she would feel more or less like herself: Leona Franks, a fallen woman who'd been lifted up and healed by her new home. As soon as she stepped inside the murky haven of the aquarium and looked up into the tall glassy blackness, she felt herself start to separate. Leona Franks was still there, but there was a new piece, a growing sliver of an alien personality that put thoughts in her mind and, as far as she could tell, lived mostly inside the cylinder. Standing before it now, she felt a tension between the two inhabitants of her body that left her feeling nauseated.

It wasn't long before the pale figures emerged, communicating again with their strange movements, pushing thoughts directly into her brain. They told her three important pieces of information:

1. Gruber had left the pit, but she shouldn't worry—he wouldn't get far.

2. The two interlopers, the older couple, would come next, and they would need to be removed. They were not wanted.

3. Two brothers would come last, and they would require careful attention. She had to make sure the trap she had set succeeded at the critical moment.

*   *   *

Leona wasn't sure how much time passed; the cylinder always seemed to steal hours from her. When she came back to herself, she pushed through the metal doors and out into the bright blue day. Her feet led her past the moldering dolphin show amphitheater, with its stale smells of popcorn and decay. She finally came to a stop in front of the pit. Her beloved pit.

She peered over the edge. As the figures in the cylinder had told her, the doctor was gone. He had left large, deep grooves in the mud as he'd slid across. Leona followed his path with her eyes, taking note of the muddy handprints on the ladder, the spots of blood on the concrete wall, the broken branches of the small tree to her left, the runty scraps of cloth littering the ground. The uneven footprints of a broken gait stumbled away, making Leona think of a wounded animal fighting for its life against some much larger predator. The thought left her feeling sad and exhilarated at the same time, a juxtaposition of conflicting emotions she was beginning to get used to.

Good riddance, a voice in her head hissed that didn't sound like her own.

Get moving, a different voice whispered. This one sounded more like her, but its tone was panicked.

She turned swiftly on one heel and let her feet take her where she needed to be. There were interlopers headed her way, and she could not suffer an interloper to live.

Their blood will nourish this earth, the not-Leona voice said, spiky with glee. *Just like all the others.*

The sun was growing hot overhead, sending beads of sweat gliding with astonishing speed down Leona's slick skull. When she reached a hand up to brush away the itchy droplets, the feel of her naked skin beneath her palm made her think of a baby, and a knotted coil of guilt and sorrow pulled tighter in her stomach. She was never destined to be the kind of mother that sang lullabies to her swaddled infant. No, she was destined to be the mother of Gullywasher's, a dark child that needed much attention—attention and sacrifice.

She continued on, back past the amphitheater again. When she reached the far side of the rusting bleachers, her feet abruptly switched direction and led her into the forest of metal struts supporting the seats. She finally stopped moving when she reached a tangle of grass, leaves, and sticks that resembled a massive bird's nest; something large and wild had crafted it long ago. The tangle of foliage was hollow, and Leona crept inside. Within the nest, she was concealed from prying eyes, but she could easily see out over the dry ground toward the drained pool.

All she had to do now was wait.

CHAPTER TWENTY-FIVE

It wasn't even noon, but the sun was already scorching as the two brothers barreled down the highway toward Savannah.

"I saw on Planet Earth that alligators have antibacterial blood. Think that's true?" Zeb asked, munching on peanut M&M's as his brother Sid piloted the rattling Civic deeper and deeper into the Georgia wilderness.

"I guess so, if you saw it on Planet Earth. I mean…that's credible, right? David Attenborough wouldn't lie to us," Sid responded.

"Yeah, that's what I figured. So, I guess if we fall into a pit and break our legs while we're out there, we just find an alligator, cut him open, and put his blood on the wound. Sound good?"

Sid side-eyed his brother through his fringe of black hair, checking for Zeb's token half-smile to see if he was joking. He was. "Sure, uh-huh. You catch the gator first, then I'll cut it open."

Zeb smiled wider. "Yeah right, like you would do that. You couldn't even dissect a rat in intro bio."

Sid frowned but said nothing. Zeb was right, after all.

The brothers fell into a companionable silence as they drove along Interstate 16 to Savannah. They'd left Atlanta on that sunny Thursday morning two hours before, leaving them about an hour and a half before they'd reach their destination. The expensive camera equipment was tucked snugly in the footwell behind Sid's seat, and the rest of their minimal baggage was crammed into the Civic's small trunk. On the back seat behind Zeb, a takeout bag was flayed open, spilling family-size bags of peanut M&M's, Skittles, Cheetos, Funyuns, and Cool Ranch Doritos onto the upholstery. Zeb reached back and retrieved the Doritos, yanking the bag open with one violent pull.

"Chip?" he asked.

"Just one," Sid said, plucking a Dorito from the bag and slipping it between his lips.

"Another?" Zeb asked, shaking the bag.

"Nah, I'm good," Sid said, swallowing. "Dude. We ate breakfast, like, less than three hours ago. How are you that hungry?"

Zeb patted his burgeoning belly with reverence, as though he were a pregnant woman. "Gotta feed the monster, my man."

Sid laughed. "Sure, but eating that much processed crap—"

"Not today, Satan," Zeb said, swallowing loudly. "When you actually graduate med school, you can try to give me advice about my eating habits."

As Zeb attacked the Doritos with almost spiteful relish, Sid thought through their plan once more. They had their cameras, portable microphones, a tripod, a telephoto lens, a few extra memory cards, waterproof boots, flashlights, cell phones, a flare gun, and an attack whistle. Not in case of an attack, just in case of…well, broken legs.

"Wait—did you pack the first aid kit?" Sid asked.

Zeb stopped chewing and thought. "Whoops," he said, shrugging.

"Come on, Zeb. Seriously," Sid huffed.

"Chill, dude. You can't prepare for everything."

"Can't I?" Sid said. "Remember that time in the woods with Dad when you got that fucking awful splinter and I was able to fix you right up because I'd brought my first aid kit?"

Zeb shrugged. "Well, yeah," he said. "But that's just because you're a good big brother. You would have found another way to do it if you hadn't had the kit."

"Oh, come on, Zeb."

"What? I got a lot of respect for you, *Doctor*."

Sid smiled in spite of himself. He took his role as big brother seriously, ever since he'd first become aware of Zeb. He remembered his mother leaning down, cradling Zeb, saying "Sid, honey, this is your new baby brother! That means you're a big brother now, and big brothers take care of their little brothers. Can you do that, Sid?" Sid had nodded enthusiastically, saying, "Yes, Mommy! I'll take care of him forever and ever and ever and ever!" His mom had kissed him on the forehead before handing him a box of animal crackers from the pantry. Ever since, he'd been watching out for Zeb, making sure he was okay even as his baby brother grew into someone brave, impulsive, and spontaneous—Sid's near-total opposite. *Big brothers take care of little brothers.*

Sid had mapped and re-mapped the route to Gullywasher's, making sure he had it just right. The path had once been well-marked and well-trodden, but these days, nobody was flocking to Georgia's former greatest water park and aquarium. Those who wanted water went to the beach, and those who wanted aquariums went to Atlanta.

It wasn't always that way. Gullywasher's of Georgia had opened in May of 1965, promising hassle-free fun for the whole family. There were pools, slides, and lazy rivers; dolphin shows and tanks of starfish you could touch; a food court and camping grounds. Famously, there was also the alligator pit.

Sid shivered when he thought about the pit. He'd been squeamish around bodies of water for most of his life, but two years ago, his fear had sprouted legs and started chasing him when he and Zeb had explored an old wildlife park and found something soulless and terrifying waiting for them in the lonely woods.

*   *   *

Two years ago, during summer vacation of 2017, Zeb and Sid had been scouring the Internet for locations that fit four main criteria: 1) they were abandoned; 2) they were interesting; 3) they were within a day's drive of Atlanta; 4) they weren't so locked down that Zeb and Sid could get arrested for trespassing. The brothers had grown up with a grisly love of abandoned places, and when they started urban exploring as teenagers, they just couldn't stop. Every school vacation, they would load up their trusty old Civic with their cameras and snacks and set off in search of adventure. They filmed their escapades, edited them into action-movie-style short films, and posted them on their YouTube channel. Their first few adventures were dull—a foreclosed house two neighborhoods over, an empty Chuck-E-Cheese in a dilapidated strip mall, a crumbling bottle factory that had nearly returned to nature after fifty years of loneliness. Despite these less-than-stellar first tries, their YouTube fanbase grew. By the time Sid started at Emory University, they had ten thousand subscribers. By the next year, when Zeb joined him at Emory, that number had tripled.

In 2017, Zeb's freshman year, Sid clicked on a Buzzfeed listicle promising the "10 Greatest Abandoned Theme Parks." Most of them he already knew about—the old Six Flags outside New Orleans that had been destroyed by Hurricane Katrina, Spreepark in Berlin that had failed thanks to the proprietor's tendency to smuggle cocaine in ride equipment—but one was unfamiliar. Mel's Wildlife Reserve was situated right on the outskirts of Hiawassee, Georgia, population 891. Further searching revealed a rather dubious blog post on an even more dubious website, which told Sid Mel's had opened in 1972 with a lion, a runty elephant, a few zebras, and an "aquarium" so small it was barely a bathtub. After visitors complained that the animals were chained and emaciated, the Humane Society stepped in, along with the local police, and shut down the park. The animals were transferred to reputable zoos, and Mel, whoever the hell he was, disappeared.

Sid sent the link to Zeb, who was just as enthralled by the park, which also happened to be within driving distance. There was a problem, though— they couldn't find any other evidence of the park's existence, and the lone photograph attached to the original blog post only showed the park's entrance: a gaudy, zebra-striped archway with MEL'S WILDLIFE PARK in block letters. Sid suggested they drive down and check it out anyway. If there was nothing there, then at least they could put their own curiosity to rest.

When they set out for Mel's on a cloudy day in July, Sid was more nervous than usual, as if to compensate for Zeb's total lack of anxiety. Sid had always secretly thought Zeb was born without a survival instinct. He never seemed to show any fear of the situations they thrust themselves into. Even when they'd been chased off of properties with shotguns, Zeb hadn't broken a sweat. Sid was the careful one—he mapped out the routes, he double- and triple-checked their provisions, and he made sure there was an extra cartridge for the flare gun.

When they reached Hiawassee, they were pleasantly surprised. The main street was quaint and clean, and the dog-walking pedestrians and cars parked along the road announced the town was happily occupied. Sid pulled into a parking spot next to, of all things, a white AMC Gremlin and cut the engine.

Zeb opened his eyes and looked around, yawning. "Are we there yet?" Another epic yawn. "Woah. Is that a fucking Gremlin?"

Sid looked up from the map he was studying and looked to his right. "Oh, yeah. I noticed that too. Weird, huh?"

"I'm surprised that piece of shit is still running. It's gotta be almost fifty years old."

"Yeah, well—I don't think this place attracts a lot of young people."

Zeb sniffed. "Well, we're here, aren't we?"

"Yup."

"You find where we're going?"

Sid sighed. "I thought we would have passed it by now, but clearly we haven't. Do you remember if that article said anything more specific about where we can find this place?"

Zeb snorted. "You act like I'm the responsible one here. I do the filming. I do the breaking and entering, when necessary. You do the reading. Let's not get confused about who we are."

Sid sighed louder. "Well, I guess we'll have to ask somebody."

Zeb thrust his chin toward a tidy shopfront with a sign: Clarence's Café. "Should we go in there?"

"We've got nothing to lose."

When they walked into Clarence's, five gray-white heads turned. Sid could feel their eyes roaming over his skin—taking him in, sizing him up. They must have decided Sid and Zeb were neither a threat nor all that interesting, because in the space of five seconds, all five heads had snapped back toward their steaming plates of food.

"Bit of a geriatric crowd here, huh?" Zeb said from the side of his mouth.

"Who else would live in such a tiny town on purpose?" Sid responded, also twitching just one corner of his lips.

Clarence's was like something out of a 1950's time capsule. A red formica and chrome lunch counter ran parallel to a high wall on the left crowded with shelves of candies, magazines, and cigarettes. To the right of the bar, red-topped tables adorned a black-and-white checkerboard floor, which ended at a row of red booths anchored to the right wall. A pharmacy counter stood at the back of the café, and Sid could see the elderly pharmacist snoozing in his drug-lined cave, head in hand. Overhead, a line of three ceiling fans spun lazily.

Sid walked to the lunch counter, where a pretty teenaged girl in a white apron and paper hat stood, counting the bills in the cash register. She was the first person not eligible for Medicare the brothers had seen since leaving civilization behind.

"Excuse me," Sid stammered, hoping the rising blush in his cheeks wasn't too obvious. "Do you think you could help us with some directions?"

The girl looked up, pushing her shoulder-length blonde hair out of her face with one hand. Her name tag read *Annie May*. "Of course. This happens all the time, although usually it's the women doing the asking. To get back on the highway, what you'll want to do is—"

Zeb cut her off, not unkindly. "Actually, Miss Annie May, we're not looking to get back on the highway. We're looking for Mel's Wildlife Reserve?"

Annie May's eyes widened, and then she laughed. "Well, I'm sorry to say fellas, but if you're looking to see some animals, you're out of luck. Mel's shut down years ago."

"Oh, we know. That's actually why we're looking for it. We kind of do the whole urban exploring thing," Sid said. Annie May raised an eyebrow. "We have our own YouTube channel," Sid offered.

Annie May's other eyebrow joined its sister high on her forehead. "So what you're telling me is you like to go to creepy old places, take some videos, and then put it on the Internet?"

Zeb said, "That's exactly what we're telling you."

Annie May laughed, the unexpected sound ringing like a shot through the nursing home atmosphere of Clarence's. The patrons either ignored it or failed to hear it and continued with their meals.

Her hair swished as she shook her head. "Boys, boys, boys. What are your names anyway?"

Zeb answered for the both of them. "I'm Zeb, and this is my brother Sid."

"Well, Zeb and Sid, I can't say I really understand what it is you're after, and why you're after it, but I'll help you out—on the condition you give me a shoutout on that video of yours. I've always wanted to be famous," she laughed.

Sid smiled. "Sure."

"Let me just get a pencil and some paper, and I'll draw you a map."

*　*　*

Twenty minutes later (five minutes for the map, five minutes for Zeb to flirt with Miss Annie May, and another ten to scarf down a couple of milkshakes), the brothers were back on the road. Sid hummed as he guided the car first away from Clarence's, then away from Main Street, and then, finally, down a rutted gravel road largely overgrown with foliage. Zeb smiled, recognizing Sid's tune: "When the Levee Breaks."

"Excellent choice," Zeb said. "Who doesn't love some Led Zep?"

"People I don't want to be friends with, that's who," Sid said. "Good music gets inside you and vibrates at the same frequency as your blood."

"Damn. That's some high-level *truth* right there!" Zeb started humming along, and the brothers' tinny duet drowned out the sounds of the forest as they got closer and closer to the big 'X' on Annie May's map.

Their humming ended abruptly when they rounded a slight bend in the road and nearly slammed into a tiny, decrepit guardhouse; the car skidded to a stop just a few feet from the base of the small building. They took note of the guardhouse's dirty, broken windows and thick layer of obscene graffiti. Zeb chuckled when he saw the large red penis spray-painted on the rotting, sloped wood of the structure's roof. He threw a gentle elbow into Sid's shoulder. "Hey, Sid. Check it out." He pointed toward the roof. Sid did not smile, or even shift his gaze.

"What? What is it?" Zeb asked.

"Do you hear that?" Sid whispered.

Zeb looked around, as if locating some sort of movement in the trees around them would help him understand what his brother was hearing. "Hear what?"

Sid sucked in a breath. "Exactly."

"What? I don't get it," Zeb said, a bit too irritated to be unnerved.

"Just listen. There's… nothing. No birds chirping. No leaves rustling. I don't hear anything," Sid said.

Zeb lifted a hand to his ear, as if to amplify any possible sounds. "Shit," he said. "Nothing."

The brothers sat in silence for a moment, their heartbeats in sync and accelerating together. Zeb was the first to break the quiet.

"Maybe we film that guardhouse?"

Sid shook his head, as if to clear it. "Good idea. Good place to start. Build up some tension for the audience."

"Yeah. I mean, with the right editing, that thing can look creepy as hell. Foreboding."

"We'll have people screaming '*No! Don't go in there!*' at their screens!" Sid joked to mask his growing anxiety as he moved to get out of the car and get the cameras set up.

Thirty seconds later, each brother held a camera in one hand and a small microphone in the other. They stood in front of the guardhouse.

"Okay, I think we should get a shot walking around the guardhouse, and maybe even a shot of the inside," Sid said.

"Works for me," Zeb flashed an awkward thumbs-up as he juggled his microphone.

They simultaneously pressed the Record button on their cameras, and twin red lights started blinking in the hazy green filtering through the trees.

"And...let's go," Sid said.

They both started rotating around the guardhouse, cameras aimed at the broken windows and vandalized walls. Zeb grabbed a quick shot of the roof-penis, trying not to let the microphone pick up his chuckle. He didn't want to ruin the eerie silence.

When they'd completed a full circle, they paused. Zeb stopped recording and lowered his camera as Sid turned his lens up to Zeb. Zeb nodded his agreement—it was time to film their customary intro clip.

Zeb waved. "Hi everybody, I'm Zeb, we've got Sid behind the camera there, and today we're exploring whatever remains of Mel's Wildlife Park in Hiawassee, Georgia. Let me tell ya, folks—this was not an easy place to find. And I don't just mean physically—there was only one article—*one!*—on the Internet about this place. Apparently, Mel's, which was started in 1972 by, big surprise, this guy named Mel, had some animals and possibly a small aquarium or something. I'm talking a lion, a couple zebras, that sort of thing. Well, it appears Mel wasn't such a great zookeeper, because visitors started complaining that the animals were all chained up and starving. So, when the Humane Society and the police stepped in, Mel stepped out." Zeb lifted his fingers and wiggled them. "And he was never seen again!"

Sid smiled from behind the camera and cocked his chin toward the guardhouse.

Zeb continued. "Sid and I started out this morning, and we drove and drove but we couldn't find this place. We ended up asking a wonderful Hiawassee girl named Miss Annie May—shoutout to you, girl!—to draw us a map. We've been driving for about fifteen minutes from Hiawassee's Main Street, and we've just come upon this lovely little guardhouse right here. As you can see"—Sid panned the camera over the guardhouse, even bringing the lens right up to a hole in the dirty glass and pointing it downwards, presumably to capture whatever crunchy nuggets of bugs and feces he could find—"ain't nobody been here for a *while*. We haven't seen a sign yet, but I think it's fairly safe to say this used to be Mel's guardhouse, where a security guard would sit with his magazine and donut and wave people through toward the parking lot—which, I think, will be our next stop."

Sid let the camera roll for another five seconds before he stopped recording and lowered the lens. "I think we got it! Nice one, bro."

"Thanks. Mind if we take a quick look? I'm worried the sunlight coming through all those leaves might make me look weird."

Sid rolled his eyes. "You looked fine. But sure, whatever. Let's take a look."

Zeb moved to stand beside his brother, their faces squished together in front of the viewfinder. Sid pressed play.

Onscreen, a miniature Zeb went through his spiel. Full-size Zeb nodded, pleased. "I'm looking *good*. Mm-hmmmm."

Sid rolled his eyes again, harder this time. Zeb stepped away, satisfied with his performance. "I think we got that good, bro. Let's get on with it," Zeb said. "I really think—"

Zeb stopped, his words caught in his throat, when he saw the stricken expression on his brother's face. Sid's eyes were glued to the viewfinder.

"What? What is it?" Zeb asked. He moved back next to Sid, following his gaze. "What—"

He saw it, too.

On the miniature screen, Sid had paused the footage at the moment when he'd pressed the lens to the broken glass for a look at the guardhouse floor. A small severed hand, resting on a bed of dead bugs and brown leaves and ragged at the edge, seemed to beckon them with its dirty palm.

Zeb jumped back. "What the fuck? What the actual fuck?"

Sid couldn't tear his eyes from the screen. "There's no way," he huffed. "That…that can't be real!"

Zeb gave him a grim stare. "We have to look." He took a ragged breath. Sid still hadn't moved a muscle. "I mean—we can't just leave that damn thing there!"

Sid finally glanced up, lowering the camera. He switched it off and set it on the roof of the car. "Christ. You're right."

Zeb mirrored his brother's action and set his own camera on the car. They both took two tentative steps back toward the guardhouse.

They stood, shoulder-to-shoulder, in front of the dirt-streaked window. The jagged hole the width of a ping-pong ball offered a clear view inside. Neither Sid nor Zeb wanted to press his face to the glass and look down, but, finally, Zeb tiptoed forward, as Sid knew he would. Zeb began to lower his right eye to the hole, squinting with his left. Sid breathed heavily next to him.

Preparing himself, Zeb leaned close and looked inside. Sid's heartbeat pounded in his ears so loudly he almost didn't hear his brother's laugh. Zeb laughed again, and Sid poked him in the shoulder blade. "What? What is it?"

Zeb stepped back. "See for yourself."

Sid, comforted by his brother's reaction, brought his eye to the window. He steeled himself and looked down to find what was, upon further inspection, obviously a doll's hand. A dirty, cracked, nibbled on, shit-smeared, doll's hand. He snorted and clapped Zeb on the back. "It's a fucking doll. How did we miss that?

"I don't know! It looked so…real on the screen!"

"Well, the frigging viewfinder is kinda shitty," Sid said.

"I've been telling you to get a new camera."

"I know, I know. But new cameras are expensive."

"Whatever. That will look good in the video! We can really scare the shit out of people."

"It really sets the stage, that's for sure," Sid agreed.

Zeb smiled, considering. "It is still creepy, even though it's not real. I mean, how did it get there? Where's the rest of the doll? Who leaves a broken doll arm in a dirty guardhouse in the middle of nowhere?"

Sid's own grin slid off his face, like unwanted food falling off a plate into the trash. "Um. Maybe we don't think about those questions until we're far away from here?"

"Fine with me."

They packed up their cameras, got back in the car, and drove on.

*　*　*

Walking. Walking. Walking. Five minutes had passed since they'd parked the car in the remains of the cracked asphalt lot and started off down the trail into the park proper. Ten minutes. Fifteen. Sid and Zeb hoisted their cameras each time they rounded a bend in the overgrown, foliage-choked gravel path, preparing for something interesting. After twenty minutes, they started to think maybe whatever was left of Mel's had decayed into nothingness, or it was so buried under the thick Georgia underbrush that no one could penetrate deep enough to find it. Sid was about to suggest they turn back toward the car and give this exploration up as a bust when they rounded a curve and came into a small clearing.

A low-slung, dirty stucco outbuilding sat like a patient spider in the tall grass. Sid couldn't put his finger on exactly what made him so uncomfortable about the building, but he knew something awaited them in there. He looked toward Zeb, and when their eyes met, Sid knew he had been thinking the same thing. Zeb took a step forward. He cocked an eyebrow at his brother. "You're not chickening out, are you?"

Screwing up his courage, Sid took two steps forward, his palms slick with anxious sweat. "Not on your life."

They hoisted their cameras once again. They'd left their microphones in the car, just in case they had to make a quick escape. Running with two hands full was difficult—Sid knew from experience. The cameras' built-in microphones would have to be good enough.

As they tiptoed closer to the building, they could make out the faded blue block letters above the wooden doorway. Zeb squinted. "What's that say?"

"I think it says…aquarium?" Sid pointed the camera toward the building. "Let's start recording here." They pressed their Record buttons, and each made a few panoramic sweeps of the building and the silent clearing.

They continued to record as they closed the distance, and when they were within three feet of the door, another set of letters came into focus. Scrawled on the door in dull red paint so faded it looked like a ghost, was "Dangerous Chemicals. Do Not Enter." Sid zoomed in with his camera.

Zeb laughed. "Come on. It's been like forty years. No way there's anything left in there. It's probably all dried up. And who knows, maybe Mel wrote this to keep dumb teenagers out after he left."

Zeb's theory didn't ring true to Sid at all, but he didn't want Zeb to see his growing fear. He balled the trembling fingers not holding his camera into a fist. "Yeah. I'm sure you're right. Plus, I mean…it's an aquarium. Chlorine would be about the only dangerous chemical that could be in there, right? And that would definitely be gone by now."

"Then let's stop standing here and give the people what they want!" Zeb said, grinning. While Sid lived for the chance to direct, shoot, and edit his own films, he knew his brother lived for the thrill of the exciting (or gross or weird or scary) reveal.

Sid unclenched his fist, put his fingers on the doorknob, and twisted.

Nothing happened.

"Oh come on," he grunted at the doorknob, twisting harder. Still, nothing happened.

"Step back," Zeb said. He handed Sid his still-recording camera and with one swift kick, he blew the door inward. Sid jumped back, just in case something was lying in wait.

"Damn," Zeb said. "That was pretty cool, if I do say so myself."

"Nice," Sid said, handing Zeb his camera back. "You ready?"

Zeb pulled a flashlight from his back pocket and pointed it into the black hole. "Now or never!"

Zeb clicked on the light and illuminated a cobwebbed hallway, the floor littered with leaves, dead bugs, and what Sid was pretty sure had been a squirrel. "Attractions This Way" was barely legible above an arrow on the wall, both in flecked blue paint. Zeb started down the hall, panning his camera to catch as many crusty details as possible. Sid followed him, doing the same.

The hallway seemed impossibly long, but it eventually opened into a large room. There were no windows, and everything beyond the weak yellow tunnel of Zeb's flashlight was pitch black. Sid hesitated, and Zeb paused, turning to face his brother. "What are you waiting for?"

Sid swallowed hard. "Nothing. Let's go."

Their feet crunched on the carpet of dead bugs and dry leaves. "Let's do a slow pan around the room, with just the night vision setting, no flashlight. And make sure to keep the camera steady, otherwise that's going to be hell for me to edit," Sid said.

"Okay, okay. Starting on the right," Zeb said, pointing his camera into a dusty corner. They both slowly panned their lenses over filthy, mold-fuzzed tanks set into a striped wall. To Sid, they looked like the eyes of corpses dumped in the forest and left to rot. The wall ended after about fifteen feet, and they panned around, exploring the rest of the room through their viewfinders. Everything looked unreal and greenish through the night vision lens. In the center of the room, a steel table with curling porno magazines sat askew. An empty pack of cigarettes lay crumpled next to the magazines, as though whoever had been here last had enjoyed just one more smoke in the damp dark, flipping through a dirty magazine as he waited for the cigarette to burn down to his fingers.

Beyond the table, rotting posters depicting fish and wildlife plastered the wall. Below them, what looked like a lobster tank sat empty.

"Nothing interesting back there," Zeb grumbled.

They continued panning both cameras, reaching another corner and sliding across the wall on their left. Sid's viewfinder revealed a colossal panel of scuzzy glass, murky liquid, and—

Sid screamed. Zeb dropped his camera and fumbled with the flashlight, managing to switch it on before it squirted from his fingers and went rolling across the carpet of decay. As it rolled, it revealed a behemoth floating in the diseased green tank. First, a sharp tail. Next, a triangular fin. Finally, a gaping, bullet-shaped mouth filled with rows upon rows of razor-sharp teeth. The flashlight came to a stop when it hit the leg of the metal table, its beam resting on the dull, dead eye of a Great White shark.

Sid and Zeb stood, speechless and motionless, for a full thirty seconds. Neither knew what to say or what to do—Zeb stared, while Sid kept his camera trained on the shark. He half-expected it to twitch a fin or close its jaws. Zeb was the first to break the silence.

"Motherfuck," he growled. "What the actual fuck is that?"

"I mean…it looks like a Great White shark?" Sid squeaked, clenching his muscles hard to keep his bladder—and his sphincter—shut.

"Again, what the motherfuck?" Zeb almost shouted. "Who keeps a Great White shark in a tiny tank in a shitty backwoods zoo? And then… who leaves it here to die?"

"Mel, apparently," Sid said softly.

"Well, fuck Mel," Zeb said. He swept his camera from the floor, then moved toward the middle of the room to pick up his flashlight. "Come over here, Sid. Let's get a closer look."

Sid's feet didn't want to move, but he managed to get them going after a brief but fierce struggle. "Sure. This might be…the craziest thing we've ever found."

"Damn straight," Zeb said. He lifted his flashlight and panned it over the twenty-foot-long tank, from left to right. First the tail, then the fin, then the gaping jaws were silhouetted in the green murk. "That is fucking freaky."

Sid's lips started to tremble, and he couldn't help imagining the flashlight going out, the cameras blinking off, and hearing a loud *crack*—the tank breaking open like an egg, spilling the needle-toothed monster into the dark…

"Sid!" Zeb yelled, breaking Sid out of his waking nightmare. "Read this."

Sid walked over, being careful not to step too close to the tank. Zeb's light was trained on a small plaque next to the glass, but the tank was somehow even more awful when Sid couldn't see what was inside.

"It says this is a preserved Great White. As in, this thing is floating in fucking formaldehyde." Zeb said, almost gleefully. "Can you believe it?"

Sid took a sharp breath. "Damn. Wonder where Mel could have found something like this."

"No fucking clue," Zeb said. He paused, considering. "I wonder if we should, like…tell someone about this? I mean, I feel like this belongs in a… museum or something."

Sid didn't think the embalmed monster belonged anywhere but the fiery cauldron of hell, but he wasn't about to let Zeb see how scared he was. "Um. Yeah. That could be a good idea."

"Man. This is gonna blow up our channel! We're gonna go viral for sure," Zeb said, grinning.

"Definitely," Sid said. "Now turn off your flashlight again and let's get a few more shots in night vision. Then we're out of here. It's getting late, and we still have a long drive back."

"Sure, sure. Just give me a second." Zeb stared wonderingly at the tank, as awed as Sid was petrified. "I'm going to name her Annie May," Zeb said. "Now if that's not a shout-out, I don't know what is!"

Sid laughed in spite of the tingling dread nudging his body toward the exit. "I'm into that," he said. "But seriously, let's move."

"Okay, okay. Keep your pants on," Zeb said, once more panning around the room. "I'll get a few last shots."

* * *

Immediately after leaving Mel's, Sid called the Georgia Aquarium. Surely somebody there would be interested in this thing in the woods. Sid's hunch proved correct, and three weeks later, bigwigs from the aquarium went to get the amazingly well-preserved Miss Annie May from the rotted ruins of Mel's. According to a news segment Sid saw on YouTube that quickly went viral, moving the shark's tomb presented a bit of an engineering challenge, but the movers managed to transfer it into a new tank of formaldehyde (Sid was glad he hadn't realized its tank was leaking while they were in that creepy cavern). The movers then drove it down to the world-renowned aquarium in Atlanta. Sid and Zeb were honorary guests when the aquarium's CEO unveiled the shark's new exhibit. News crews were on hand, and the brothers gave a dozen interviews to various reporters, although, as usual, Zeb did most of the talking. They made sure to reference their YouTube channel in every conversation.

Subsequently, their video, which they titled "Finding PRESERVED GREAT WHITE SHARK at Mel's Wildlife Park," did, in fact, also go viral, even more so than the initial news segment. They gained nearly one million subscribers over the next month, prompting Sid to reconsider his expensive and difficult medical career path when vlogging could be so illustrious instead.

Sid and Zeb were thrilled with the success and influence the whole experience had brought them, but that didn't stop Sid's nightmares. Every night, Sid dreamed of the dead shark. Except in his dreams, it was very much alive—alive and hungry.

Sid tried to push the memory out of his mind as he and Zeb sped down the highway toward Gullywasher's.

CHAPTER TWENTY-SIX

Sam was scrolling through emails on her phone as she and Lucas walked from the hotel lobby toward his Jeep, appearing engrossed to discourage him from starting a conversation. Her personal email held few messages of interest—discount codes for cheap tennis shoes, new sales at Bed Bath and Beyond, a few irrelevant Notes to Alumni from her alma mater. She swiped to delete them all, then switched over to her work inbox.

That was a different story. She was inundated with status reports for various projects, data sets to review, analyses from student researchers, and the other administrative minutiae that demanded so much of her attention that she rarely got to do much actual work these days. Scrolling, she read the subject lines of each, just to make sure nothing was so urgent she needed to delay their departure—such as a response from Gruber. No dice. Satisfied she wasn't neglecting any urgent tasks, she popped her phone back in her pocket.

The car beeped as Lucas hit the unlock button on his key fob, and he pulled Sam's door open for her in a studied imitation of chivalry. When they were both settled in the car, he gave her a toothy grin that turned her stomach.

His finger stabbed the ignition button, but the Jeep remained silent.

"Uh oh," he said, frowning.

"What is it?" Sam asked.

"Umm…I'm really no expert with cars, but I know enough to say this baby isn't purring like she should."

"Yikes," Sam said. Maybe they wouldn't have to go to Gullywasher's after all?

He stabbed the button again. The result was the same: nothing.

"Shit," he murmured. "I think we're out of luck."

"Too bad," Sam said softly. "No theme park today, I guess." She tried to hide her elation; she felt as though a deity had swooped down to save her.

That deity clearly had other plans, though. Lucas scrunched his mouth to one side of his face and said, "Well, there's really no reason we still can't go through with that. I'll need to get this car fixed before we can leave Savannah, anyway. Why don't I just call Triple A, and we can get an Uber to take us to Gullywasher's? It'll be better than sitting around in a mechanic's shop, waiting for what I'm expecting will be a hefty price tag to fix this baby up."

"I think it would be prudent for us to head over to the hospital—"

"Oh, live a little, Clements! A cab is probably better anyway to get to Gullywasher's. Then we don't have to worry about parking. I'll call Triple A—we'll see what the time estimate is for them to get here, hopefully it's quick—then we can call an Uber. We'll probably still get there before it even opens."

"I really don't know—"

"Well, I do. It's the best course of action, and we're taking it!" Lucas said with finality. Clearly, once again, he wouldn't be swayed, and he was pushing so hard that any further objection on her part would just be awkward.

"I'm going in search of more coffee while you take care of that," Sam said, unbuckling her seatbelt and hopping out of the car in one swift motion, relishing the fresh air.

"Get me a venti almond milk latte with four shots, would you?" he hollered after her as she walked away.

"Fine," she said, trying hard to keep the anger out of her voice.

"You can Venmo me for the cost," he added.

"Alright," she said through gritted teeth, praying that Triple A would be late, that they wouldn't be able to find an Uber, that Lucas would get a spontaneous bout of food poisoning—anything to prevent their trip to Gullywasher's. There was nothing professional about it, and she felt powerless to stop it.

Again, the deity had other plans. Triple A was hooking up Lucas' Jeep to the tow truck when she got back with his coffee.

*   *   *

"Wow, that was fast," she said, gesturing with her cup toward the truck.

"This is why I pay Triple A the big bucks," he said, winking. "Thanks for the coffee."

"Yep."

"I owe you one."

Sam shook her head. "You don't owe me anything. It's just coffee."

"I'll pay you back one day, just you wait," he said. "Maybe dinner and a movie?"

"Hey, Mr. Lucas?" one of the Triple A men called, saving Sam from having to answer.

"What's up?" Lucas said. "And it's Dr. Lucas, by the way."

"Sorry. Dr. Lucas. We're gonna take your Jeep over to Tucker and Sons— it's near Forsyth Park, on Montgomery. They do a good job over there, and it'll be cheaper and quicker than the dealership service department. They'll probably get her up and running by the end of the day."

"Alright, that's not too bad," Lucas said.

"They'll give you a call when she's all fixed up." The man rummaged in his pocket and pulled out a slightly rumpled but still serviceable business card. In artless script on the front, it said Tucker & Sons Service Center. He pressed it into Lucas' outstretched hand. "Just ring them up if you need anything in the meantime."

"Thanks. Appreciate y'all coming out here this morning."

"No worries, Dr. Lucas. You have a good day now."

"And yourselves, too."

Both men gave Lucas friendly nods and climbed into the cab of the tow truck. With a roar of the engine, they scooted away from the curb, dragging his car along behind them. The smell of motor oil and gasoline bloomed in the wet air.

Lucas turned to Sam, who was furiously sucking down the last of her drink and trying to fortify herself with the caffeine. Today was not going to be easy, that much was clear.

"Well," he said, grinning. "Let's get that Uber and continue on our quest to play hooky even though we're adults with mortgages and 401(k)'s."

"I don't have a mortgage, but sure," she said.

"Well, then you're far more responsible than I am."

"Right." That was probably the truest thing Lucas had ever said to her.

"Call us that Uber, will you?"

Sam was about to offer a last protest when, down the street, a yellow taxi turned the corner and started coming straight toward them. "Hold up," he said, pointing at the taxi and raising his arm. "No need for an Uber—looks like we got lucky today."

The cab driver, seeing Lucas' outstretched arm, put on a blinker and pulled up in front of them.

"Hey folks," the driver said as they scooted into the back seat. "Where y'all headed this morning?" His name tag, which read 'Eugene Frasier,' hung from the rearview mirror.

Shit, Sam thought. *Looks like I'm headed to Gullywasher's.*

*   *   *

Lucas was chortling with a childish glee Sam found repulsive as he said, "Gullywasher's of Georgia, please."

Eugene whipped around to face them, his eyes bright. "Gullywasher's?"

"You know the place?" Lucas asked.

"Of course I know it," Eugene said amiably, turning back toward the road as he pulled away from the curb.

"Good place?" Lucas asked.

Eugene chuckled, and it put Sam on edge for reasons she couldn't articulate. "Oh yeah," he said, wiping his nose on the back of his hand with a perfunctory snort. "Great place."

Doubt crept into Sam's mind, and she thought back to the discount offer text she'd gotten from the unknown number. Something was wrong here. What was she missing?

"Usually crowded this time of year?" Lucas asked, still smiling as the taxi glided past ornate old houses. The droplets of humidity in the air caught the morning light and sparkled like diamonds.

"Heh," Eugene said, merging onto the highway. The houses gave way to ugly strip malls and gas stations, tall signs for fast food, then acres upon acres of thick, swampy forest. "Not usually, but it's been popular recently."

What is that supposed to mean?

"Huh. Good news for us then, eh?" Lucas said, raising an eyebrow at Sam. That was definitely not good news; she much preferred to be around Lucas only when there were as many other people around as possible. She didn't trust him, especially not after the way he'd invaded her privacy so brazenly that morning.

"Sure," Eugene said, reaching up to adjust his rearview mirror. "Although, I wouldn't have taken you two for the Gullywasher's type."

"Why not?" Sam asked, failing to keep a faint note of worry out of her voice.

"Let's just say you look a little more... respectable than my usual passengers." Eugene laughed, a nasty choking noise more reminiscent of anger than mirth.

"Well, we are very respectable," Lucas said, smiling. Sam could tell he was playing along, thinking the cabbie was just another colorful Savannah resident, harmless. Sam wasn't so sure.

Trees whizzed by, and Eugene flipped on his blinker, exiting the highway.

"Now, we're almost there. We just need to discuss my payment."

"Uh…okay," Lucas said, consternation creeping into his voice.

"I handle everything for Leona—you'll pay a flat fee for the stuff, then a small commission and transportation charge for myself. I guess I should have said this before, but cash only, please. How much are you folks lookin' to get?"

"Excuse me?" Sam asked.

Eugene's eyes flicked over their curious faces in the rearview mirror. "You know, a quarter gram, a half, a whole gram, what?"

"A gram of what?" Sam said, frustration pushing her voice an octave higher than normal.

"Lady, the only people who go to Gullywasher's are looking for a fix. Please tell me you know that?"

"Jesus," Lucas mumbled under his breath. More loudly, he said, "We're just looking for a fun day at an amusement park. We don't want any trouble."

Seat creaking, Eugene turned to look at them, risking an accident as the cab lumbered over the bumpy road toward Gullywasher's. "Um," he said, frowning. "Hate to break it to you folks, but Gullywasher's shut down about fifteen years ago, now."

"That's impossible," Lucas said. "I checked the website today. Everything looked completely up to date."

"Heh. Believe it or not, I've heard that one before."

"What?"

"Look, you don't have to beat around the bush with me. I'm not here to bust you or con you or anything. I'm just the driver." Eugene brought his hand up to scratch a patch of dandruff in his greasy hair, but in the rearview mirror, his eyes gleamed with suspicion.

Sam started wringing her hands in her lap, her teeth digging into her lip. Lucas contrived to move his leg to touch hers, and when she glanced at his face, he was looking out the window, smiling innocently. She scowled in response, pulling her leg away.

With a snort, Lucas leaned forward, trying to look casual. The car was slowing as it approached a decrepit archway. "So," he said, directing his voice up at Eugene. "How long have you been working for Leona? Have you taken many people here?"

Sam and Lucas were thrown into the seats in front of them as Eugene slammed on the brakes, bringing them to a painful stop directly below the arch that had once welcomed people to Gullywasher's of Georgia.

"Just who the fuck are you," Eugene said, turning to face them with a snarl. A blade appeared in his hammy fist.

Lucas threw his hands up, his attention now completely on the unexpected threat. "Woah, woah, woah," he said.

"You cops? Narcs? What?" He was waving the blade, each pass causing the light filtering through the canopy of trees to glint off of its sharp edge. Sam felt sweat sliding down her back.

"We're just scientists!" she blurted, her hand creeping toward the door handle as quietly as possible.

Eugene stopped waving the blade, taken aback. "Scientists?"

"We're from the CDC," Lucas said, his hand reaching for his door handle just as Sam reached for hers, both of them eager to leave this dangerous man in the dust.

"CDC?" Eugene repeated. "Why?"

"There's an outbreak investigation going on," Lucas said. "We're here for support."

The cloud of confusion on Eugene's face cleared. "Huh," he said. "That son of a bitch."

Sam's hand was clenched around the door handle, and she was ready to spring out when the moment was right.

Eugene continued, not waiting for a response. "I knew he wasn't looking for a fix."

Sam was about to bolt when Eugene turned again to face them with such speed that flakes of dandruff flew off his head in snowy cascades. "Forget everything I said before. Gullywasher's is great. In fact, I dropped your friend off here yesterday. Twitchy little guy."

Sam's eyebrows shot up in shock. "What are you talking about?"

"Forties, balding, sweaty, tight-assed. Ring any bells?"

Sam sucked in a breath. "Gruber was here?" she asked.

"Didn't tell me his name. Just wanted to visit Leona. Now you both go on and get out. It's time I went on my way."

"What? Can you at least drive us to the main entrance?" Lucas said.

Eugene's voice turned stony. "I'm exercising my rights as a taxi driver in the city of Savannah to politely ask passengers to remove themselves from my vehicle when the ride has concluded."

"Um…alright, of course," Lucas said nervously. Sam thought getting out right now was a wonderful idea, far preferable to staying in this cab for another minute with a dandruff-laced, potentially homicidal stranger.

"Out! Both of you!"

Sam didn't need to be told twice. She sprang out of the car, whipping around to slam the door. Lucas clambered out more slowly and walked over to join her near the base of the arch.

Eugene honked his horn once, then flipped the cab into reverse and accelerated backward down the path, popping up and down rhythmically over potholes. He hadn't even asked them to pay the fare.

When he was out of sight and the dust had settled, Lucas turned to Sam.

"Well. That was…weird."

"It was terrifying, that's what it was," Sam said, closing her eyes and shaking her head.

"Aw, look at you. It's okay. I'm so sorry you were scared," Lucas said, sidling closer. Before Sam could react or step away, his arm was around her, squeezing. "It's all good now. You're safe here with me."

That was the biggest load of crap Sam had ever heard, and she hurriedly slipped out of his grip. She pulled her phone from her pocket, every muscle in her body tense. "I'm going to call an Uber." She navigated to the Uber app on her phone and clicked to call a ride.

Nothing happened.

"What the hell?" Sam said, worry burrowing deeper into her voice. "Shit."

"What is it?"

"Do you have service out here?"

Lucas slipped his phone from his pocket and cursed. When he turned the phone around to face her, she saw where the four white AT&T bars should have been, there were words instead: No Service.

"Shit," Lucas said. "What do you propose we do now?"

Sam was still staring at her screen. Her phone had downloaded a new email from the server, apparently before they'd left the range of cell service. As she read, her eyes grew wide.

"What?" Lucas asked.

"I just got an email from Flora, one of the EIS officers on the Savannah investigation. Apparently Patricia Dalco just died."

"Seriously?"

"Yep."

"Lung failure?"

"They're not quite sure yet, but that's my guess." Sam's fearful expression turned thoughtful. "You know, I've given this some thought, and I'm trying not to jump to conclusions or say 'zebra' when I hear hoofbeats, but… botulism is a real possibility here."

Lucas shrugged. "It definitely could be. How long do you think it'll take for the autopsy?"

"Flora said they've put a rush on it—hopefully we'll have something by the end of the week."

"Well, that's good news."

They stood in silence for a moment as Sam processed. She didn't have many choices, but she knew she didn't want to prolong the forced alone time with Lucas. "So maybe right now we go in search of a signal, or even a payphone?"

"Alright," Lucas said.

Shoving her useless phone back in her pocket, she walked under the archway, past a guardhouse, and down the path into Gullywasher's, Lucas following slightly behind.

CHAPTER TWENTY-SEVEN

Lucas followed Sam through the cracked parking lot, down a path choked with dying trees, and toward the ticket booth. Sam half-expected to see a short line of children curled into adults, herded in by metal guardrails painted a bright blue, all waiting to purchase tickets from bored, gum-popping teenagers in candy-striped uniforms.

What she saw instead was far more interesting. Sam had always harbored a secret passion for abandoned places; she thought the stories they held were fascinating. As a teenager, she'd explored an abandoned soap factory near her neighborhood, spending the entire day absorbed by the derelict beauty of it all and snapping photos with her disposable Kodak. Now, seeing the Gullywasher's ticket booth ahead, her steps quickened in anticipation. The building was decrepit, covered in rude graffiti, left to rot. Sam felt a smile spread across her face.

"What are you so happy about?" Lucas asked.

"Nothing. It's just so…interesting here."

Lucas snorted. "Interesting? Really? I would say it's more…disgusting? I mean, come on—I'm pretty sure that's black mold right there."

Sam didn't want to share anything with Lucas, didn't want to invite him into her inner world, but her fingers were vibrating with the urge to take pictures, to capture everything around her, to explore. He would invariably be tagging along behind her. Best to get everything out of the way as quickly as possible.

"There's just something so fascinating about exploring a place people and time have left behind. When I was younger, I was a bit more adventurous, and I'd go out searching for falling-down places. I usually brought my camera, and I actually got some good pictures."

"Wow. I didn't realize I was in the company of an artist." Lucas let out a long, low whistle that made Sam's skin crawl.

Sam chuckled humorlessly. "Hardly. I don't do it much anymore. Turns out wandering around in condemned buildings and crawling under fences with 'No Trespassing' signs isn't exactly the safest of hobbies."

"I would think not. You don't have to worry now, though—you know I can protect you out here, of course." Lucas winked.

Sam ignored him and continued. "I let the Internet do my exploring for me now."

"That's a thing?"

"Sure. Urban exploring is extremely popular."

"I guess I never really thought about it."

"Most people don't. One of my favorite things to do—when I'm not working, of course—is watch these two brothers on YouTube. They have a channel where they go and explore abandoned places. They're actually pretty famous. Maybe you've heard of them? Sid and Zeb Barkov. They found that preserved Great White that's now at the Georgia Aquarium."

Lucas squinted, thinking. "You know what? I think that does ring a bell. There was a big ceremony or something, right? It was on TV?"

"All over the news. It was incredible." Sam remembered the media coverage fondly. She'd even recorded the segment so she could watch the dead shark being unveiled over and over. She never grew tired of seeing it.

"Hm. Okay. So that means bringing you to an abandoned amusement park is actually more exciting for you than if it was operating?"

Sam shifted away from Lucas. "I suppose so."

"Well, then I'm glad this place is shut down."

"Maybe I'll get some good photos out of this," Sam said, speaking more to herself than Lucas.

"We should take some selfies, too. I'm going to let you lead the way. I've got no experience with this stuff. Show me what you love about this urban exploring thing." He smiled, showing way too many teeth. "I love to see a woman so passionate about something."

Sam coughed to hide the sound of her gagging.

*　　*　　*

"So," Lucas ventured as they made their way around the ticket booth and into the heart of the park. "What did you make of that psycho cabbie talking about someone named Leona?"

"I'm not sure. What did you think?"

"Probably bullshit—pardon my language. The guy didn't exactly inspire confidence, especially after pulling a knife on us and leaving us stranded with no cell service."

"What does that mean for Dr. Gruber?" Sam asked, uneasy for so many different reasons.

"What about him? Sounds like, worst case, he is into some stuff we definitely did not expect. I hope he didn't come here to buy dope. As his direct supervisor, you'd have to take action—it could be the end of his CDC career. Best case, maybe he got that fake ticket discount email, too, and he realized pretty fast this isn't everything it's cracked up to be."

"Maybe," Sam said, her voice pregnant with discomfort. "What if he's in trouble here? This is all just so unlike him."

"Maybe, maybe not. How well do you really know him as a person? Not just as an epidemiologist and a colleague and, I guess, as a teacher?"

Sam considered. "I've known him for a long time. He's not as bad as everyone thinks, at least that's what my gut tells me. Plus, I'm pretty sure he watered my office plants for me while I was gone."

"Well, that's not exactly a ringing endorsement—the custodial staff probably watered your plants. If there is some slim chance that he's still here, all we can really do is go search around anyway." Lucas shrugged, peeking at her from the corner of his eye.

"That's true," Sam said, pasting a thin smile on her lips. This was going to be a long day, and she needed to keep things as pleasant as possible if she was going to survive with her career and her reputation intact.

She turned away from Lucas to survey the scene before her, which kindled a fire of childish joy that balanced out the dread she felt at being alone for an extended period of time with Lucas.

The sun was rising steadily in the sky, and the humidity was starting to make Sam's hair fuzz, forming a gentle halo around her face. The park still smelled of decades-old hot dogs, greasy funnel cakes, sticky-sweet ice cream cones, and burnt popcorn. Out of the corner of her eye, Sam could just make out a large sign to her right that read 'Food Court.' Sam's palms itched for her camera as she headed in that direction, not looking back to see if Lucas was following.

"This is pretty neat, I guess," Lucas said, running to catch up. He pointed toward the food court. "Hungry?"

"Ha. I'm going to look around there first, maybe take some pictures. It's been a long time since I've been someplace this interesting."

She started walking again, but stopped short as her eyes fell on the broken bridge straddling the lazy river. Lucas groaned like a walrus.

"I don't think we're going anywhere with the bridge like that, I'm afraid," he said.

Sam shook her head at him. "How easily you give up." She didn't wait for a response. She jogged toward a clump of blistered, broken trees. Her biceps popped as she pulled a log from the bunch, kicking at the base to separate the last few roots connecting it to the ground. She had already dragged the log back over to the bank of the river before Lucas bothered to lift a finger.

"Need a hand?" he asked.

"It's a little late for that, but you can help me set this up over the river."

Lucas bent down, his knees cracking violently, and gripped one end of the log. Sam balanced the other end between her hand and her hip.

"Alright," she said. "I'll count to three, and then you'll push up while I set this down. If we time it just right and push hard enough, we can somersault this up and over the river."

"I must admit, I'm extremely impressed with your handiness," he said, a leer souring the compliment.

Sam choked back her disgust. "Ready?"

When Lucas nodded, she called, "One… two… three!" She lodged her end of the log into the grass about a foot from the drop-off into the concrete channel at the same time as Lucas launched himself out of his squat and shoved the log high up into the air. It wavered for a second at the top, balanced on its new ragged base, before falling over neatly to the other side.

"Timber!" Lucas yelled, lifting his hand for a high five.

Sam really didn't want to oblige, but she held her hand up anyway. He slapped it and squeezed before letting go.

"Let's keep going," Sam said, wiping her palms on her pants.

"Don't you think—" Lucas started, but Sam was already on the other side and nearly at the Food Court.

She passed under its sign and into a small courtyard rimmed with food stalls. A rotating hot dog warmer, its glass panes smeared, sat on one counter; in another stall, a slushy machine tank was stained red, a relic of all the cherry drinks park patrons had ordered over the years.

"Abandoned places always look like the people left in a hurry," Sam said, awestruck.

"Huh. You're right," Lucas said, out of breath after hustling to catch up with her.

She headed toward the nearest stall; a molding sign overhead read 'Funnel Cakes.' Behind the scarred counter, they could see a row of rusty deep fryers lined with oil so old and clotted it looked like enamel. To the left of the fryers, a few bags of prepackaged funnel cake mix had exploded at the tiny hands of curious wildlife; the mix had left layers of dusty powder along the counter. Sam thought she could see a few small clumps of feces mixed in.

"I loved funnel cake as a kid," Lucas said. "Like doughnuts, but better."

"Cool," Sam said, ambling deeper into the food court.

At one stall, she was surprised to find a massive, desiccated pretzel hanging all by its lonesome from a metal hook in a rectangular glass case. Her fingers itched for her camera; it would be a perfect picture. The hardy foodstuff had aged from its original caramel color to a chocolate brown, which set off the white flakes of sea salt much more starkly.

"Dare me?" Lucas asked, his eyes lusty.

"Dare you to what?" Sam asked, bewildered.

"Dare me to take a bite?"

"Of that?" Sam asked, gesturing toward the pretzel. "You can't be serious."

"Oh, I'm serious."

"No, I don't think so."

Lucas considered, but not for very long. "Oh, you're no fun. I'll dare myself."

She raised an eyebrow, a smirk on her face. Maybe if Lucas broke his teeth, he'd spend more time complaining than trying to seduce her. "Alright. Go ahead."

"What'll you give me if I do it?"

"Nope. You dared yourself. You don't get anything in return."

"Well, once again, you've outsmarted me."

Sam didn't really think Lucas was going to go through with it, but he surprised her. He inhaled sharply before scrambling over the counter.

With a hard yank, he pulled open the door at the back of the glass case. He licked his lips, enjoying his own performance. "Mm. Smells good."

"Uh huh," Sam replied, frowning.

Lucas reached inside and grasped the pretzel. At his touch, the pretzel dissolved into a pile of dust and crumbs so suddenly he gasped.

"Damn!" he said, pulling his hand back.

"Too bad," Sam said over her shoulder. She walked on, not waiting to see if he was following.

*　　*　　*

Sam passed back out under the decaying 'Food Court' arch, Lucas trailing in her wake. In front of her, the remains of the water park sprawled like a dead spider—slides jutted from empty pools, standing water covered jumbles of discarded lounge chairs, a rust-streaked grotto served as a gravestone for the waterfall that had once gushed from above. A lifeguard chair, rising high into the air, leaned at a precarious angle out over the gulf of the main pool. Whereas the food court had been amusing, Sam found the remains of the pool simultaneously unsettling and intriguing.

"Wow," Sam breathed, as she came to a stop at the edge of the large gulch, its plaster falling away from the concrete walls in powdery chunks. "I really wish I had my camera."

"Can't you use your phone?" Lucas said.

Sam blinked, taken aback. Of course she could use her phone—why hadn't she thought of that? "I completely forgot I even had it." She pulled it from her pocket, glancing at the screen.

She froze.

Lucas, who had been studying the strange scene in front of them, turned toward her and moved uncomfortably close. "What is it?"

"Um." Sam gulped, the saliva forcing itself around a large lump in her throat. "I have a new email."

"Huh? So you have service?"

Sam squinted down at the screen. "No," she said slowly. "It literally says 'No Service.'"

"Then how did you get an email?"

"I don't know."

"Well, what does it say?"

Sam entered her phone's passcode and clicked on the email.

"It's from the Savannah Coroner's Office. I think this is Patricia Dalco's autopsy results…wait, there's an audio recording."

"Well, play it!"

"I'm going to," Sam said, irritated. She pressed play, and the air filled with the sounds of the autopsy theater.

"This is Dr. Angus Burroughs, senior forensic pathologist for the city of Savannah. The time is 1:34pm. On the table, I have Patricia Dalco, Caucasian female, age twenty-five. Eyes, green. Hair, light brown, shoulder-length."

"Agreed," came another male voice. "She's a looker."

"Felix, please," said Dr. Burroughs.

"You said CDC put a rush on this one?"

"Yes," Burroughs said.

"So… think we'll be out of here by four today?"

A heavy sigh crackled though the speaker before Burroughs said, "We're not going to do a rush job on this just because you want to go home early."

"Woah, no…I was just wondering, since. You know. I have an appointment…"

"Uh huh," Burroughs replied. "It takes however long it takes. For God's sake, Felix, we're still recording. We'll have to cut all this before we send it to CDC."

"Right, sorry."

"I trust you've read her medical records?" Burroughs asked.

"Yep."

"Excellent," Burroughs said. "Then let's begin. Again."

The sound of disposable gloves being adjusted snapped through the speaker.

"So," Burroughs said. "Here we have Patricia Dalco, age twenty-five, Caucasian female. Eyes, green. Hair, light brown, shoulder-length. Wounds consistent with drug injection on the backs of both hands, inside both elbows, and between the hallux and index toes of each foot. Beginning internal examination with the initial incision at the left shoulder joint."

The squish-squash sound of a cadaver being opened filled the stale air.

"It's so weird how they don't bleed," Felix said.

"Felix, hush! Starting second incision at the right shoulder joint."

"Woah, her nipples are almost black," Felix said. "Is that normal?"

"Can the comments! You're here to observe and learn. Finishing the trunk incision," Burroughs said. "Felix, picture," he snapped.

The sound of a camera clicking bellowed out of the speaker.

"Opening the Y-cut," Burroughs said. "Pinning the skin flaps of the Y-cut open using surgical pins."

Another camera click punctuated the silence.

"You know, Felix, there are two ways to open a chest cavity. One is cutting between the cartilage and ribs so the bones can be cracked open like a walnut, if you'll forgive the simile. The other option is to cut along the outer edges of the chest cavity, severing the ribs while leaving them attached to the breastbone. Then, I can pull out the entire apparatus and set it aside. I prefer this approach. Watch carefully."

The cracking of bones came next, followed by a dry sucking sound as the chest plate was removed.

Another camera click before Burroughs spoke again.

"Severing internal abdominal attachment tissue," Burroughs said. "Removing the intestines."

A wet plop came next—Sam assumed it was Patricia's viscera.

"Removing the spleen."

Camera click.

"Removing the liver."

Camera click.

"Removing the heart."

Camera click.

"Removing the stomach."

Camera click.

"Removing the lungs."

"Uh-oh," Felix said, his voice squeaky.

"Damn," Burroughs said.

"Is her lung supposed to bleed like that?"

"Of course it's not supposed to bleed like that. Cadavers don't bleed, Felix."

A few seconds of silence passed before Burroughs spoke again. "Get a picture," he hissed, then said loudly, "Accidental puncture of right lung has resulted in a slow bleed."

"That doesn't look like blood," Felix said.

"Well, what else could it possibly be? Hm, Felix?"

"I mean, it's brown. And chunky."

Burroughs snorted and then said, "Blood appears to be of an unnatural brownish color, with a…chunky consistency. Get a sample, Felix, quickly."

"Okay, okay," Felix said.

"God Almighty, what is that smell?" he said, so quietly Sam could barely hear him.

"It's coming from her!" Felix said.

"I really don't think that's possible…dear God, take a video of this, Felix! It's coming out of her eyes, her nose, her mouth…"

The men stopped speaking, and Sam thought she could make out a slippery squelching sound in the background, like toothpaste being squeezed from a tube. She felt sick.

"Oh my God," Burroughs said after a long silence.

"What happened?"

"I—I don't know," Burroughs said. He sounded spooked. "Um. Let the record show the body appears to have become…How to describe this? For lack of a better term…the body now appears…mummified. The circumstances of mummification are unclear. The epidermis has become dry and wrinkled and has taken on a grayish hue. The, um, the blood-like substance that issued from her facial orifices has evaporated. Oh my God—"

The recording cut out.

* * *

"What the hell was that?" Lucas asked.

"I don't know, and I can't understand how this recording possibly downloaded onto my phone with no cell service," Sam said.

Lucas shrugged. "Well, I think it's safe to say there won't be an open casket at her funeral."

Sam recoiled, disgusted. "Are you—"

A beep from her phone interrupted her.

"Oh God, what now?" Lucas asked.

"It's a text," Sam said, clicking on the alert and reading it aloud. "Outbreak at Gullywasher's amusement park. Biohazard suspected. Area being evacuated." In the distance, a crow cawed, sounding almost like laughter.

"Huh?" Lucas said, baffled.

Sam was shaking her head, her eyes closed. "What the hell? Nothing makes sense. I still don't even have service!"

"Does it say anything else?"

Sam opened her eyes, bringing the screen closer to her face to read the tiny text. Just as the words began to come into focus, her screen went blank and her phone shut off.

"Well," Lucas said. "Let's forget the weird autopsy recording for a moment. I'm sure there's a simple explanation. As for the text, I think, since there's nobody here and we don't have any cell service, that it's safe to say… it wasn't real?" He was trying for bravado, but not quite succeeding.

"What do you mean not real? We both saw it."

"Yes, we both saw it, but I think it was some sort of joke, or phishing scam, or something like that."

Sam sighed, her breath heaving from her chest, squeezing around the lump still sitting like wet burlap in her throat. "You don't really believe that, do you?" she said. "Anymore than you believe that autopsy wasn't highly unusual?"

Lucas tried to grin, but it looked more ghastly than amused. "No," he said in a small voice.

"We should leave," Sam whispered, the words paining her even as she said them. There was still so much to explore, and she hadn't yet seen a trace of Gruber.

"We still don't have cell service, so no way to call an Uber or a cab. Even if we leave, we can't really leave. How would we get back to the city?" Lucas said. She wondered dimly how a guy like him ever made it to such a position of authority in the CDC. He had zero problem-solving skills, his resourcefulness was negligible, and he was, for lack of a better word, a creep.

"We'll have to find another way out, then," Sam said. "Even if we have to walk all the way back to Savannah." In her mind's eye, all she could see was chunky mud oozing from Patricia Dalco's dead eyes.

"You know what I think?" Lucas asked, putting one heavy palm on her shoulder. "I think maybe we just content ourselves with the very plausible idea that that was some strange spam text. Didn't you tell me you've gotten one before?"

"Yeah. But that was a discount offer."

"To a park we now realize hasn't been open for years. Clearly somebody's messing with us."

"How would anybody know we're here? No one at the CDC, unless you told them without my knowledge, knows where we are. And who could possibly send a biohazard message when there is *no fucking service*?"

"It's just spam," Lucas said again, a broken record.

"Spam," Sam said, spitting the word out with venom. She pressed her fingers to her forehead, breathing deeply, trying to regain control of herself. "I guess…Ugh. I don't know. As for the autopsy—"

"Let's put that aside for now," Lucas said. Sam could hear the fear in his voice. "Maybe we just continue on, keep an eye out for a payphone or radio or something, but then head back out to the main road. Don't worry, I got you. You're safe with me."

Sam had never heard such a bald-faced lie in all her life, but she kept her misgivings to herself. "I mean, I guess we could always hitch or something if we have to."

Lucas snorted. "Hitch? Yeah, right."

Sam scowled. "It's an option."

"Hitching isn't safe for a young woman like you," he said, sidling closer.

"I'm just fine on my own," she said, and continued walking around the rim of the pool. She wondered if Patricia Dalco's body would ever be claimed by any family members.

As Sam walked around the pool, stepping past overturned lounge chairs, dry slides, putrefying dead things in the dark greenish standing water, a creeping terror started to envelop her.

When she reached the baby pool, which sat to the left of the main pool and was hemmed in by a low fence, Sam paused.

A child's teddy bear lay facedown in an inch of murky water, its fur matted with grime.

"What…" Lucas said, catching sight of it over her shoulder.

"I think maybe it's better to not ask questions," Sam said.

Somewhere ahead of them, a crow cawed.

CHAPTER TWENTY-EIGHT

Even though no families were merrily caravanning to Gullywasher's anymore, and hadn't been for nearly fifteen years, the Internet had not forgotten about the once-beloved park. Compared to the single blog post Sid and Zeb could find about Mel's, the Google-generated cache of results on Gullywasher's was a veritable treasure trove. There were fan websites lamenting its closure, nostalgic blogs with pictures of families in hideous 70's swimwear floating down the lazy river of their youth, and the official Gullywasher's of Georgia page was even still alive and limping onwards. The graphics were primitive, and the home page sported a large "After nearly forty years of aquatic fun, we regret to inform you we are no longer in business. Thank you for your patronage over the years." Surprisingly, the link to the park map still worked, and Sid was very thankful for that small courtesy.

Sid and Zeb had actually visited Gullywasher's when they were barely old enough to swim without floaties, their parents pulling them into big boy swim trunks and lathering them in thick white sunscreen that made them look like Victorian ghosts. Sid could faintly remember sitting in his mom's lap as they floated down the lazy river in a hot black inner tube, his brother in a similar position with their dad. That was nearly everything he remembered about the park—the lazy river, the inner tubes...

...and the alligator pit.

Sid didn't want to think about that. They had just exited the freeway near a crumbling billboard which still beckoned hot and thirsty travelers to "Gullywasher's of Georgia—Wet n' Wild Fun for the Whole Family!" The blue and white paint was sunbaked and fading, but the message was clear. It gave Sid the creeps.

"Getting so pumped right now…we're almost there!" Zeb said. He'd worked his way through the entire family-size bag of Cool Ranch Doritos with minimal help from Sid and was now reaching for the Funyuns. "Gotta fuel up!" he said, noticing Sid staring at his not-quite-plump hand pawing at another bag.

"Uh-huh," Sid said, rolling his eyes. "If we have to crawl through any fences to get there, you might be out of luck."

"Fuck off," Zeb said, laughing. "I can make myself very tiny when I so choose."

Sid laughed in response, and the brothers turned off the smooth pavement onto cracked asphalt, still usable, but rapidly deteriorating after nearly fifteen years of neglect under the unforgiving Georgia sun. The car bumped and bucked like an angry steer, and Zeb spilled a few Funyuns onto the floor.

"Watch it!" Zeb said. With a look of longing, he zipped up the resealable bag and placed it in the back seat with the others, then wiped his fingers on his shirt.

"Chill, I think we're almost there," Sid said, struggling to weave the car between ruts and potholes.

Zeb pulled out the map, tracing his finger over the broken road they'd taken.

"Okay. We're about to come to the entrance," Zeb said.

"How much farther?" Sid asked. "This is starting to make me a little carsick. And I didn't bring those motion sickness meds."

"I don't know, maybe an eighth of a mile? Three minutes or so?" Zeb said.

Sid grimaced, but said nothing.

The car jerked around for a few more minutes until they came to a shaky halt in front of a high, rickety archway. Arcing across the rotting wood were dark blue plastic letters that had once spelled Gullywasher's of Georgia but which now had more in common with a decaying typewriter, missing a handful of letters and spelling out nothing in any coherent way. Faint glue outlines remained where the letters had been. Sid wondered if some kid stole the missing letters, and if so, what he could have spelled with them. Rule? Where? How? Whore?

Sid's gaze fell from the decaying arch to the ugly structure beside it. A gray cinder block guardhouse, about fourteen feet square, squatted there like someone about to take a dump. Even though Sid found this unlikely comparison hilarious when it popped into his head, his good humor was shadowed by the memory of the small, sinister guardhouse at Mel's. The dirty doll hand still waved to him in nightmares, except in the nightmares, the doll hand grew straight out of a bullet-shaped shark's head. Sid shuddered.

"Hey," Zeb said, as if reading his brother's mind, "That guardhouse remind you of anything?"

Sid swallowed, loudly. "Kinda. Maybe the one at Mel's?"

"Yeah, maybe," Zeb said absentmindedly, as if lost in uncomfortable reveries of his own. Zeb gulped, and Sid wondered if doll-armed dead sharks swam through his nightmares, too.

Zeb clapped his hands, as if to dispel an unwelcome miasma. "Well," he said. "Do you want to get some footage of this bad boy?"

"Yeah. Maybe a few pans with audio intro and a few still shots of the arch," Sid said. "We can do another audio intro in front of the ticket booths, but we might as well get more footage than we need."

"Agreed," Zeb said. The brothers started unloading and preparing the camera equipment, the routine so well-worn it was graceful, almost ritualistic.

Sid's hands were full of equipment, so he let Zeb take the keys.

"Lock up, okay?" Sid said.

"You really think car thieves are gonna be skulking around here? You think they want your Civic?" Zeb teased.

"Shut up," Sid said as they walked the short distance to the guardhouse.

"Do you want to do the intro this time?" Zeb asked. "I feel like I'm always doing it. Which is fine, just wasn't sure if you'd rather get some screen time. Show the world that handsome mug of yours." Zeb reached up to pinch his brother's cheek, and Sid flinched away, leaving Zeb's fingers to grasp at the air.

Sid considered. Finally, he shook his head. "Nah. People are used to seeing you, and that's been working for us. Might as well stick with it."

"Fine by me," Zeb said. He set down his camera on the hood of the car and stepped beneath the arch, stopping in front of the dented metal guardhouse door. "Ready when you are, bro."

Sid moved back so he could get the entirety of the arch and the guardhouse in the shot. As he brought the camera into focus, he examined the scene with an artist's eye. He may have been studying biology in the pre-med track at school, but he was a filmmaker at heart—as well as a pragmatist. Filmmaking would probably never pay the bills, even with millions of YouTube subscribers, so a bachelor's degree from a great university (and, hopefully, an MD from a good medical school) was a much better bargaining chip for future employment. Zeb was less discerning, having finally settled on Italian Studies after a year and a half of, as their father called it, 'dicking around.' When Zeb announced his major, their father still proclaimed this 'dicking around,' but at least it was dicking around with a goal in mind.

"Yo," Zeb said. "You ready or what?"

Sid gave his brother a thumbs up and pressed the Record button. When the red light started blinking, Sid counted down three, two, one on his thin fingers, then pointed to give Zeb the go-ahead.

Zeb cleared his throat. "Hey everybody! As you know, you've got Zeb here, and my lovely brother Sid is behind the camera. Today, we're at one of the most well-known abandoned landmarks in Georgia. Any guesses?" He paused for dramatic effect. Sid thought it was a bit much, but whatever. Zeb was Zeb. He continued: "I'll give you a hint. We're just outside of Savannah, at a place known for its water park, aquarium, and roller coasters…but probably most famously for its *alligator pit*." Zeb emphasized this last piece in a deep voice, fingers raised and wiggling, as though tickling a ghost. "That's right folks, we're at Gullywasher's of Georgia! Which maybe you guessed from this crusty old arch above me, even with most of the letters missing. In case you're not familiar with Gullywasher's, I'll give you a bit of history. Once upon a time, which was 1965, this place opened, and was *the* place for family fun in Georgia. Sid and I even came here when we were little to ride down the lazy river, eat some cotton candy, and look at some big-ass gators. Fast forward to about fifteen or so years ago, and the park's owners really dropped the ball. The park was getting pretty gross and falling apart—I even heard a dolphin died because of some toxic mold or something. We also found in our research a young kid named Brandon Meyer died on the Gullywasher roller coaster in 2003. Apparently he was too small to ride the giant coaster, but the operator let him on anyway. One minute, Brandon was happily screaming with his hands up next to his dad, and the next minute he was just screaming, and then he was gone. There were a whole bunch of lawsuits and some criminal charges. Then, as if that wasn't bad enough, the Georgia Aquarium opened over in Atlanta in 2005. Gullywasher's lost a ton of business—people who wanted water went to the beaches nearby, and people who wanted aquariums went to Atlanta. The park officially closed in 2005." He paused dramatically. "But, that's not the end of the story. Apparently, there have been quite a few disappearances around this area since the park closed. Not all of them made the national news, but if you're a Georgia local and you read the papers, you probably remember hearing about Patrick Fenwick. He was the park's last security guard. He had four children at home. Reporters thought it might have been suicide because he was about to lose his job, but his wife never believed that. Plus, police never found his body." Zeb paused again, gesturing at the arch. "And he was just one of the disappearances connected to this park. Don't believe me? Go do some Googling yourself. I'll wait." Zeb paused again, smirking, before lifting up his hand in a welcoming, circus barker-style gesture. "And now, we're going to give you an inside look at what fifteen years of abandonment does to a place like this." Zeb smiled. "Let's get going."

Sid let the camera run for a few more seconds, zooming in on Zeb and then sweeping across the guardhouse. As Sid stared through his viewfinder, he noticed something odd. The guardhouse was encircled almost entirely in windows that started about chest-height, except where the opaque metal door interrupted the glass. Most of the windows were grimy, coated in nearly fifteen years of dirt, dust, and bug shit. Below the windows, uninspired teenagers had graffitied lumpy penises and, in one unusual case, an innocent-looking angel. Sid's gaze settled on the angel, outlined in blue, and then lifted upward to the window above the angel's halo.

Directly above the angel, an unmistakable handprint left a clean spot in the dirty glass. Sid zoomed in and thought he could see a faint red tinge at the fingertips.

"Hey! You still recording?" Zeb asked.

Sid sucked in a breath and pressed the red button. He lowered the camera. "Zeb," he whispered harshly. "Come over here for a second."

"What?"

"Just come here," Sid said, as he started walking toward the angel. He stopped in front of it and Zeb joined him, puzzled.

"Okay, what is it?" Zeb asked.

Sid pointed at the handprint, struggling to keep his finger from shaking. "Do you see that?"

Zeb followed Sid's finger, his eyes landing on the window. His eyes widened. "Damn," he said, almost reverently. "You get that on camera?"

"Well, yeah," Sid said. "But that's not really the point."

Zeb turned to look at his brother. "Then what is?"

"Anything look weird to you about that handprint?"

Zeb took a step closer, squinting a little to examine the print. After a few seconds of inspection, he stepped back. "Nope. Why? What am I supposed to be seeing?"

Sid sighed. *I'm not going crazy*, he thought. *This is just like with that fucking doll's hand. It's like I want to be scared, so I'm seeing scary things. It's just a handprint. There's no blood. No fucking blood at all.*

"Nothing," Sid said. "I guess something just looked a little wonky through the lens. Let's move on."

"Alrighty," Zeb said, always agreeable.

Sid didn't try to peek inside the guardhouse this time. Even though he could explain away the handprint easily enough—*just some stupid kids, looking for a place to hook up and smoke weed*—he wasn't willing to look any further. He and Zeb had investigated enough before coming here; he'd stayed up late into the night, reading newspaper articles about the disappearances of Katrina Ryen, George Bigby, Gina Choate, and of course, Patrick Fenwick. All those lost people, all tied to this decrepit park. Sid gulped and tried to put the black-and-white newsprint photos out of his mind. He wasn't afraid, but he wasn't entirely unafraid, either.

The brothers loaded their cameras back in the car and climbed in, headed for the parking lot.

CHAPTER TWENTY-NINE

Sid and Zeb cruised through the Gullywasher's parking lot, where long-dead industrial streetlights listed precariously to the side. With the windows down, Sid could hear the eerie sound of beer cans rolling in the soupy breeze. They stopped near the crooked asphalt path with a remarkably well-preserved sign pointing to the ticket booths and got out, stretching their legs.

"Alright," Sid said with a gulp. "Now comes the real fun." This last sentence came out as more of a question than a statement.

Zeb high-fived him. "I'm so excited I might piss my pants."

"Maybe don't do that."

"I do what I want," Zeb said, and hawked a loogie onto the ground to prove his point.

"And that's why you don't have a girlfriend," Sid said.

Zeb mock-gasped. "My my, that's some big talk coming from my bro who *also* has no girlfriend."

Sid chuckled. "Touché."

Zeb clapped his hands and rubbed them together. "I'm assuming you've got the map?"

Sid pulled the tightly rolled tube from his pocket where he'd stuffed it for safekeeping. "Of course I do." He unfurled it and held it up so his brother could see. "Looks like the first thing we'll come to is the ticket and admin building."

"Not sure if we'll see much exciting stuff there. Since we already filmed at the guardhouse, you cool with skipping the ticket booth unless we find something worth filming?" Zeb said.

"Yeah, that works," said Sid. "Although, you never know—remember when we found that collection of vintage celluloid reels in the ticket booth at the old movie theater? Now that was a pretty cool shot—zooming in close, then zooming back out, then I put that filter on it, and made it look like something out of a 1980's Japanese art house film…"

Zeb laughed, the sound bubbling up from deep within his considerable belly. "Oh yeah. That was pretty sweet."

They removed their equipment from the car, pulled cameras out of cases, attached microphones, reapplied deodorant and bug repellent, checked sound and video quality, and stuck water bottles in their back pockets, all of their movements efficient and graceful, choreographed by years of experience.

Fully outfitted, the brothers set off down the asphalt path toward the official entrance to Gullywasher's.

*   *   *

At first glance, the abandoned ticket booth was as uninteresting as the brothers had expected. Soaped-over windows, peeling paint, rotting wood, and the ubiquitous genitalia-inspired graffiti. As they got closer, discomfiting signs of recent human habitation materialized. There were the letters 'BTH' scratched into the window grime; a broken padlock on the side door; a shiny plastic barrette beneath the awning. Separately, none were enough to frighten Sid, but together, the signs formed a breadcrumb trail that led him down a dark path. Thoughts of serial killers, dope dealers, and severed hands danced through his consciousness, taunting him. He batted them away and grew frustrated with himself for falling into the fear trap Zeb so effortlessly avoided at all times.

"BTH?" Zeb said. "Hmmm…. I'm going with Billy Trent Huckins. That sounds redneck, doesn't it?"

Sid tried to laugh but couldn't quite make it sound natural. "It really does. But I think it's more of a Betty Trina Hathaway."

Zeb raised an eyebrow. "That's either Anne Hathaway's hot younger sister or a wrinkly sack of grandma."

"I'm glad that came across. I was going for wrinkly grandma."

Zeb clapped him on the back. "You're nasty, dude."

Sid grimaced and said nothing.

"So, not much to film here then, huh?" Zeb asked.

Sid frowned in thought and surveyed the crumbling building more closely. "I mean, I don't *think* so, but maybe we just get a quick pano shot. May be worth splicing it in later to give more of a journey vibe, like the audience is there with us—kind of like I did with that old arcade last year."

Zeb nodded. "Works for me. I'll take care of that; do you want to scout out what's next? I won't be long."

Sid really didn't want to venture off on his own into this godforsaken place, but he wanted his brother to call him a coward even less. "Yeah, okay."

As Zeb got his camera ready, Sid walked timidly around the side of the building. Sections of rusted metal railings were the last vestiges of evidence that crowds large enough to need corralling had once come here. He lifted his foot high and could just barely step over the railing, feeling as though he were crossing a divide with no easy return.

Continuing around the side of the squat ticket building, the first thing Sid found was a concrete channel that wound across the park in discordantly elegant arcs. Muddy water, dead leaves, and discarded plastic bags jostled in the bottom of what had once been the lazy river. Directly in front of him, a small wooden bridge had collapsed. Next to its jagged remains, some intrepid visitor had improvised a path across using an old log that barely traversed the channel below.

A bird cawed somewhere off to his right, and when he snapped his head in that direction, he noticed a woman's high-heeled shoe tangled in a clump of weeds growing through the concrete near the remains of the old bridge. Sid shivered despite the sauna-like heat.

"Sid!" Zeb called. "I got the shot! I'm coming around now. You find anything interesting?"

To his frustration, Sid struggled to respond in a voice not choked by unease. "Um," he tried. "Maybe?" This last came out as a squeak, which Sid prayed his brother would not notice.

No such luck. "You finally going through puberty?" he asked as he followed Sid's steps over the metal railing and to the bank of the lazy river.

Sid ignored the comment. When Zeb arrived at his side, he pointed one slightly trembling finger toward the shoe. "Does that look new to you?" he asked.

Zeb shrugged. "Kind of, I guess? Who cares, though?"

"Doesn't it make you even a little bit nervous to think that some woman was here and in such a hurry to leave she didn't even stop to grab her shoe when she lost it?"

Zeb shrugged again, a gesture Sid found increasingly maddening. "Not really. I mean, how many times have we found crap people have left behind? It was probably someone who was high, or a couple of kids out here to bang, or just some piece of trash. And what's the big deal if it isn't as old as all the other shit here?"

Sid frowned. "I don't know. It just gives me the creeps, is all."

Zeb gave him a reassuring smile. "Don't worry! You know how many times I've gotten the creeps on one of these adventures of ours?"

"What?" Sid said.

Zeb raised an eyebrow and gave Sid a pensive look. "Of course I get a little nervous sometimes. I just try really hard not to show it."

Sid blinked. "Huh." He blinked again, processing this unexpected information that shed new light on his unflappable brother. "Well. You do a very good job of hiding it."

Zeb shrugged yet again, but it bothered Sid less this time. "When in doubt, make a dick joke."

Sid laughed, relieved, as the dark feeling of unease receded. "I'll keep that in mind."

"As best you should."

Sid gestured toward the broken bridge and its rickety but usable replacement. "What do you make of that?"

"Looks like some nice fellow has laid out the red carpet for us. I say we take advantage of his generosity and get on with it."

"I don't know. It looks…unstable."

"So what? Don't you want to get over there and explore?"

"I mean…yeah," Sid said. "But I'm going first, to make sure it's safe."

Big brothers take care of little brothers.

* * *

They tiptoed across the log, balancing their camera equipment, with a false bravery so brittle it nearly broke apart. They filmed the lazy river from the other side in sweeping arcs, and then continued onward.

Old gravel and new filth squished under their shoes, reminding Zeb of the Russian camping trips their father organized when they were kids. Valentin Barkov was not rich, and what intelligence he possessed lived in his hands instead of his head. He was a brilliant woodworker, carpenter, and builder, but his unkempt beard and sandpaper-rough hands often put people off. He didn't look like the sort of person who could create immaculately carved dining sets or intricately detailed armoires.

In hindsight, America was probably never a good idea for Valentin. He was a man of the forest, of the snow, and of the dirt—but when Amelia Acker caught his eye and held it at his favorite bar on the outskirts of St. Petersburg, he forgot himself in an instant and became a man of her denim blue eyes, her milk-pale skin, her long, shining hair. Amelia was studying abroad, reveling in a semester away from the beautiful but claustrophobic bubble of Georgetown University. She was twenty; at thirty-five, Valentin didn't believe he had anything to offer that she would want.

He was wrong. Amelia was forthright, unabashed. Like a homing pigeon, she glided toward him from her seat across the room and sidled next to him at the bar. She smiled, and in barely accented Russian she asked, "What are you drinking?"

Valentin must have looked completely shocked, because Amelia threw her head back and laughed like a hyena. That laugh—it scared Valentin, but it also aroused him with its reckless music. He told her he was drinking *kvass*, the most patriotically Russian drink there was. She laughed again and ordered one for herself from the scruffy bartender. When he placed it in front of her, she clinked her glass against Valentin's and took a large gulp. When she raised her eyes to his, they were sparkling.

They barely made it out of the bar fully clothed. Amelia had an animal magnetism that enraptured Valentin; in her presence, he was powerless. He was lost. He was deliriously happy.

It was March. Amelia was so bundled beneath layers of coats, fleeces, flannels, and thermals that Valentin could barely feel the shape of her body. She took him on a short, slippery walk to a squat concrete apartment building, pulled him up the stairs, and yanked him through her door. Like someone dying of hypothermia, she ripped her clothes off frantically. Valentin was swept up in the moment; he matched her energy and did the same with his shabby coats. Soon, they were both naked, appraising each other like predator and prey. Valentin wasn't sure which role was his, but he didn't much care.

Their relationship blossomed from that point onward, despite Amelia's return to the States in July looming. Valentin wrote her love letters in poetic Russian, carved her small animal figurines and Pan flutes, and took her to authentic restaurants where *babushkas* in splattered aprons dished out steaming plates of *pelmeni* dumplings and cabbage. They drank liters of *kvass* and barely spent a second apart.

One morning in April as they lay entwined in each other's limbs, Amelia sat up with a jolt and sprinted to the small bathroom in the hallway. Valentin could hear her vomit splashing into the toilet through the thin wall. When she came back, paler than usual and smelling of bile, she simply said, "*Da.*" Yes.

Later that day, a doctor confirmed what they both already knew: Amelia was pregnant.

He didn't want to, but he had to ask. "Do you want to keep it?"

She looked up at him through her thick lashes, tears turning her denim irises into glimmering discs. "How could you even ask that?" She wasn't angry. "Of course, we will keep this baby."

Her silken fingers threaded through his rough ones, and she squeezed. He said, "I love you." She said, "I love you, too."

They were married shortly thereafter with little fanfare, and she became Amelia Barkova. She wrote home to tell her parents—not just about the marriage, but about their incubating little chick of a grandchild, and she signed the letter with a kiss and her new name. Valentin was surprised by her candor; his own mother, had she still been alive, would have sucked in breath after breath to fuel the disapproving tirade to come. A baby out of wedlock. An American girl more than a dozen years his junior.

In July, Amelia finished her classes. Valentin loved to lay his hands on her abdomen, very gently, and feel the life blossoming within. It was almost time for her to leave; Valentin was despondent. His indulged his grief because he knew it wouldn't last forever—in a few months, when his visa was approved, he would join her in the United States.

Valentin listened to English language tapes on the flight to Atlanta, mouthing the words silently. *Please. Thank you. I am from Russia. I am working on my English. I would like a vodka.* By the time he landed, he could passably sit in a bar and have a decent experience.

When Amelia came to pick him up from the airport, baby Sidney dangled from her front, snug in his carrier. Valentin, naturally stoic, could hardly contain his joy.

Six weeks later, Amelia was pregnant again. Her second pregnancy was not as easy as the first; by the time Zebediah was born, the twin tolls of childcare and cultural dissonance had shaken the marriage. Valentin couldn't bring in any money until his work visa arrived, and Amelia's parents had had to support her growing family. Her husband grew sullen. He wasn't able to provide for his family, and he couldn't navigate the English-speaking suburbs of Atlanta without her. Plus, he wasn't much use as a caregiver to children only interested in breastfeeding, sleeping, and squeezing stuffed animals. Amelia dropped out of school. Their marriage fell out of love, and Valentin booked a ticket back home, mourning in his silent way. Amelia was more devastated by the realization love wasn't enough than by her husband's impending return to Russia. He was never abusive, but his withdrawal of affection felt like the worst kind of torture.

By the time the boys were five and six, their father was barely in their lives, aside from a few vacations. Plane tickets were expensive, and Amelia's earning potential was limited by her lack of a college degree. Zeb and Sid were her whole world, but sometimes she felt even that wasn't enough.

Zeb didn't know much about the difficult parts of his parents' lives. When he was younger, he saw his few summers in Russia with Sid and their father as amazing adventures: camping in the thick black forests, cooking dumplings and cabbage over roaring fires, and practicing his Russian with a man who would carve him baseball bats and toy cars while he tried, as best he could, to explain how their lives came to be.

When he was older, Zeb saw his summers away for what they were: chances for his mother to take a break. She tried taking classes to finish her degree, but she didn't have the stamina for those kinds of pursuits anymore. She wasn't a sad woman, but everything she did was tinged with a lovely regret that, at first glance, people took for grace.

All in all, Zeb considered his childhood happy. He had his brother, who had always been his best friend. He had a mother who loved him, and whose failures made her especially supportive of her sons' educations. He had fairytale summers in Russian forests with a mysterious but loving father.

The dark jungle of Gullywasher's took him back to those thick copses of trees—green everywhere, nature given free rein. The faint smell of fried meat and fat, which he wasn't entirely sure he hadn't imagined, intensified the nostalgic, forbidding feeling spreading through his chest.

He wasn't scared—but he wasn't *not* scared, either.

*　　*　　*

On the other side of the bridge, they headed toward a large red cross with a promise of First Aid that would never be fulfilled. As they walked, Sid also thought of his father and their camping trips. Zeb may have remembered them fondly, but Sid's memories were sharp-edged things that threatened to draw blood if handled carelessly. Camping for Sid meant tall trees crowded together so solidly he couldn't see five feet in front of him, strange animals either hooting a predatory victory or howling with pain, and floury dumplings that collapsed on his tongue, turned to paste, and choked him.

Valentin wanted his sons to earn his love through tests of masculinity and bravery that Zeb found amusing and Sid found abusive. Figuring out how to build fires with no fire starter and wet wood; racing to shoot the most rabbits, then skinning them just as quickly, their feet still jumping as if trying to escape, even in death; carving their own walking sticks with dull knives that slipped and cut deep; stitching up wounds with improvised thread pulled from extra shirts and bone needles from his father's backpack.

Those same feelings of helplessness, fear, and a dull, burning panic climbed Sid's throat with ragged fingernails as he and Zeb continued onward. The First Aid building was unremarkable: a cube of white concrete with faded red lettering and a padlocked metal door. Through a check-in window at the front, Sid could see a jumble of chairs, cots, shelves, and, covering the mess, a snowy layer of spilled cotton balls.

There was also an upturned red box of needles, the sharps strewn across the floor, illustrating the panic of the searcher. A few needles were broken, but none looked dusty, nor were they covered with cotton balls. Sid felt sick.

Zeb coughed and pointed at a puddle coagulating on the floor near the needles. Sid was surprised he hadn't noticed it at first. The puddle was almost perfectly circular, rust-colored at the edges where the substance was dry, and black in the middle. Sid knew if he touched it, his fingers would come away tacky and red and smelling of iron.

Instead of insisting they leave immediately, call for help, or even search for whoever was clearly injured, Zeb said, "This'll make a good scene. You think anybody will buy we didn't fake this?"

Sid was incredulous. "Are you serious? That is clearly fucking blood. And it's still wet. Do you get what that means? Two options: somebody accidentally hurt themselves pretty badly, or somebody else did that to them. Either way this means there is something wrong here." Sid was breathing heavily; he didn't notice until Zeb set down his camera and put two meaty hands on his brother's hunched shoulders.

"Chill, dude," Zeb said. "It could have been an animal. Or, more likely, somebody using drugs by the look of all those needles. But, since I'm not seeing a body, I'm going to go ahead and say whatever bled here got away and is fine."

Sid glared. "That's irresponsibly optimistic."

Zeb shrugged, an irritating smile stretching his lips. "What can I say? I've always been a glass half full kinda guy."

When Sid continued to scowl, Zeb picked his equipment back up and walked over to the padlocked metal door. "So. We can run away and miss out on what is clearly gonna be some sick footage, or we can act like real adults, be brave, and get on with it." Zeb didn't wait for an answer; he knelt down to inspect the padlock. "This lock is broken," he said, mostly to himself. He kicked at the lock and it fell in a rusted heap into the weeds below. With a quick tug, he yanked open the door and stepped inside.

Sid took a deep breath, which felt more like hyperventilating than relaxing, and followed his brother.

Once inside, Sid found the horror of the scene he'd glimpsed from the outside diminished. The pool of blood was smaller than he'd thought, no more than the width of a man's wrist. Zeb was already filming, twisting the camera this way and that in wide arcs. He gestured to his microphone and turned it on, beginning to narrate.

"What we've got here, folks, is all that's left of Gullywasher's First Aid building. Weirdly enough, it looks like someone has come here seeking just that—check out all these needles. The really creepy part, though, is over here. Does that look like blood to anybody else?" Zeb paused for dramatic effect. "Not even a hundred yards into this park and already we're seeing some eerie shit!"

Zeb snapped the microphone off and stopped recording. He turned to Sid. "I think that'll do for in here." Sid could feel the frown still pasted on his face. Zeb said, "Listen up. I'll make you a deal. We see any other creepy shit in here, we'll leave."

Sid raised an eyebrow, skeptical. "Just like that?"

Zeb nodded. "Just like that. Not gonna lie, I'm a little creeped out too, but come on—this is the coolest place we've gone in months. This could be our next big thing! Who knows—do a good job with this and you might even have Steven Spielberg knocking at your door!"

"Hmph."

"That's the spirit! Now let's get on with it. Even I don't want to be here after dark."

CHAPTER THIRTY

As the Barkov brothers walked along the weed-choked path that wound parallel to the dry lazy river, Sid struggled not to tense or gasp at every bird call, leaf rustle, or cricket chirp. Zeb was whistling "Like a Virgin."

"Can you stop?" Sid asked.

"Stop what?" Zeb said.

"The goddam whistling," Sid snarled, anger obscuring the fear in his voice.

Zeb stopped short, his shoes flinging missiles of gravel dust into the air, and turned to face his brother. "What is your problem?"

Sid closed his eyes, trying to calm himself. "Look," he said. "I'm sorry. I'm not trying to be a dick."

"Could've fooled me," Zeb mumbled.

"I'm just…really fucking anxious. I know this is gonna be probably our best episode ever, but come on—I mean, we found syringes and pools of blood in a building that should have been empty for over a decade. And, not to get too weird, but can't you feel something off about this place?" Sid paused, nearly panting. He gripped his camera hard to still the trembling of his fingers.

Zeb knitted his eyebrows together and and tilted his head, considering. After a moment, he looked back toward Sid. His eyes revealed a deep well of empathy most people wouldn't have thought Zeb possessed. "Look, bro," he said, almost sadly. "I get it. I really do. Like I said before, I'm creeped out, too. But we've been in creepy situations before. I was terrified at Mel's when we found that shark, but I pushed through it and look at us now! That pretty much launched our channel to viral status. You know that as well as I do."

Now it was Sid's turn to look thoughtful. "Yeah," he said slowly, drawing the word out. "I know you're right." Sid paused, looking around. "I guess I'm just extra jumpy today for some reason."

"Not for 'some reason,' it's because of this place. Let's respect that and just move on carefully. Maybe we act a bit more cautious than usual. I'm sure this place is no more dangerous than Mel's or the Georgia Girl Drive-In or Central State Hospital. But, just for the sake of argument, we'll pretend it is. Does that work for you?"

Sid exhaled long and slow, like a balloon deflating. "Yes. Yes, that works for me," he said. "Thanks."

Zeb smiled. "You know I got you."

A blush of shame flitted across Sid's face as Zeb turned back around. Zeb shouldn't have to be the one consoling Sid. *Big brothers take care of little brothers.* Sid swallowed the dread and embarrassment creeping up his throat, and they started walking again.

Over the tops of ragged bushes, they could see an oval concrete slab ringed by a crumbling railing and topped with a half-collapsed metal roof. At the edge where the roof was still standing, Sid could see skinny metal poles that stretched down from the roof into the faded metal-and-rubber husks of bumper cars. The cars were faded and the rubber around the rims was cracking, but they otherwise looked hungry for passengers. The image of a small child climbing into one of those cars and zooming straight into the collapsed part of the roof flashed through Sid's mind. He felt sure if he concentrated, he'd be able to hear that child scream.

Zeb interrupted his thoughts, and Sid was grateful. "Oh, check that shit out!" Zeb said, gleeful. "Now that's the kinda stuff our viewers want to see. An abandoned place that isn't so old it's all trees, but not so new it still looks like somebody could save it. Just perfect."

"Let's stop and get a few shots, then?" Sid said.

"Definitely. I'll do a quick narration, too."

Sid trained the camera on his brother and pressed Record. Zeb burped and cleared his throat. "Now, ladies and gentlemen, *this* is the kinda thing you come to us for. Sid and I have been walking along the path toward the midway, when, bam! Half-collapsed bumper cars. You can't make this shit up, folks. Think about how many kids climbed up into those cars and tried to ram each other. And now, nothing. Definitely makes you think." Zeb gave Sid the signal to cut away and get a close-up of the bumper cars. Sid stepped closer and zoomed in gradually, making the focal point a bumper car that was now pink, but had probably once been red. He pulled in tight, tighter, tightest, until the back of the pink bumper car completely filled the viewfinder. In the split second before he looked away to stop recording, a small, dark hand flopped up and over the back of the seat. It was missing all five fingernails.

*   *   *

Sid didn't realize for a full twenty seconds the screams he was hearing were his own. His eyes were clamped hard against the tiny, blood-tipped hand, but the afterimage glowed on the backs of his eyelids. From a dark corner of his mind he tried to keep padlocked at all times, a similar image of a horrifying severed hand surfaced. He was haunted by hands.

When Zeb pressed a firm finger on his shoulder, Sid screamed even louder.

"Dude," Zeb said. "What the fuck?"

Sid opened his eyes tentatively. At some point during his fit, he'd dropped his camera. He hunkered down to retrieve it without looking back toward the pink bumper car. He wiped away the dirt on the black plastic with sweaty fingers.

Zeb prodded him with one sneaker. "Sid?" he said. The worry in his voice made Sid even more anxious. Zeb was supposed to be the solid one.

In between shallow breaths, Sid said, "I'm okay."

"Want to tell me what happened?" Zeb said, his tone more annoyed now that he was sure his brother wasn't hurt.

"Um," Sid tried. "I… saw something."

Sid could tell Zeb was trying not to sigh in exasperation. "Well, what did you see?"

"There was," Sid gulped. "A hand."

Zeb's face scrunched with confusion. "What do you mean, a hand?"

"In the bumper car. I saw a hand," Sid said quietly.

"Like at Mel's?" Zeb said. Goosebumps erupted on Sid's bare arms despite the sickening afternoon heat.

"No, not like at Mel's."

"What was it like, then?"

"I was zooming in on the pink bumper car," Sid said. "Right before I turned away, there was this hand that popped up over the seat."

Zeb scoffed. "Sid, I think you're seeing things."

"It was missing all its fingernails," Sid said.

Zeb didn't have a witty retort; as Sid stared at him, his brother's face drained of color.

"Zeb?"

"That's fucking creepy," Zeb managed in a hoarse voice. He squinted, closing one eye, looking toward the bumper cars. A bit of color filtered back into his face when he said, "But I don't see anything there now."

Sid wasn't sure if he should feel relieved the nightmare claw was gone, or terrified because Zeb actually believed him.

"Let me see that," Zeb said, gesturing toward the camera. "We've got the proof right here."

Sid handed over the camera but didn't move to watch the small screen with his brother. He didn't need to see that image again.

Zeb found the footage, pressed play, and bit his lower lip. Sid could hear his brother's voice squeaking from the speakers. Then, silence. Zeb's face did not change as the footage concluded.

"Man," Zeb said. "I hate to tell you this, but… I didn't see anything."

Sid was once again faced with a painful war of emotions. He was happy that the nightmare wasn't real, but he was also terrified by his imagination's ability to creep into his waking life so insidiously.

"Oh," was all Sid could manage.

"You okay?"

"Uh-huh."

Sid felt numb. He remembered the camping trips his father imposed on them when they visited him in Russia, feeling the familiar helplessness creeping through his body. He needed to outrun whatever was pressing its nails into him before it broke the skin.

Zeb handed the camera back to him and they continued down the path.

*   *   *

They didn't have to walk far before the tented roof of a carousel came into view. There was a narrow but navigable break in the brush, and Zeb waded through it without hesitation.

When Sid saw Zeb crunch through the scruffy foliage, his first instinct was to cry out and pull his brother back by the shoulder, but the numbness creeping up his body had reached his hands. Instead of grabbing Zeb, his fingertips pushed aside sharp leaves, clearing a path for him to join his brother in front of the carousel—where he came face-to-face with the aggressive wooden teeth of a horse.

Sid knew immediately there was something off about the carousel—not just because he'd been spooked since they arrived, but because of the grotesque modifications the horses sported. Zeb was reaching out to touch the horse nearest to him, which had balloon-shaped eyes the size of softballs that bulged out of its head as though someone in the saddle were squeezing far too hard with their legs.

"Woah," Zeb said. "The fuck is this? You seeing this?"

"Yeah, I'm seeing it," Sid said.

"No way this carousel always looked like… this, right?"

"I mean, we were here a long time ago. I think we rode the carousel. And no way Mom would have put us onto something that looked like that?" Sid meant to sound definitive, but the declaration came out as a question.

"No, no way," Zeb said. "I mean, just look at this motherfucker!" Zeb made a wide sweeping gesture, and Sid followed Zeb's hand as it passed over the rest of the horses. Although 'horse' could only be used in the loosest sense.

Next to Mr. Balloon Eyes was a white horse that was slowly turning yellow with decay. The body was normal, four horsey legs and a horsey torso, but the face could only be described as human. Two blue eyes, which had curiously retained their strong color, stared back at Sid and Zeb. A sharp nose jutted from beneath the eyes, bordering a set of full red Angelina Jolie lips. The effect was almost more disturbing than the phantom hand in the pink bumper car.

"Jesus," Sid whispered.

Next to Angelina Jolie was a black horse with the segmented body and antennae of an ant, complete with large, liquid dark eyes. Following the Ant was a horse that had once been pale brown but was now horribly charred where the saddle should have been. To Sid, it looked like an extremely unfortunate rider had spontaneously combusted to the tune of jaunty carousel music. Next was a horse that was normal…except for its four missing legs. Where they had been cut off, the paint was red and looked wet, ready to drip.

"Well," Zeb said, breaking the silence. "This is nasty. But, on the bright side, this shit will make our video seriously gold."

Sid nodded, trying to force himself into feeling more confident than he was. "Right. Let's film this and move on."

Sid got everything ready, and Zeb launched into his spiel.

"By now, you've seen some pretty wild shit here at Gullywasher's, and you're probably thinking, 'How can it get any weirder? Maybe I've seen all there is to see and should just go make some Pizza Rolls and catch up on *The Bachelor*.' But no. Let me stop you right there. Because what I have behind me is fucking creepy, my friends." Sid panned the camera across the carousel, zooming in on each freakish horse's mutated face. "Now, I'm sure you're wondering, just as we were: 'How could any parent possibly let their child ride on a carousel where the horses look like *this*?' My answer is simple: they wouldn't. The horses were *not* like this back when families still flocked here. Somebody came in and did this deliberately, sometime in the past fifteen years. Avant-garde artist or seriously disturbed delinquent? You decide!" Zeb gave the signal for Sid to cut.

When the red recording light blinked off, Zeb said, "This is some ridiculously good shit here. Just think about how many new subscribers we'll get!"

Sid tried to smile. "A ton!" His voice sounded fake to his own ears. He hoped Zeb wouldn't pick up on it.

"I can't wait to see what else we've got going on here," Zeb said. "And just think, we haven't even *seen* three quarters of the park!"

Sid gulped. "Yay," he said weakly. He pressed his fingers hard against his camera once again to stop their trembling.

*　*　*

They walked on, the carousel horses smirking as the brothers passed. A series of striped tents in varying stages of decay coming up on their left signaled they had reached the Midway.

The Midway was one of the few things Sid remembered clearly from his childhood visit to Gullywasher's. He'd walked up to one of the booths, his chin barely reaching above the counter. The barker sidled up to him, thrown his mom a wink, and asked him if he'd like to try his hand at popping a balloon with a dart. The barker was missing several teeth, and his fingernails were rimmed with grime. Sid looked eagerly to his mom, who smiled and gave a small nod, reaching into her purse for a few dollars. Little Zeb stood next to her, cheerfully stuffing his cheeks from a paper cone of cotton candy.

After the money changed hands, the barker gave Sid a set of three brightly colored darts and told him if he popped even one balloon, he'd get to pick out a prize. Sid's eyes narrowed and he stuck out his tongue in concentration. His first throw hit between two balloons. His second was a fumble; it didn't even make it to the back of the tent. He screwed up his face with worry and tried so hard to land the third shot, squealing when he was rewarded with a satisfying pop! He turned back to face his mom and brother, his face beaming. They both smiled back at him, and his mother even clapped. For his prize, he picked out a green and yellow stuffed dragon.

Despite the ragged state of the park now, the sweetness of the memory overcame him, and he swore he could smell caramel and fresh popcorn drifting through the heavy air.

"It still smells like popcorn," Zeb said, startling Sid so badly he nearly tripped.

"I was literally just thinking the same thing," Sid said. "I thought I was imagining it."

"Not so, bro," Zeb said. "I definitely smell that, too. It's making me hungry."

"Everything makes you hungry."

"I'm a growing boy," Zeb said, patting his belly.

"Right. I wonder if the balloon booth is still standing," Sid said, half joking.

"We should totally find it! That would make a great shot. You could do the narration there!"

"Okay."

They wandered up and down the aisle of tents, passing moldering stuffed animals, rotting canvas, and a medley of darts, balls, hoops, and baskets. They'd just about decided to give up when they came upon the very last tent. The board was pockmarked with ancient dart holes, and flaccid scraps of faded balloon hung from a few pushpins. Miraculously, one lone balloon near the edge of the board remained weirdly taut.

"Dude!" Zeb said, pointing at the survivor. "There's actually one we could still pop!"

"Huh," Sid said.

"I'm gonna see if there are any darts we could throw. I think it would be a great scene if we could film you with your narration talking about your experience here when we were kids, then throw a dart and pop that last lil motherfucker, eh?" Zeb smiled wide.

"Huh," Sid said again. "Yeah, I guess that could work."

"Oh, it'll do more than work. It's gonna conquer."

As Sid set his own camera down and smoothed his shirt, Zeb hefted himself over the counter and knelt down. "Found one!" he called out, raising one hand high. Huffing, he lifted himself up and climbed back over, handing the rusty dart to Sid. Sid rolled the dart between his fingertips as Zeb set up his microphone. When he was ready, he gave Sid a thumbs-up and pressed Record.

"Hi, everybody," Sid started, a bit shaky. "I'm here in front of Gullywasher's famous Midway, where thousands of kids came to play for prizes while their parents got ripped off." He paused, cleared his throat, and started again, trying to keep his expression neutral. "Zeb and I actually came here, to this exact booth, when we were kids. I had two bad throws before I finally popped one of the balloons and won myself a stuffed dragon. Everything looked so different back then—first of all, there were tons of people around, and nothing was molding or rotting or decaying. But this is what happens when we abandon things and nature starts to take back over." Sid paused, and Zeb nodded, encouraging him to continue. "And, since we're here, I figured I'd try one last time to hit a balloon on the first try. Zeb found an old dart behind the counter here, and crazily enough, there is one balloon left standing after all these years." Zeb gave him another nod of encouragement, and Sid lifted the dart. Zeb zoomed in on his brother's body, catching the moments when he lined up the shot, tensed, and released. His camera followed the dart through the air and then to the board, where it collided with the balloon with a wet pop both brothers found disproportionately loud.

The balloon exploded, spewing scarlet drops of blood in a hundred different directions.

CHAPTER THIRTY-ONE

The Savannah Tribune, August 29, 2009

ANOTHER DISAPPEARANCE LINKED TO GULLYWASHER'S OF GEORGIA

Forty-six-year-old Gina Choate was reported missing by her parole officer, Gary Dancy, last week. According to Dancy, Choate is required to meet with him weekly to satisfy the conditions of her parole. She was released late last year from Pulaski State Prison in Hawkinsville after serving two years for solicitation and drug possession.

Irma Wells, Choate's landlord, told investigators she saw Choate get into a taxicab on the evening of Tuesday, August 18. Wells, whose boardinghouse often serves as a halfway house for women transitioning back into society, keeps close track of her tenants and was able to give investigators the make, model, and partial license plate of the taxi.

Police questioned Eugene Frasier, the taxi driver, about Choate's disappearance. Frasier confirmed he picked up Choate on Tuesday night and drove her to Gullywasher's of Georgia. When pressed, Frasier admitted he knew the park was closed, but he took Choate there anyway. When questioned about her mental state at the time, Frasier remarked she "was dressed like a streetwalker" and was "pretty jittery, like she was on something." Frasier said after paying her fare, Choate walked through the park's entrance, and that was the last he saw of her.

Investigators searched the area and found a pair of stockings near the old ticket booth, along with a set of fake eyelashes and a small pool of blood, which DNA testing has identified as Choate's.

The authorities urge the public to come forward with any information that could help the investigation.

CHAPTER THIRTY-TWO

On the opposite side of the park, Sam walked past the baby pool, trying to keep her eyes off the drowned teddy bear. She hoped no irresponsible parent had actually brought their child to this place, not in its current state. As fascinating as she found Gullywasher's, she also felt an undercurrent of malevolence, as though she were walking all around a sleeping, scaly creature, and one wrong step would send it snapping at her ankles.

"What next?" Lucas asked, coming up behind her.

Sam stopped, staring ahead. "What do you think that is up there?"

Lucas squinted, shielding his eyes with his palm. "Huh," he said. "Maybe…" He paused, thinking, before snapping his fingers suddenly, making Sam jump. "You know what? Maybe Gullywasher's used to do those dolphin shows. I guess everybody thinks those are unethical now, but I really don't see the problem. Anyway, looks to me like this place fits the bill."

Sam nodded, looking out over the open grave of the watery stage, the rusting metal bleachers climbing into the sky on impossibly spindly legs. The entire tableaux looked like it could collapse at any moment. Anxiety twisted through Sam's stomach; her lips pulled down at the corners in a frown.

Lucas put a meaty hand on her shoulder, and Sam frowned harder. "You alright?" he asked.

Sam shrugged away from Lucas' touch. "Yes," she said. "It's just been a long time since I've been near structures like this, where I actually thought,

'You know what? That might collapse and take me with it.'"

Lucas took a step closer to her. "Yeah, you're right. That really doesn't look like it belongs in the land of the living." He laughed, a harsh sound, almost like a crow's caw scraping against the air. "You know I got you, though. That thing isn't going to take you anywhere." Sam wanted to run far away from him, but his phrase 'land of the living' stopped her cold and sent a chill like static electricity across her skin.

When she felt capable of movement again, she headed off toward the dolphin arena. She'd much rather face an abandoned, dangerous structure than be in Lucas' company. He was far more insidious.

As she walked, her thoughts returned to Gruber. Was he still here? If he was, where?

Sam was lost in her own thoughts, trying to think of scenarios that didn't spell something horrible for Gruber. Perhaps that was why she didn't notice the ragged, sticklike figure popping out from under the darkness of the bleachers until it was too late to change course. When she finally did comprehend the reality of the situation, she could only watch in horror, momentarily paralyzed, as a zombie-like woman leapt at her with surprising agility, fraying strips of clothing swinging with the force of the movement. The nightmare figure brandished two fistfuls of syringes, each needle arrayed between her knuckles like a hypodermic Freddy Krueger. She charged, screeching and swiping wildly with her needle claws.

If Sam had seen her even a second earlier, she might have been able to pull away in time. As it was, Sam wasn't aware of the imminent danger until she heard Lucas' sharp gasp. An acicular claw ripped across Sam's arm, leaving long, pencil-thin streaks of scarlet. She clutched her arm to her chest, staggering backward and letting out a low, terrified wail as the deep scratches welled up with thick beads of blood that began running in rivulets down her skin.

The ragged assailant was still coming at them, both needle-clawed hands flailing wildly, seeking purchase in human flesh.

"Run!" Sam screamed as she stumbled back, trying not to fall—but Lucas had quickly abandoned her. He was already yards away, in headlong flight, his feet hammering the pavement. Some protector.

As Sam fought for balance, the woman in front of her slowed, her footsteps growing shorter and more tentative as she moved forward.

Sam regained control and was just turning away to follow the spineless Lucas when, without warning, the raging woman halted, arms outstretched, needles clenched in her fists, and collapsed to the ground, sending up a cloud of hot Georgia dust.

*　　*　　*

Sam's legs gave out, and she slumped to the ground a few yards away from her attacker. Sam was panting, clutching her bleeding arm to her chest. After a few moments, Lucas reappeared at her side, pale and shaken.

"What the hell just happened?" she asked between ragged breaths.

"Christ if I know," he responded. His face was a mask of blank shock, his jaw unhinged. He was completely useless. For all his bravado, all his incessant insistence he would keep her safe, whether she wanted him to or not, he had fled at the first sign of danger, abandoning her to her fate. It was clear: Lucas was both a creep and a coward.

Her arm throbbed, and a tiny sob issued from her mouth. She bit it back harshly before it could turn into blubbering—she didn't want to give Lucas any conceivable reason to touch her. She stood up slowly and turned shakily to face him. Blood was seeping through the thin fabric of her shirt in stripes where her arm pressed against her ribs, a white-and-scarlet zebra.

Lucas reached his arms out, gesturing for her to let him have a look at her injuries. She clutched her arm closer to her chest.

"I can handle this," she said, almost snarling.

"Come on," he said. "Those cuts can't be too deep, at least," he said, a wary smile touching his lips.

Sam knew the cuts were, in fact, deep, and she met his smile with a scowl. "Don't do that. These are absolutely deep cuts, I can feel them, and plus, we both know what made these cuts, and we both know what needles can mean." She stopped abruptly, breathing heavily.

A weighty sigh escaped Lucas' mouth before he could smother it. "No way."

"I have to think about that possibility. I don't know where those needles came from, what was in them, who they were in first…"

"You can't let yourself go down that rabbit hole. We can't know anything for certain until we get you to a hospital."

Sam let out a shuddering sob masquerading as a breath. "Of course we can't, but that really doesn't help me now."

"Well, all we can do is try to stop the bleeding. Then…then we'll get you to a hospital."

Sam thought he was going to try to touch her again; when he didn't, she ripped the sleeve from her shirt, which had already been perforated by the needles and came away easily. Blood gushed from the cuts now that they were fully revealed, and Sam's vision began to swim.

She must have swooned, because Lucas did touch her then, putting a palm on the small of her back to steady her. He pulled the ripped shirt from her hand and tied it tightly around her arm, for which she was grudgingly grateful. She slipped out of his embrace as quickly as possible.

"Alright, then," he said. "Let's go."

Even in her daze, Sam felt her medical training kick in. "What about her?"

They both turned to look at the woman splayed on the ground, the eight needles that had been clutched in her fists sprawled out next to her, many of their tips bulbous and scarlet with Sam's blood like early-spring flower buds.

"I have no idea about her," Lucas said, wiping his nose with the back of his hand. "But I need to get you out of here."

Sam ignored him and crept a few steps closer to the prone figure, studying her. The shininess of her bald head suggested some underlying ailment. The gangrenous smell of rotting flesh drifted off her, telling Sam the story of a woman who must be close to death.

"We can't just leave her here," Sam said.

"What are we supposed to do, exactly?"

"She's obviously in need of medical help."

"Sure, but you're injured, so we can't really haul an unconscious, murderous transient out of an abandoned amusement park that has no cell service."

Sam chewed her lip, thinking. Despite the injuries this woman had given her, Sam still felt an urge to help. Unfortunately, Lucas was right—there wasn't much they could do for her now, not without backup. "Fine. We'll just have to send help here after we get out," she said, sighing.

"That's all we can do," he said, his voice smacking of mock sincerity as he slipped an arm around her hunched shoulders.

"This doesn't feel right. Not at all." She shrugged out from under his bicep.

"Nothing about this place feels right."

"Ouch," Sam hissed as Lucas brushed against her arm.

"Ah, sorry," he said. "You alright?"

"Fine," she said, her mouth tight. "Let's go."

She set off back the way they'd come, Lucas once again following behind as she retraced their steps past the dry pool, with its broken slides rising up like searching tongues. As she walked past the food court, the previously pleasant smells turned sour—funnel cake to rotten batter; pretzels to burned dough; popcorn to old cheese.

There was no question in her mind she was done with urban exploring.

*　*　*

Sam passed the First Aid station again and briefly considered stopping to scavenge some supplies, if any still existed. She thought better of it as they neared the structure and the phallic graffiti, dust-smeared windows, and formidable weeds came into focus; she'd be more likely to contract a new infection from such a place than to treat any current ones.

"Jesus, this is really starting to sting," she groaned, clutching her bandaged arm.

"If only we had a field kit. There'd be bandages and some proper disinfectant. We're really not on our game as epidemiologists today, huh?"

"No," she snapped. "Besides just, you know, getting the hell out of here, do we have a plan?" She felt chilled despite the overwhelming heat.

Her footfalls crunched over gravel and dry grass as they passed the First Aid station and the lazy river gulch came into view. The log they'd laboriously commandeered as a makeshift bridge was still there, but now it looked a bit more skewed than it had before. Sam couldn't put her finger on it, but the log had a traveled look that made her feel uneasy, as though they weren't the only ones who'd taken advantage of it. Maybe the poor woman now collapsed back by the bleachers had gotten in this way?

"Well," Lucas said, "we start by crossing this river. Then, we get to the parking lot. Then, we walk down the path until we find someone who can drive us away from here or—"

"Fine, fine," she said, cutting him off. Lucas was just parroting back what she'd already told him, and the sound of his voice was getting on her nerves.

"Maybe if we walk down the path far enough, we'll have service," Lucas said.

Sam didn't know the status of Lucas' phone, but her own sat useless in her pocket, drained of battery.

"My phone's dead. What about yours?" She tried to keep her sentences short; the effort of speaking was sucking up too much of her dwindling energy.

Lucas pulled his phone from his pocket and looked down. "Shit," he said quietly. "Mine's dead, too."

"Great," she said, fighting back a sob. Even though she was now in serious pain and terrified for her life, she didn't want to look weak to Lucas.

"Well, we'll do what we can," he managed after a few moments of silence.

They reached the log and paused, their feet nestled in the crispy grass.

"Do you think you can manage?" he asked, nodding toward the log.

"Yes," Sam said, but she didn't like how her voice shook as she said it.

"Do you want to go first?" he asked.

She didn't say anything; she just stepped onto the log, took a deep breath, and pulled her injured arm closer to her ribs. Leaning forward, she crossed the distance in a few brisk strides, hopping off the end on the other side with a relieved exhale.

Her breath caught in her throat, and she leaned over, huffing. When she stood up straight again, Lucas was at her side.

"There may be another option here," he said.

"What?"

"It's a long shot, but maybe that old guardhouse we passed before we got to the parking lot still has a radio or a phone?"

"A radio or a phone? That still works?"

"Like I said, it's a long shot, but this place is weird anyway, so who knows? Something has been sending texts and emails from somewhere."

Sam sighed. "We can try it."

They walked past the ticket booth in blessed silence and continued on down the tunnel-like path to the parking lot.

*　*　*

Sam and Lucas reached the dismal parking lot, dirt bleeding through the fissures ahead of them, the scene a cameo of misery as they emerged from the leafy tunnel. Sam's fist, which she hadn't even realized she'd been clenching, uncurled slowly at her side. Nothing about the day had been right. Interesting, for sure, but tinged with a sour wrongness that seeped up through the ground, settling in her pores. It made her feel sick and old.

Useless stadium lights spiked up from the parking lot, reaching into the white-blue sky, their bulbs long since broken.

Immediately to her right sat a Honda Civic.

Lucas had seen it as well, stopping abruptly. "Sam?" he asked, as though he had no faith in his own judgment. "That wasn't here when we came in. It must be that woman's, right?"

Sam sucked in a breath, with effort. "Did she look in any condition to drive to you?"

Lucas frowned. "Maybe?"

Sam shrugged, the motion sending a twinge of pain through her arm.

"Who else would be showing up at an abandoned theme park in the middle of a spanking hot day?" Lucas asked.

"Didn't that cab driver say Gruber came here to meet somebody?"

"Yeah…"

"Remember her name?"

"Do you honestly think anything that guy said was true?"

"Doesn't matter," Sam said, her words coming slower.

"I guess not," Lucas said.

"You remember what he said about Gruber?"

"Something about him coming here for drugs, but that just didn't seem believable to me. It still doesn't."

"If it's true, Gruber came here and somehow went to look for something— maybe drugs, maybe not…" Sam trailed off, perspiration beading on her brow.

Then, it hit her like a physical blow.

"Leona," she said. "That was the woman's name."

"Oh, right," Lucas whispered.

"She needs serious help, that's for sure."

"So do we," Lucas said.

Sam thought for a moment, then asked weakly, "Know how to hot-wire a car?"

"You can't be serious," Lucas said. "What makes you think I'd know how to do that?"

"You have a better idea? You're smart, you can figure it out," Sam said, raising her injured arm, trying to keep the panic from her voice.

"We still don't even know whose it is!"

Sam exhaled sharply, irritated. "It doesn't matter. I'm losing blood. I don't know how much farther I can walk, and we don't have a working phone. I need your help, for God's sake."

Lucas tried one more time, limply. "Maybe somebody else will come along?"

Sam said nothing, just glared. She never thought she'd be in a position like this—prodding her superior to take charge. Her arm throbbed, reminding her of the exigent circumstances. Her head swimming, she longed for the sanctuary of her home, Shmoo in her lap.

"Okay," Lucas said finally. He clenched and unclenched his fists at his sides. "I guess I can try?"

"Thank God," Sam said. She turned toward the Civic as her arm began shaking violently.

"What if it's not unlocked?" he said, right as Sam yanked the handle and the passenger door yawned open without protest. She collapsed into the car.

"Well," he said. He closed the distance quickly, shutting Sam's door behind her. She relaxed back into the seat as much as possible, trying to regulate her breathing.

"Now, I wouldn't say I know per se how to even start hot-wiring a car…" Lucas said, slipping into the driver's seat. Sam wasn't paying attention; she leaned forward to root around in the glove compartment. A few seconds later, she grunted in triumph and lifted a small object out of the compartment.

"Spare key." She dangled it over his hand until he opened his palm, then she dropped it.

"Right on," Lucas said.

As he plunged the key into the ignition, he gave her good arm a squeeze he probably meant to be reassuring. Instead, Sam felt dizziness closing in over her. The car's engine roared to life just as her eyes rolled back, and the darkness enveloped her.

CHAPTER THIRTY-THREE

"Well," Zeb said, staring at the burst balloon in the dilapidated midway booth. "That was certainly something."

Sid was silent, his eyes following the comet tails of blood across the wall, the floor, the striped canvas of the tent ceiling.

"At least we both saw it this time, right?" Zeb said, nudging his brother with an elbow.

Sid turned to face him, his mouth slack. "I don't know what I'm seeing anymore."

"Don't worry about it, dude. This place is creepy and weird. I bet a lot of randos come here to fuck shit up. Some kid probably filled that balloon with red paint to freak out future intrepid explorers such as ourselves."

Sid nodded, even though the explanation didn't ring true for a second. "Sure."

Zeb started fussing with his camera, adjusting the zoom and remounting the microphone. "Are you in still in this with me?" he asked.

Sid sighed. "Yeah. I mean, I can't just leave you here." *Big brothers take care of little brothers.*

Zeb smiled. "Like you would dare."

Sid's smile in return was weak. "Can we move on?"

"Yeah, just give me a second." He was still fiddling with his camera when they heard the laughter.

It was subtle at first, an electric undercurrent in the air. It grew steadily, the tinkling sounds vibrating until they were almost an assault on Sid's ears. He clapped his hands to his head, grimacing. Zeb's scrunched face mirrored his brother's, but his hands stayed planted on the camera.

When the laughter subsided, Sid's hands dropped to his sides and he stood silently, staring off down the Midway.

"The fuck?" Zeb said. "This place is just full of surprises, huh?"

Sid swallowed. "That was creepy, just too goddamn creepy, fucking laughing, the park is fucking laughing at us—" His voice rose to an octave it hadn't hit since before puberty.

"Woah, woah!" Zeb said. "It's not that big a deal!"

"Not that big a deal?" Sid echoed.

"No, it's not. Remember when we watched old reruns of Three's Company with Dad during the summers? Jeez, that had to be the only American TV show we could get over there."

Sid did remember, but he'd always preferred watching medical procedurals with Mom, snuggled on the overstuffed couch in their cozy Georgia living room, usually with a bowl of mint chocolate chip ice cream or popcorn balanced on his lap. The austerity of Dad's Russian cabin in comparison, where they huddled on spindly wooden chairs near the boxy, ancient television as Dad nursed a beer and Sid and Zeb tried to split a piece of tough jerky, was not favorable in Sid's mind. Whereas Zeb had loved that rough little cabin, Sid had found it claustrophobic and unbearable.

"Well," Zeb continued. "You know all those cheesy laugh tracks on sitcoms? I heard those were all recorded in the 50's or something. Which means that every time you hear the audience laughing at a stupid joke, you're hearing dead people's laughter."

"Why would you tell me that?" Sid said.

"Well, I mean, you said you heard laughing, and obviously, there's nobody here. Maybe it was an old laugh track or something coming through speakers around here. I was just trying to make you feel a little bit better."

"Now I'm just thinking about dead kids laughing."

"That's fucked up," Zeb said.

"So is your morbid little fun fact!" Sid shouted, his fear bubbling up in his throat, turning to anger on his tongue.

"Like I said, just trying to lighten the mood a bit and make you feel better."

"Does everything have to be a joke to you?" Sid said. He started walking past the striped tents of the Midway, pointed in the direction of the teetering, eponymous Gullywasher roller coaster.

Zeb jogged to catch up. "What is your deal? Come on, for real, why does everything have to be so serious?"

Sid wheeled around just before reaching the first of the wooden roller coaster struts. The coaster's shadow cast both of them in shade, and the wind whistling through the rotten wood hurt Sid's ears. "Because one of us has to be fucking serious! We go into some dangerous motherfucking places, and if I don't cover our asses and be cautious and prepare for everything, you'll get us both arrested! Or fucking killed!" Sid started panting, his rage blossoming into a poisonous flower, sitting heavy on his lungs. "And it's my job to take care of you!"

"I don't think that's fair—" Zeb started. He was interrupted by a groan from the roller coaster that ripped through the charged air like a scream. The sound of splintering wood followed the groan, and before Sid could move, or shout, or protect his brother, a massive, spiky chunk snapped off the rotting coaster, hurtled down to the earth with shocking speed, and impaled Zeb through the chest.

A rattling groan escaped Zeb's lungs as he fell to the ground with a heavy thud.

Sid stood, unmoving, for a few seconds before the shock receded. Then, with an agility he didn't know he had, he surged forward, tossing his camera aside into the dirt. His hands grabbed the wood, and even though the rational part of his mind told him he should leave it where it was, he couldn't stop himself from lifting and pulling to get it out of Zeb.

This doesn't belong here, it doesn't, I have to get it out. If I can just get it out, he'll be okay. He has to be okay.

When he finally succeeded, he stared down at his brother.

Zeb's face was calm. If it weren't for the wide circle of blood seeping through the front of his shirt, Sid would have thought he was just sleeping off a hangover.

CHAPTER THIRTY-FOUR

In the moments after the jagged shard of wood slammed through Zeb's chest, smashing him to the ground, time slowed to a crawl. Sid tossed his camera aside, dropping to a crouch over his brother's prone body. He felt himself lifting up Zeb's shirt to check the wound, then wincing when he saw the circle of raw hamburger between Zeb's pectoral muscles. He knew he ripped off the sleeve of his own shirt to staunch the bleeding, pressing it fiercely into the gushing wound, but nothing felt like a conscious decision. He didn't think, he just did. *Big brothers take care of little brothers.*

He stroked his brother's head, muttering "Zeb? Zeb, wake up now. It's alright, you're fine, you're going to be just fine." In response, Zeb's eyelids fluttered, and his breathing hitched. All the air he fought to inhale guttered out in a sputtering exhale, sending a mist of fine blood droplets into the air, which fell back to rest on his face. If Sid squinted, he could pretend the specks of blood were just remnants of Zeb's furious teenage acne.

Sid shook his head and continued to soothe his brother with soft pats. "Shh, don't try to talk. I'm here. It's going to be fine." The words came out slow as molasses, the vocal equivalent of walking through quicksand. Sid pressed two fingers to Zeb's neck, checking his pulse. It was thready at best. "Wait, I'll call 911! I'll get you an ambulance, don't worry!" Sid thrust his hand into his pocket and pulled out his phone. He punched the numbers and held the phone to his ear before he realized he didn't have service. The phone beeped once, then went silent.

"It's okay, it's okay," Sid said, mostly to himself. "My phone isn't working, but I'll try yours!" He fished around in Zeb's pocket and repeated the procedure with the same result. "Fuck!" he screamed.

In spite of the blood now pooling in his throat, Zeb managed to choke out "Sid—"

The unnatural composure that had guided Sid snapped, and time sped up. Sid was standing up, throwing his arms in the air, slapping his palms to his face, sobbing like a child just waking from a nightmare. On the ground, Zeb was convulsing, thick scarlet rivers rushing from the corners of his lips and pooling in the cups of his ears. The shirtsleeve Sid had pressed to his brother's belly was soaked through, and Sid could imagine the bloody tampon joke Zeb would make if he were standing next to him now, instead of writhing on the ground.

Sid remembered the ever-present clump of emergency Band-Aids in his back pocket and grabbed for them. Why hadn't he insisted on a fully stocked first aid kit after Zeb forgot to bring one to Mel's? How could he have overlooked it again?

With trembling fingers, he ripped the bandages open, sending sticky bits of paper fluttering down on Zeb like snow. He knelt to press a few Band-Aids to Zeb's wound. At his touch, Zeb cried out, and blood immediately saturated the bandages. Even if Zeb had brought the first aid kit, Sid wouldn't have been prepared for this.

For the first time, the thought that Zeb was dying alighted in Sid's mind like a hornet, buzzing around, causing panic, and threatening a painful sting. If Sid let that hornet pierce him, he knew he would die right alongside his brother.

Zeb let out one last shuddering exhalation, blowing a bubble of blood through his lips. The bubble popped, sending another spray of scarlet across Zeb's face. Eyes that had once held unmatched mirth grew dim. As Sid watched, Zeb's corneas filmed over. A mosquito dove onto Zeb's face, proboscis thrusting into the feast of blood before it.

Sid crouched, motionless, empty. He might have stayed there for the rest of time if one thought hadn't started pulsating in his head louder than his heartbeat: *Big brothers take care of little brothers.*

Sid spurred himself into action, murmuring, "It's alright, Zeb, I'm just going to get you more comfortable while I go for help, don't worry, it's going to be alright, it's just a scratch, really, you're fine." He fastened his fingers around Zeb's ankles and pulled him into the shade of the ring-toss booth's tattered awning. He moved around to Zeb's torso, gripped his shoulders, and hoisted him into a sitting position. Zeb's body slumped against the booth, the shade reaching to his waist. It would have to do.

Sid ran back to the cameras, which they had dropped by the roller coaster, and picked them up. Slowly, he walked back toward his brother and placed his camera gently in the crook of his arm.

"Just in case something interesting happens while I'm gone," he said, feeling numb. "You were right. We're getting some awesome footage, and if anything happens, you just record it from right here. I won't be long. You'll be just fine." *Big brothers take care of little brothers.*

In the distance, a crow cawed.

CHAPTER THIRTY-FIVE

Leona had revived enough to creep slowly back to the pit, head hung in shame. She'd left the hypodermics scattered where they had fallen, and the bruises on the insides of her fingers where she'd clutched too hard were already fading. She took that as a good sign that the pale figures in the cylinder hadn't given up on her.

The pit was just as she'd left it, empty and forlorn. Somehow, she managed to negotiate her wisp of a body down the ladder, knees knocking together like a baby's rattle. Reaching the bottom, she let herself fall, coming to rest with a wet squelch into the muck. Tarantula thrashed briefly, acknowledging her return like a dog wagging its tail.

"Hey," she croaked with affection. "How you doing?"

Tarantula didn't move in response, but the crow, alighting at the edge of the pit, cawed harshly. Its blue-black feathers glistened in the glare of the hot sun; Leona was grateful she was ensconced in the cool damp of the pit instead of that hot nest of sticks under the bleachers. Or, worse, stuck somewhere at the hands of those horrible interlopers. They'd come into her home, disturbed her peace, touched her things...

A sharp jolt of electricity shot through her body, starting at the soles of her feet and reaching its painful apex in the middle of her skull. Her territorial thoughts evaporated, replaced by one pulsating word: *Ours.*

"I'm sorry, I'm sorry!" she whimpered, regressing into the small, scared child she'd been as she'd bounced around foster homes. Even now, she was still essentially powerless. Any authority she thought she had was simply borrowed from the primal forces governing the park, and she'd do well not to forget that.

The pain in her skull dissolved as quickly as it had arrived, and the bold reprimand was replaced with a much gentler missive: *Stay. Recover.*

She did.

She stayed in the pit, squeezing mud through her fingers and toes, smearing layers of it onto her exposed skin like armor. She stayed there until she heard what she'd been waiting for: the low groan and sharp crash from the Gullywasher roller coaster. Above her, the crow cawed, and she knew it was time to get moving again.

*   *   *

Leona stood, letting excess mud drip from her like blood. The deep aches in her joints had disappeared, and the bruising between her fingers was completely gone.

Lifting each foot carefully, she made her way back toward the ladder. At the electrical box, she paused, as if listening to a soft sound traveling on the blistering breeze. After a few seconds of consideration, she flipped the switch to 'On.' Tarantula sprang to life, thrashing his tail and snapping his jaws with such ferocity it seemed like he would be able to break away from his moorings and swim away, like his scale-and-bone brethren.

Leona smiled and continued on to the ladder, where she climbed up with the agility of a child sprinting up a tree. She felt light and buoyant, completely refreshed.

The crow cawed gently, and she turned toward it with a curious look on her face.

"What?" she said.

The crow said nothing, but flapped its wings, lifting off and landing a few feet away, where a dark jumble of wood that had once been benches for the audience lay. Message received, Leona flitted behind the rotting, splintery pile and crouched down to wait.

The crow cawed its approval.

CHAPTER THIRTY-SIX

Sweat slithered from Sid's short hair, down his spine, and pooled in the small of his back as he first walked, then trotted, then ran from where he'd left Zeb's body propped against a midway booth, limp fingers splayed on a camera.

Must find help must find help must find help…

Sid refused to believe his brother was dead. During their harrowing camping trips with their father in the Russian wilderness, Zeb always sprinted toward what Sid considered inarguable danger. Zeb climbed tall, spiky trees, even going so far as to shimmy along the toothpick-thin limbs; he bounded into caves that smelled of rotting meat, disregarding the possibility of awakening a hungry bear; he balanced on splintered logs as he crossed rushing rivers, laughing when he stumbled instead of crying out in fear. Sid always tried to dissuade his brother, but it never made a difference. He had to settle for being prepared to react to accidents instead of trying to prevent them. Despite Sid's obvious intelligence, he knew their father had loved Zeb more for his bravery, even though Valentin had never said anything of the sort.

It should have been me, Sid thought. The idea pierced a hole in his heart, and memories flooded out as he ran: Zeb at five, tying a string around a loose tooth, smiling as he prepared to slam the door and send the tooth flying. Zeb at eleven, talking his way out of detention by explaining he had a medical condition that required him to eat something sweet every few hours, which was why he'd stolen Katie Tompkin's Hershey bar right out of her hand. Zeb at eighteen, joining Sid at Emory. Zeb at nineteen, exploring everything, right by Sid's side.

One memory stuck out, demanding his attention. Zeb was twelve, Sid thirteen, when they decided to build a fort in their backyard. Zeb ran around on the dry grass, looking for sticks, leaves, and anything else that could act as building material. Sid stationed himself in the middle of the yard, looking through his dad's old toolbox, creating a blueprint in his head. Zeb wandered over with an armful of sticks and plopped down next to his brother.

"Can I help?" Zeb asked, eager.

Sid gave him an appraising glance. "We agreed you'd find the wood and stuff, and I'd use all the tools."

"Sid! Come on! That's not fair!"

"We agreed!" Sid said, his face growing red.

"Whatever," Zeb grumbled, ambling away to look for more sticks.

Sid was focused on the large toolbox, rooting around for the electric nail gun that should have been there, when he heard the cry. He whipped around and saw his brother holding the nail gun in one hand, the other pierced by a nail that fastened it to a thick stick. Blood flowed down Zeb's hand, pooling at his bent wrist. Sid could just make out the shiny nail head jutting from Zeb's palm.

"Sid! Help!" Zeb cried, panic turning his voice into a squeak. "It hurts!"

"Hold on, hold on!" Sid yelled, running over to him. The wound was even worse up close, the flesh around the nail head growing purple and swelling fast. "Just let me—"

"What's going on here?" their mother asked, emerging from the kitchen door, blinking in the harsh sunlight. "Who's hurt?"

"Mom!" Zeb screeched. "Help me!"

Amelia ran over, terror clouding her vision. "Oh my god," she said, seeing Zeb's hand up close. "Oh my god, Zeb, how did this happen?"

"I—"

Before Zeb could answer, Amelia wheeled on Sid. "Sidney, how could you let this happen to your brother? Big brothers take care of little brothers!"

Sid was crying, fat tears coursing down his cheeks. "I'm sorry, I—"

"Enough," Amelia said, rising to her feet. "I'm taking your brother to the hospital right now. You stay here and clean up this mess." She swept a hand around the backyard, encompassing the ratty pile of sticks and the old toolbox spilling bits and bobs onto the grass. "And you just better think about what happened here. Don't you ever let that happen again!"

Now, in the defunct park, his brother once again injured, Sid moved quicker, hoping to outrun the painful memory. Despite what he'd promised his mother that day, he had let something horrible happen to Zeb again. He'd failed in his duty as a big brother, and now there was no guarantee he'd ever make new memories with Zeb. Would he ever see Zeb at twenty-one, Sid taking him to a bar for his first legal drink? What about Zeb at twenty-nine, marrying an easygoing, happy girl like himself? Or Zeb at thirty-eight, watching his kids play with Sid's, both sipping beers and reminiscing?

Big brothers take care of little brothers.

The world upended with an unexpected thump, and Sid was splayed on the ground before it even registered that he was falling. His camera once again went skidding through the dirt as his cheek rammed into the dust. He laid there for a moment, finding a a modicum of relief in the numbness that settled on his body before the inevitable pain came.

When the pain did come, after what seemed like only a few merciless seconds, he sat up. His fingers crept over his cheek and came away red; he must have cut his face on a piece of gravel.

Wiping his fingers on his now-filthy shirt, he looked around. In his panic, he'd managed to run the entire length of the creaking Gullywasher roller coaster, the opposite direction from the way he'd wanted to go, finally coming to a stop in a small clearing. Behind him, the roller coaster soared, touching the sky. To his left, he could just barely make out the concrete banks of the lazy river. To his right, he could see the planks of rotting bleachers that were the only remnant of the dolphin show arena that had once housed cheering families, children squealing with delight and wonder as the dolphins danced before them.

In front of him, an ominous sign read 'Alligator Pit. Danger.'

Somewhere nearby, a crow cawed.

*   *   *

Alligator pit. Those were two words Sid hated separately; squeezed together like that, they threatened to annihilate Sid's sanity entirely. No good could come from alligators; they were cunning, powerful, dangerous beasts that surely wouldn't hesitate to drag Sid through the mud, drown him like an animal, and crunch his skull between their jaws. As for pits, anybody who'd read *The Pit and the Pendulum*, as Sid had, would have reservations about going anywhere near such a thing. Pits promised tortures all the more horrible because they were utterly unknown and unknowable.

Despite his fear, his disobedient feet slapped the sticky ground, drawing him closer to the pit against his will. He could hear a mechanical thrashing, feel the pull and suck of the earth, even smell the fetid stench of an animal's den—but he felt completely divorced from himself, as though he were sitting on the comfortable futon in his dorm room, watching a movie where a hapless victim walks right into the arms of danger. Sid felt his throat constricting with the words he wanted to cry out: *No! Don't go that way! Don't you know that's where the murderer is?*

He continued, his movements artless like a sleepwalker. The air was heavy on his shoulders, adding even more weight to each step.

A crow cawed again, much closer this time, snapping Sid out of his trance. The stench was stronger now, assaulting his nostrils, the scent particles burrowing into his sinuses. He wanted to gag, or faint, or turn around and run back out of the park, the way he'd meant to go, but he felt powerless to do anything other than walk closer to the pit. The metal-on-metal screeching grew louder, and he resisted the urge to slap his hands over his ears.

When he reached the rickety metal bars surrounding the lip of the pit, he paused, resting his hands on the railing. Flakes of rust bit into his palms.

His first mistake was looking down. Angling his eyes into the pit, he saw the massive, prehistoric monster undulating ferociously in the mud. His next mistake was crying out, a sharp sound that stabbed the atmosphere. His last mistake was stepping backward in horror, right into a pair of outstretched arms.

CHAPTER THIRTY-SEVEN

Sid's body flooded with adrenaline as the scrawny but powerful arms encircled him; at first, he thought maybe Zeb had followed him and was now there to comfort him just like he'd always done.

Sid turned his head slightly to catch a glimpse of whomever was behind him. He took in the brown, cracked face, the smoldering eyes, the unsettling bald head, the rags, the filth, the unholy smell.

Just before he fainted, he felt the flapping of large wings near his head and turned slightly to see a greasy black bird. He heard a caw cracking through the hot air; he saw a jelly-like grayish object, striated with red and dotted with a large black circle, plop from the crow's beak and into the now open palm of his captor, who was still pinning his arms to his sides. The blob landed with a *squich*, the black circle staring up at him.

It looked an awful lot like an eyeball…oh God, Zeb's eyeball?

Sid tasted bile, and then he was out.

CHAPTER THIRTY-EIGHT

The way the sallow boy's feet bobbed and bounced on the gravel as Leona dragged his limp body mirrored Gruber's experience almost exactly, except Leona was taking this one to the aquarium instead of the pit, and he wasn't injured. Yet.

He also wasn't conscious. Leona guessed the shock of seeing the eyeball dropping into her hand had been too much for him to handle.

Leona heaved breath after gasping breath as she pulled the boy along. He was bigger than the doctor, and she wasn't entirely prepared for the strain. She had her left hand gripping his left, her right hand squeezing his right. Walking backwards, she was afraid of stumbling, so she tried to balance the need to be careful with the overwhelming urge to hurry. Even though she was still a ways away, she could feel the pale denizens of the cylinder pushing that word *hurry* into her mind over and over, like a server glitching and sending out the same repeated message again and again.

The crow hopscotched his way beside her, flying from one outstretched, scraggly branch to another. He cawed occasionally, adding even more urgency to the cylinder's message, like an avian siren.

"I'm coming!" she panted. The jubilance her voice had carried just a few weeks ago had been replaced by a frantic, high-pitched anxiety, making her sound like an adolescent boy on the cusp of puberty.

Finally, a cool shadow hit her back and she knew she'd reached the aquarium. The metal doors had been propped courteously open, flat rocks wedged under their jambs to keep them wide. With palpable relief, Leona crossed the threshold, then yanked the boy inside with one last powerful pull. She collapsed on the ground next to him, on the verge of hyperventilating with exertion.

Her head nodded down, and she thought she might pass out herself. *That would be just peachy, wouldn't it?* A small, nasty voice whispered in her ear. *Fall asleep like the boy, laze about while he escapes and takes the other with him?*

An electric jolt, now a familiar sting, ping-ponged through her body, hitting her bones, shocking her muscles, and rattling her soft tissue. She closed her eyes when the room started shaking so she wouldn't be sick.

"I'm going!" she screamed, hot tears stinging the backs of her eyelids. "I promise I'm going, you don't have to hurt me no more!"

Abruptly, the electricity halted. On unstable legs, Leona rose slowly, gripping a nearby discarded chair for balance. She opened her eyes, and the tears spilled fat and boiling down her cheeks. "I'm sorry," she whispered, her throat choked and painful with a repressed sob. "I'm doing the best I can."

No figures appeared pale and dreamlike in the cylinder, but their words pulsed in her brain: *Do better.*

The crow cawed beyond the metal doors, and Leona shambled outside to meet him.

*   *   *

The walk back across the dry earth toward the alligator pit was much easier without the boy's dead weight slowing her down. The crow flew ahead of her, stopped to let her catch up, then flew on. She followed obediently, her feet light and quick once again.

A ticking sound invaded her brain, soft at first, but growing louder and louder until it was all she could hear. Even the crow's caws couldn't break through. Time was running out, and Leona needed to move faster, think smarter, do better.

She passed by the alligator pit on her right. The ticking drowned out any sound Tarantula might have been making. Leona's gut told her he'd stopped thrashing—he'd completed his job, after all. He'd distracted that sallow boy.

Her feet crossed larger distances with each step, and she leaned forward to capitalize on any forward momentum she could generate. The Gullywasher roller coaster rose up on her left; she couldn't hear its structural groaning, but she felt the vibrations of its instability travel along the ground and up into her bones.

She entered the wide pathway between the Gullywasher roller coaster and the rows of moldering midway booths. The crow finally stopped moving, coming to rest on the faded awning of the ring-toss booth.

Slumped below the crow in the rapidly shrinking shadow of the booth lay a pudgy young man, his corpulent belly straining at his too-tight t-shirt. Where the shirt had rucked up around his middle, Leona could see a forest of thick black hairs. Identical strands stuck up straight in the back and on the sides of his head. Despite the gaping red hole where his stolen eye had previously rested, Leona could see the family resemblance. This boy, the one the cylinder wanted so badly, was kin to the sallow, skinny one she'd left in the aquarium. Brothers.

"You must be the one," she croaked, groaning. "Fuck if you're not twenty pounds or more heavier than that brother of yours."

The crow cawed, as if to silence her complaints. *Hurry.*

Leona plastered a beauty-queen smile on her face, the kind of smile that said *This ain't no thing for a girl like me.*

She squatted, gripped one of the boy's hammy ankles in each fist, and started to pull.

Gonna need a long time in the pit after this one, she thought, feeling something straining and splintering in her lower back. *Shit.*

CHAPTER THIRTY-NINE

The first thing that pierced the veil of Sid's unconsciousness was a black glow. Even with his eyes closed, it crept under his eyelids, filtering through his thick lashes. It rested on his eyeballs like oil on water, eventually forcing him to blink, trying to clear it.

Everything was blurry when he opened his eyes; a sudden fear sent goosebumps down his arms when he remembered his last few moments of consciousness. That hideous pit, the disgusting creature thrashing like a dying, scaly bug, the thin white arms trapping him…the gelatinous mass of eyeball, of *Zeb's* eyeball—what else could it be?—thwapping into a stranger's palm.

He leaned over and threw up, a violent projectile stream of mostly bile. When he was done, he wiped his lips on the inside of his shirt. His mouth tasted like Doritos; the thought almost made him retch again, but he swallowed it all back down with one big gulp.

"Fuck," he whispered, hoarse. His throat stung; he wished desperately for water.

Falling back against the ground, he rubbed his eyes with his fists. He tried to assess the situation rationally, but he couldn't find anything logical to use as an anchor. Everything circling through his head was awash in a haze of unreality that made him question whether or not he was dreaming.

The pain in his throat and behind his eyes insisted he wasn't; he figured he could cross dreaming off the list of explanations for what was happening.

What did that leave? What did he even know for sure? He tried to tick things off mentally: *Zeb and I came to Gullywasher's to shoot a video; I saw some fucked up shit Zeb didn't see, for whatever reason, and some that he saw, too; we argued; something fell out of the sky and skewered Zeb; he fell over; I left him in the midway so I could get help…*

And a fucking crow stole his eyeball.

Sid nearly laughed at the humorless absurdity of it all; he stopped himself, knowing any laughter he let escape would quickly turn to a raging, mad scream that would rip his sanity to shreds. If a goddamned bird had—Jesus Christ— pecked out Zeb's eyeball, then the chances of him still being alive were…

No. He couldn't go down that path, he just couldn't. He peeled his fists away from his face and tested his vision again, prying open first one eye and then the other. Things were a bit clearer now, and he was able to survey the scene in front of him. He was sprawled on a hard cement floor; in front of him and a little to his left, a cylindrical tank rose up from the floor all the way to the ceiling high above. Spindly spiral staircases connected the upper floor catwalks that ringed the building's interior like a wedding cake. Set into every wall, the blank, molding glass of drained fish tanks stared back at Sid like dead men's eyes. He thought of Zeb again and his gaze wandered over to the closed double doors off to his right.

How did I get here?

He thought back to the outstretched arms, the upturned palm that caught Zeb's disembodied eyeball. Had that person, whoever they were, brought him here?

Panic surged up his throat. *If someone brought me here*, he thought, *when will they be back?*

*   *   *

Sid wasn't sure what to do. His assessment of the situation was bleak at best, fatal at worst. He figured he was still on the Gullywasher's property, but there wasn't much else he could be sure about.

His head was roiling with unanswered and unanswerable questions. No course of action he could think of seemed right. He grew increasingly frantic, but he managed to hoist himself into a seated position with his legs crossed like a kindergartner at story time. He had no conception of how much time had passed; his fainting spell and the general lack of sensory information in this strange place left him unbalanced and disoriented.

A crow's sharp caw and a syncopated crunch-swish of gravel brought a decisive end to his frenzied introspection. His inability to decide what to do had been a decision in itself: he was staying put. For now, he thought it would be a very good idea to play unconscious; he could hopefully avoid further attention from whomever was returning to their lair, while at the same time gather some bit of information about what the fuck was going on.

He fell backwards into a sprawl, eyes closing, just as he heard a loud "Fuck!" and the squeal of metal hinges. Bright light filtered under his lids as he heard the doors screech open. A series of muted thumps and heaving breaths came next, punctuated occasionally by a crow's caw.

Goddamn crow, he thought, making a mental note to rip the throat out of whichever piece of shit crow had stolen his brother's eyeball.

He forced his breaths to come slow and regular, praying his captor wouldn't notice his puddle of fresh vomit. Right now, his best friends were stillness and silence.

"Fucking hell," came the voice again. The panting that followed made Sid picture a hefty woman, bent over, elbows on knees, trying desperately to catch her breath. He resisted the urge to open his eyes and look his tormentor in the face.

Another, heavier thump resounded through the echoing chamber.

"My back," hissed the voice. Sid could almost feel the venom spitting from the woman's mouth, which made it all the more surprising when her next words came, a few moments later, in a simpering whimper: "Time to go where?"

CHAPTER FORTY

A sharp pain in her abdomen jolted Sam awake. When she managed to open her eyes, she saw the seat belt clamped around her middle.

"What?" she said. Her voice was thick, and she felt as though she was speaking around mouthfuls of food. How long had she been out? Something must have gone wrong, because the car wasn't moving and they were still on the rocky path.

Groggy, she glanced down at her clothing to make sure everything was still zipped, buttoned, and in place. A sigh of relief burst from her lips when she saw everything was as it should be.

Then, the memory of their ordeal came flooding back.

"Out of gas," Lucas said. "We barely got a hundred yards down the road before the damned car stopped dead."

"What?" Sam said, more clearly. "Seriously?"

Lucas let out a suffocating, lung-clearing whoosh of breath. His head fell forward against the steering wheel, setting off a blaring horn. Sam squirmed to cover her ears, forgetting that one of her arms was out of commission.

"Stop!" she snapped, trying to push Lucas up with her good arm.

He sat back slowly, a look of fear and defeat twisting his features. "Sorry," he said, so softly Sam almost didn't hear him. For a second, she wasn't sure if he was talking about the car or something else she hadn't yet grasped. Her stomach lurched.

Sam turned her head back and forth, like a beacon searching for a signal. "Where are we?" she asked. "Are we out of the park?"

Lucas stared down at his hands, fiddling anxiously in his lap. "We're not even past the entrance," he said.

"Oh," Sam said, her voice small.

"Yep."

"So, what do we do now?"

Avoiding her question, Lucas asked one of his own. "How's your arm?"

"It's fine," she said, even though it ached horribly. She didn't want him to know how bad it really was. Her words weren't very convincing, though, and the lie hung in the air between them, polluting it, making it poisonous.

After a few seconds of silence, Lucas said, "It's not really, is it?"

Sam gulped. No point in continuing the lie. "No," she admitted. "It's bad, but I'm dealing with it."

Lucas turned to face her. "I wish I could do something. I'd take away all your pain if I could." Something about his declarations felt greasy, and Sam squirmed.

Ignoring him, she surveyed the scene around them. Her gaze caught on something a few yards away, and her heart started beating at a rapid clip. "Wait a minute!" she said. "Look over there!" Lucas followed the tilt of her head, looking out the passenger side window. They had managed to come to a stop near the guardhouse.

"A radio! Or maybe a phone!" he blurted.

"Yes!" Sam said, nodding furiously.

"Remember, there's no guarantee there's one in there," he said.

"I know," she said, with a touch of irritation. "But finding a radio or phone is our best bet, short of walking all the way back to Savannah, wouldn't you agree?"

"Yeah," he said, chastened.

When he still didn't move, Sam unbuckled her seat belt. "Come on," she said wearily.

Before Lucas could stop her, she pushed open the door and stepped gingerly out of the car.

"Let's go," she prodded.

Sam heard Lucas open his car door as she walked haltingly over to the guardhouse. She reached the guardhouse door, pulling it open with her good arm. Thankfully, it wasn't locked. She allowed herself to hope that maybe everything would be alright after all.

She peeked inside and registered the scene before a scream ripped out of her throat, the sound shattering the unnatural quiet like a sonic boom.

*   *   *

Lucas rushed to her side, shouting something incomprehensible. She was shaking, her hands glued to her eyes, when she felt his unwelcome touch on her shoulder.

He wrapped himself around her, and a bolt of pain shot through her arm. She struggled to free herself, but he was strengthened by his own overwhelming fear as he surveyed the scene, and she couldn't shake him off.

Below them, Dr. Archibald Gruber was sprawled among the dirt and leaves. One leg was sticking out at an unnatural angle; it must be broken. One of Gruber's hands was resting on his abdomen, the other was outstretched, as though he'd been grasping for something just out of reach. Rust-colored streaks and speckles wallpapered his shirt. The face was ghostly pale; in the crook of one elbow, Sam could see a nasty abscess turning black around the edges.

Immediately, Sam had wanted to scream and run, to shout and thrash and jump away, but she didn't. Now, she stood still, her reason reasserting itself. She downloaded all of the details, forcing herself to assess the situation objectively, even though thinking clearly was becoming difficult. She hoped her thoughts were being jumbled by fear instead of fever.

"I'm going to check for a pulse," Sam said, finally extricating herself from Lucas.

She took a few steps forward and pressed her fingers to Gruber's neck, right below his ear. Beads of sweat rolled down her neck; the little building acted as a greenhouse in the heat, trapping it and sending the temperature soaring unbearably high. After a few moments, she dropped her hand and stood up.

"No pulse," she said, her voice flat. She wondered if Gruber's body would start to leak like Patricia Dalco's had, if that bizarre autopsy recording were to be believed. The thought made her want to scream.

"My God. Gruber," Lucas said. "Commander Clements. I...I don't know what to do now."

Sam shrugged, then winced, pulling her injured arm back against her chest. A tear drifted down her cheek, pooling in the corner of her mouth. "Me neither."

Lucas sighed, his entire body lifting up into the inhale and slumping back down to earth on the exhale. He looked decades older than when they'd set out that morning, and the smarmy smirk and lusty glint in his eyes were gone at last.

Regaining some professional poise, Sam asked, "You see that abscess in the crook of his arm?"

"Yeah," Lucas said.

"Not that I'm putting any stock in what that cab driver said, but that really does look like something a drug user would have. I've seen a ton of botulism patients with abscesses just like that, and they were all black tar heroin users."

"Huh," Lucas said dully.

Sam went on anyway, her voice far calmer than she felt. "Remember when I sent that email to Gruber earlier? Asking him if he needed any help investigating? Well, I think he came here because he found some sort of clue from Patricia Dalco. As far as we know, she was a drug user. Maybe he figured he could find the source of the epidemic if he came here and got a sample of the drugs."

Lucas didn't even look up. "Yeah, maybe."

Her gaze shifted to Gruber's face, and her thin veil of composure abandoned her. Tears started rolling more freely down her cheeks. Sure, she'd seen plenty of cadavers in medical school, and later on outbreak investigations in the field, but this was her colleague. She couldn't dissociate herself like that. Gruber didn't deserve to die, and he definitely didn't deserve to die here—alone, sick, probably terrified.

The hot air was beginning to reek with the stench of decomposition, and Sam stepped back toward the door, thirsting for a clean breeze. She was about to walk outside to regroup when a scratchy crackle shattered the funereal silence.

* * *

"What was that?" Sam asked, taking an involuntary step closer to Lucas.

"I don't—" he started, but another crackle, louder this time, split the air and cut him off.

The sound crackled on, intertwined with garbled noises that could have been words.

Sam wracked her brain, listening intently. *What is that?*

"Hah!" she shouted, recognition and relief rolling over her.

"What?"

"It's a radio! It has to be!" Sam rose up to her tiptoes, then fell back to her heels, over and over, a cautious substitute for jumping.

"Damn," Lucas said, a grin stretching out his lips. "Who knew? I was right!"

Sam rolled her eyes and bounded forward, reverently stepping around Gruber's corpse. A flicker of agony passed across her face, a mixture of physical pain due to her injuries and grief over her dead colleague, the man who'd taught her the basics of epidemiology before becoming her prickly but trusted subordinate.

"Come over here," she said to Lucas, her voice now hushed even though she knew Gruber couldn't hear her—not anymore.

"Coming," he said, his voice too loud.

When he drew up next to her, she was tossing aside papers, pen cups, and other detritus that littered the narrow counter ringing the perimeter of the small room, searching desperately for the source of that radio static.

"Sam?" he said.

She ignored him, absorbed in tossing aside food wrappers, dry leaves, cigarette butts, and empty cans of spray paint. The level of junk that had accumulated in this lonely space was nothing short of astonishing. If Sam hadn't been so hellbent on finding the radio, she might have stopped to survey the scene with interest. As it was, she continued to search, growing more frantic with every rat-gnawed cereal box and crusty candy wrapper she shoved aside.

"Care to help?" Sam asked, after noticing Lucas hadn't moved to assist her. He was looking out the grubby windows, his head cocked to one side.

"What are you doing?" she asked.

There was an odd look on his face. "Don't you hear that?" he asked.

She stood up and stretched her neck. "Hear what?"

"Listen," he said, gesturing vaguely toward an area of the guardhouse where she'd just been searching.

Sam sucked in a long, silent breath and closed her eyes, concentrating on picking out whatever strange noise was putting that look on Lucas' face.

After a few seconds, she heard it.

The sound was faint, tinny; it reminded her of what would come out of an old-timey gramophone. A goofy voice was rising and falling in pitch, beckoning like a carnival barker. When Sam's ears adjusted, she could just make out the words:

"Hello, folks! Have you heard about the newest attractions? That's right! After fifteen years, Gullywasher's is opening its doors once again!"

Goosebumps broke out on Sam's skin, and the gashes in her arm began aching with fresh violence. Lucas still looked lost in a dream, his expression blank. Sam wondered if he was hearing the same things she was.

"We were down, but we weren't out, folks! They tried to close us up, tried to take us away from all of you forever, but we won't let them!"

Sam's stomach churned, and for a brief moment, she was sure she was going to vomit. Everything stayed down, but a painful queasiness settled in her chest. Lucas still hadn't moved or changed his expression.

"That's right, folks! We're back and better than ever. We've got a brand new power source and we'll be bringing you that sweet, sweet medicine nonstop! Come ride the bumper cars, the Gravitron, the mighty Gullywasher roller coaster! Come burst our blood balloons and swim in our pools! See our dolphins jump and die! Take a spin round the alligator pit—Tarantula won't mind!"

The voice was rising toward a terrifying hilarity. Sam's stomach clenched again, and she hunched in a protective crouch, narrowly retaining control over her body.

When she stood back up a few seconds later, Lucas snapped out of his trance and rushed toward her.

"Are you okay?"

"Did you hear that, too?" she asked, putting her uninjured arm out to keep him from touching her.

"The radio! That horrible—"

It came again, louder now. "We've got a special discount for our first batch of visitors! That's right, we're talking to you, Samantha Clements and Theodore Lucas! Once you come in, you'll never want to leave!"

The voice devolved into a shuddering succession of high-pitched giggles that made Sam's ears ring. Lucas flinched beside her.

She was done with this. If someone was out there playing a trick on them, it ended now. "We're leaving," she said, putting as much force into her voice as possible. "Now."

Sam was stepping back past Gruber and toward the doorway when a thin, reedy voice said "Clements?"

When Sam's head jerked round to locate the source of the voice, desperately hoping it wasn't coming from the horrible phantom radio, her gaze locked onto Gruber.

His eyes were open.

*   *   *

"Shit!" Sam screamed, jumping back into Lucas and nearly knocking him down onto the litter-strewn floor.

"What?" Lucas said.

She turned to face Lucas, staring into his eyes, searching. "Didn't you hear that?"

Lucas stared back at her, his eyes blank. "No," he said, shrugging his shoulders. "Nothing besides that horrible radio."

"It was Gruber!" she said, whipping her head around and pointing a shaky finger at the body sprawled below. Lucas turned his head, but she couldn't be sure if he was seeing what she was seeing.

Gruber's eyes were open, the irises slowly clouding under a layer of corpse fog. If Lucas couldn't see it, then Sam might have to reevaluate her own sanity. She wasn't sure if it was the greenhouse-like atmosphere of the guardhouse, but her entire face felt as though it was being held over a hot stove.

Finally, Lucas asked, "Were his eyes like that before?"

"No!" Sam said, violently relieved that what she was seeing was real. "And he said my name."

Lucas sucked in a breath. "He spoke to you?"

Seeing Lucas' obvious incredulity, Sam's certainty wavered. "I mean…I heard something. It sounded like 'Clements'…"

"Are you sure it wasn't the radio?"

She wanted to be angry with him for questioning her; she wasn't out of her mind… or so she thought. "No, I'm not sure," she said at last, her voice a whisper.

Together, they stared down at Gruber; Sam's mouth twisted into a grimace. When she glanced at Lucas, his lips held the same expression.

"It's been awhile since I've seen a cadaver," Lucas said, gulping.

"I'm not sure I want to refer to him as a 'cadaver'," Sam said, her voice shaking at the edges as she thought again of Patricia Dalco and the strange autopsy audio recording. "We knew the man. He was our colleague."

"Yeah, I guess so." Lucas hung his head.

Sam looked up, as though the peeling paint on the guardhouse ceiling might hold answers to their predicament. *Samantha Clements, what is wrong with you?*

Normally, as a Commander, she was so decisive, so eponymously commanding. She could lead a research study in a war-torn, disease-ravaged country while directing a team of EIS officers and serving as a mentor to armies of student researchers from Emory's public health school next door. Her abilities to lead, decide, multitask, and think strategically had all paved the way for her quick ascent through the CDC ranks. What she was feeling now, this near-paralysis, was so alien it threatened her entire sense of self. She just couldn't seem to access the real Sam Clements, who was buried somewhere beneath the avalanche of insanity that had started the moment they entered this godforsaken park.

She didn't have much choice but to revert to their original plan, even though leaving Gruber felt like a betrayal. "Back to Plan A."

"Remind me?" Lucas said.

"We walk until we find the road."

"Do you feel good enough to walk? I'm not sure how far it is, but that cab ride felt pretty long. I could carry you."

Sam stood up straighter and lifted her chin in what she hoped was a posture of power and defiance. No matter what happened, even if she lay unconscious on the ground, she didn't want Lucas' fingers on her skin. That was a stain she would be hard pressed to scrub away. "I'm fine."

She took a deep, cleansing breath. She was prepared to call the shots; they had a plan, and while she felt less than great, she was okay enough to execute on that plan. Everything was going to be all right. They just needed to start walking.

"Let's go," Sam said. She stepped back over Gruber, lifting her feet unnecessarily high to avoid coming anywhere close to the body. A childhood fear of having her ankles grabbed by the monster under the bed tickled at the back of her mind, and she couldn't help imagining Gruber's cold, dead hand reaching up and gripping her foot like a shackle.

Lucas followed, stepping over Gruber without incident. When he reached the doorway, they both paused, looking back.

"It's a shame," Lucas said, shaking his head. "He was a great epidemiologist."

"It's just so strange," Sam said. "I don't know why he did all of this…or why he let it go this far."

"Looks like we'll never know," Lucas said. "Damn shame. Better start looking for his replacement."

What an ass. The poor dead man was right there, not even buried yet, and Lucas was making gauche remarks about personnel changes. One day soon, she was going to rise above him and get out from under his thumb. She would not let Theodore Lucas have even the tiniest bit of control over her life.

She turned around to finally leave the guardhouse, which had taken on the odor of an abattoir.

Without warning, the metal door that had been propped against the outer wall shook, then slammed in her face. Lucas let out a sharp cry as they were sealed into the hot gloom.

CHAPTER FORTY-ONE

Leona had dragged the heavy boy as quickly as she possibly could, pushing her body to the absolute breaking point. Reaching the doors, she banged the curve of her spine into the metal, sending twangs of electric pain scuttling through her body.

"Fuck!" she yelled, nearly dropping the boy's ankles.

The crow cawed at her fiercely, and the word *hurry* flashed like an ambulance siren in the middle of her brain, the unbidden messages coming more insistently now from the pale figures in the cylinder. She managed to yank the doors open, dragging them outward and sending sharp bits of gravel and clouds of dust flying in all directions.

She pulled the boy hard up and over the threshold. With a few more quick tugs, he was all the way inside, and she dropped him unceremoniously on the floor like a burlap sack of potatoes. The doors caught on the rucked-up runnels of gravel and stayed open, welcoming heat and moisture into the aquarium.

Straightening her back was torture. Slowly, she rose, letting her head lift last. When her eyes adjusted to the gloom inside the aquarium, she could see that the skinny boy was still out like a goddamn light, which was good. The cylinder, however, was wide awake.

In front of her, the tank bubbled and churned, the pale figures now twisting violently as though in the grip of grand mal seizures. Gone was the body language of gentle sways and graceful dances. If the cylinder's previous mode of physical communication had been a ballet, this was a war march.

Leona recovered from the initial shock and began absorbing what the cylinder was telling her.

Give us the boy.

Leona nodded, her mouth slack. A string of drool dangled from her lower lip.

It's time to go.

Nothing was making sense to her. She'd brought the heavy boy. She'd done everything the figures had asked of her. What more could they want that she hadn't done? Where did she need to go?

After several long moments of slack-jawed gaping at the churning inside the cylinder, Leona managed to eke out, "Time to go where?"

A lazy prickling in her toes, like her feet were coming back online after being asleep, made her look down. Her face stretched into a mask of horror; a warbling scream caught in her throat, threatening to choke her.

Her feet were dissolving.

CHAPTER FORTY-TWO

As her feet dissolved, Leona's latent scream became a giggle. The sensation tickled; she would have expected it to be unbearably painful. In a way, she was relieved. She knew, deep down in her heart, her delusions of grandeur had gotten her here. Maybe, if things had been different, if *she* had been different, she would have been allowed to stay, to continue her work. To treat the endless stream of broken people who came to her for help.

Who would help them now?

The tickling crept past her toe knuckles; her toeless bare feet now looked like stiff wooden paddles. She found she could still feel her toes, though, and if she flexed and relaxed her feet, the dirt where her toes should have been shot up in tiny puffs.

Under her gaze, the balls of her feet, then her arches, then her heels evaporated. When she didn't fall over, she realized all of her parts were still present, just not entirely visible. Once again, she felt the strange feeling of division wash over her. The Leona Franks who had traveled down the river in an inexplicably available rowboat was being flushed away, like so much unnecessary waste. Her spiteful inner voice of self-loathing laughed, telling her that was exactly what she deserved.

In old Leona's place, the Leona who belonged to the cylinder started to grow. The two pieces that lived inside the stick-thin, sucked-dry body pulled apart as though they were being unzipped—one half discarded, falling away to the floor, the other chained to the black glow of the cylinder.

I don't live here anymore, she thought, mentally tapping a dirty finger to her forehead. *I live there.* Her mental finger pointed toward the cylinder.

While the dissolving had tickled, the separation hurt; her brain ached and bobbled in her skull as the transformation continued. The woman she had been—a junkie, a failed would-be mother, a scared, shivering child—faded. The woman she was becoming—malevolent, slippery, entombed—took over. This was her reckoning.

Leona wasn't a child of the park, or its custodian, or its queen—she was its sacrifice.

On some level, she was grateful. Her old identity was painful, constricting and irritating her like an itchy sweater. Now, her pale face watched the dissolving body from within the cylinder. This was exactly what she needed to be. That sense of rightness, of belonging, began to subsume the pain of her old self's death.

As she stared out from the cylinder with gleaming black eyes, she watched old Leona's body, now no more than a useless husk, evaporate.

Good riddance, she thought.

CHAPTER FORTY-THREE

Sid tried to resist the wild cawing of the crow, but after several moments of hearing nothing from the woman near him, he cracked open one eye to see what could possibly be so upsetting it would send a crow into a frenzy.

Directly in front of him, the woman was indeed hunched over, as he'd pictured. But her position was the only thing about her he'd imagined correctly; where he'd thought she was hefty and older, she was actually thin as a Q-tip, bald, and, from what he could tell through one eye, relatively young, but terribly wasted. Her face was turned away from him, and she was facing the cylindrical tank that thrust up out of the floor. It reminded Sid of tanks he'd seen in the Georgia Aquarium, filled with colorful tropical fish darting to and fro.

This tank, in stark contrast, was completely black. Sid figured when the owners had left the park to rot, they'd decided against emptying it, probably to save money. In Sid's estimation, the tank was now coated within from top to bottom in some sort of mold or algae, rendering it opaque and, frankly, horrible.

As Sid watched, the woman straightened up and stared, transfixed, into the dark cylinder. Sid followed her gaze, and realized, after a few moments of holding his breath, the tank wasn't completely black, nor was it unoccupied.

Something—or, more accurately, somethings—fish belly-white and sinuous undulated through whatever filthy muck was still enclosed in the tank. The way the shapes bobbed in the forsaken liquid reminded Sid forcefully and viscerally of the preserved Great White he and Zeb had found at Mel's, the way the bullet-shaped head had emerged from the blackness under the thin beam of the flashlight. He felt sick again and tried desperately to gulp everything back down.

Zeb, he thought. *Goddamn.*

The woman in front of him was still captivated by the tank. Sid's eyes wandered around the room. He took in the walls lined with broken tanks, the narrow second-story catwalk, the pile of blankets in the corner.

And near the entrance…could it be? Dear God, it was.

Zeb.

He glanced over at the woman, confirming she was still hypnotized by whatever unfortunate creature—or creatures—lived in the tank. Seeing her so preoccupied and motionless, he dared to crack open his other eye. Squinting, he looked at his brother.

Zeb was lying face-up in front of the doorway, his arms above his head. It wasn't a stretch to deduce he'd been dragged, much as Sid himself had. Zeb's shirt was splattered with blood that had dried to a deep scarlet. Sid was grateful Zeb's face was turned away; he didn't think he'd be able to bear looking into a red-raw eye socket.

Looking at Zeb's prone body, Sid couldn't fool himself anymore. No amount of magical thinking was going to bring Zeb back; he was clearly dead. Sid choked back a wail. If he had the good fortune to escape this place alive, he would have to face life without Zeb by his side. He would have to live with his unforgivable failure, the failure of letting his brother die, the failure of not protecting him when he needed it, the failure of—*Big brothers take care of little brothers.*

The thought ratcheted up his nausea and self-loathing, and he flicked his gaze back over to the woman.

She was gone.

Jolts of panic shot through Sid's body. *Where did she go?*

Then, as his eyes jerked around the room, he stopped, inhaling so sharply he felt a stabbing pain in his lungs.

She wasn't entirely gone. Suspended about five and a half feet in the air was the woman's head.

As Sid watched, her shiny, egg-shaped skull began to disappear from the chin up, as though her entire existence was nothing more than an Etch-a-Sketch drawing that could be obliterated with one swipe.

The last silver-white sliver of cranium winked out of existence. Sid blinked. Surely what'd he'd just seen couldn't be real. *I must be dreaming*, he thought. *All of this. The park, Zeb dying. Wake up, wake up*, he silently pleaded.

When nothing happened, his eyes flicked back to the cylinder.

A ghostly face was staring back at him, its features smooth, its scalp bald.

CHAPTER FORTY-FOUR

The Leona who now lived inside the tank peered through the thick glass with her reptilian eyes. The others gathered around as her body pieced itself back together.

Now, when the voices came, hers was a part of the melee.

The boy.

On the ground where the old Leona had left him, the fat boy lay sprawled, arms above his head. The ugly red hole the crow had left behind when it tugged out the boy's eyeball glared up at them like an accusation.

Around her, the others began to dance. Without having to think, or feel, or breathe, she joined in. Her movements were familiar, automatic, as though she'd finally found the one thing in life she was perfectly suited for; the one place she belonged. Finally, everything felt effortless.

They were still chanting, churning the black water with their graceful figures.

The boy.

Their movements and their twisting voices conjured up the old hatred, the evil that had suffused the land since the beginning. That evil had been fed by the men and women with black hearts and a demon to please, then by the years of park guests full of delicious fear and loathing, ripe and ready for harvesting. Now, the land would feed once again.

On the ground, the boy's body began to quake; the shudders began in his fingertips and traveled in spasms down his arms and across his shoulders, shooting up into his face and sending his teeth chattering. His spine heaved, sending his body into an arched rictus. His pelvis shook up and down suggestively, a repulsive simulacrum of sex. As they watched, thighs shook, knees rattled, ankles snapped back and forth. Toes curled.

At last, the boy sat up and turned to face them.

CHAPTER FORTY-FIVE

Sid presumed the denizens of the cylinder were so focused they didn't notice him staring in wide-eyed horror at the Frankenstein reanimation of his brother.

Sid's tongue lay dry and heavy in his mouth. He couldn't wrench his gaze away from Zeb's body convulsing on the floor like a fish flopping about in the dirty water at the bottom of a boat. Everything about the entire scene was so fundamentally wrong it threatened to shatter Sid's sanity and leave him broken and useless. With every ounce of strength left in him, he steeled himself against madness and suspended his disbelief.

A low thrumming was now coming from the cylinder, but Sid didn't turn to look at it. The sound was like the toneless vibration of some infernal engine; deep, resonant, but indecipherable.

After several painful moments of impossible thrashing, Zeb sat up. Then his dead brother swiveled his head in Sid's direction.

The angry red hole where his eye should have been gaped at Sid. Fresh runnels of blood trickled out of it like tears.

The room grew uncomfortably hot. The thrum from the cylinder crescendoed into a screech, and Sid could now make out the words, "The boy."

Sid couldn't bear to watch, but he couldn't look away, either. The screeching sounds seemed to be injecting energy directly into Zeb, restarting his shriveled heart and sending blood gushing back through his veins. His skin lost its gray pallor, instead taking on a feverish pink glow.

Within the red hole of his empty eye socket, a miniature white balloon began to inflate. It grew until it was the size of a large grape. As Sid watched, the gelatinous white balloon rolled this way and that, shaking around in the socket until it rolled forward, tattooed with Zeb's unmistakable black iris.

Screams, vomit, and breath fought violently in Sid's throat, all trying to get out of his body at once. They ended up killing each other in the skirmish, leaving Sid paralyzed and silent on the floor, playing the voyeur as his dead brother came fully back to life.

CHAPTER FORTY-SIX

Sam had been trapped in the guardhouse with Gruber's body and the useless Lucas for nearly an hour, but it seemed much longer. The door refused to budge, and, after much pounding, Sam had accepted that the windows were shatterproof. She focused her energies on finding other ways out of the hellhole that was starting to feel like a boiling outhouse.

In many ways, the sealed guardhouse reminded Sam of an escape room. She'd solved her first escape room with her old EIS friends, and between the six epidemiologists, they'd solved every last clue and burst out of the room in a blistering twenty minutes, forty-six seconds. Since then, Sam had been hooked.

"It's like we're stuck in an escape room," Sam mumbled, mostly to herself.

"What?" Lucas asked from his position in the corner, where he stood fanning himself.

"Have you ever done an escape room?"

"Yeah, once. It wasn't really my thing."

"Oh. Well it feels like we're in one right now." Sam's arm throbbed.

"Kind of? Except in a real escape room, we're not trapped in the room against our will with a corpse." Lucas' voice was almost a whine, and she struggled to push down the bitter disgust flowing through her.

Sam could see Lucas was close to the breaking point. The coping mechanisms that a CDC director like Lucas should have had were seriously underdeveloped. Without warning, he pressed his back against one rough wall decorated with a startlingly accurate piece of penis graffiti and slid down with his head in his hands, coming to rest in a pile of dead leaves and God knew what else.

"Fuck," he said, his muffled voice traveling out between the crooks of his elbows. "I'm out of ideas."

"No kidding."

His voice was rising, coming faster and faster. "What are we going to do? What are we going to actually, realistically do? Gruber is dead. We're trapped. We don't know what happened. We don't have cell service. It's boiling in here, I—"

"Hold on," Sam said, cutting off what threatened to become hysteria. She felt herself rising to the challenge, taking control in the vacuum left by Lucas' disintegration. "I'm trying to tell you what we can do." She heard Lucas' derisory snort through his elbows. "Really. Yes, this is a horrible situation, but we'll get out of here. Somebody will come along, I'm sure of it."

Sam spoke with far more confidence than she felt; in reality, she wasn't at all sure another person would travel down this lonely lane, much less stop to check in the guardhouse even if they did make it this far. That thug of a cabbie wouldn't come back looking for them, that was for sure. There was also the gruesome fact of Gruber's decomposition, which, in the sweltering heat of the guardhouse, was becoming unbearable. Sam's face was burning, and her throat was dry despite the humidity. She fervently wished for some water.

Lucas ignored her, but his words seemed to echo her thoughts. "It's hot as hell in here, and Gruber's starting to turn," he said petulantly. At least his voice wasn't warbling like a scared child's anymore, and if he was feeling any panic, it wasn't evident. Sam took that as a good sign. "I'm so thirsty," he whined. "Really wish I had my good old CDC-issued reusable water bottle right about now." He tittered.

The reusable water bottles were a running inside joke; when CDC had given them to everybody in the department, encouraging them to be sustainable and stop drinking out of plastic, the reaction had been enthusiastic. That enthusiasm dissolved when the first group of go-getters filled their bottles from the water fountain and found that some sort of manufacturing error had given the inside of the bottles a gritty texture that sloughed off into whatever was poured inside. One research administrator with a particularly sensitive stomach had even vomited after one sip from the bottle. After that, most of their colleagues had thrown the bottles away, but a few of them had kept theirs, referring to them often and laughing.

"Yeah," Sam said, her voice croaking out of her parched throat. "I'm thirsty, too."

"So, what's our course of action, then? You're in charge now."

"What else can we do? I'm going to keep looking around for clues, or a way out, or something," Sam said.

"Let me know if you find anything," Lucas said, remaining firmly in his spot on the floor.

"You're not going to help me?"

"I can't even help myself right now. I'm two seconds away from banging on that jammed door and screaming until someone comes to find us."

Sam raised her eyebrows. "Seriously? For God's sake, you were deployed during Ebola! Why is this so different?"

Lucas threw up his hands. "Two words. Dead. Fucking. Gruber."

"That was three words," Sam said, exasperated. Clearly, she had to be the one to keep a cool head.

After ten minutes of fruitless searching for a way out, her fingers skating along dirty surfaces and tugging on long-stuck drawers, she finally gave up, sinking into the leaves as far away from Lucas and from Gruber's body as she could get.

"I guess we wait," Lucas said.

"I guess we do."

CHAPTER FORTY-SEVEN

Sid's eyes bulged as vitality flowed into Zeb, reanimating him as the shapes in the cylinder churned the black water to froth. Sid remained motionless on the aquarium floor, once again frozen with indecision.

Think, he told himself. *What the hell is happening?*

He screwed his eyes shut, trying to block out the insane nightmare playing out in front of him. *Think!*

Okay. Possibilities: One, this is all a ridiculously vivid nightmare, and I'm about to wake up in my own bed. Two, this is not real, and I'm going insane. Three, this is real, and I'm going to die here. Four, this is real, and my brother is dead, but I'm going to get out of here. Five, this is real, Zeb is alive, and we're both going to get out of here.

Sid's head started to ache as he thought through every possible combination of truths, lies, and misconceptions—every forecast, prediction, and analysis of the situation and what might lay ahead.

He liked possibility five the best, but he knew it was the most unlikely. That didn't stop him from trying to will it into reality; he and Zeb could walk out of this wretched place together. *Big brothers take care of little brothers.*

Okay, let's say possibility five is true. Now what?

The thrumming from the tank continued to grow in volume, threatening to drown out his thoughts with *'The boy.'*

Now what? he asked himself again. *Lay here until I know what's happening and Zeb's fully healed? Get up and try to pull Zeb out of here? Run out on my own and go get help for Zeb? Will any of that work?*

In front of Sid, his brother was coming back from the dead. Nothing in his life—or his imagination—had prepared him for something like this.

As Sid wrestled with his thoughts, which still had to compete with the thrumming that was nearing a painful volume, Zeb rose to his feet.

The body standing in the middle of the cacophonous concrete tomb of the aquarium had longish dark hair, greasy with blood and sweat, a tight, red-splattered shirt, torn shorts covered in coal-dark dirt. He looked like Zeb. There was no doubt about that. But when Sid saw the black eyes, staring straight ahead, he knew.

Whatever now inhabited his brother's body wasn't Zeb. Something else had crawled inside him, using his body as nothing more than a human suit.

The thing that was and wasn't Zeb locked its eyes on what had become a maelstrom of motion in the cylinder. Sid followed its gaze, watching the furious movements of whatever hideous creatures were stuck inside. Impossibly, the thrumming grew even louder, crashing around through the aquarium like a ricocheting bullet: *The boy the boy the boy the boy the boy.*

Sid became so enraptured, so distracted by the sound and the motion, that it took several moments for him to swing his gaze back toward the thing that used to be his brother.

Something dark and intelligent seemed to spark in Zeb's eyes, and a glimmer of hope twisted through Sid. Maybe his brother was in there, after all.

The tone of the thrumming changed, and Sid couldn't pull the words out of the new rhythm. Zeb was nodding, as though confirming receipt of some message the cylinder was transmitting.

It's telling him something, Sid thought, *and he's listening.*

Suddenly, with an abruptness that left Sid's ears ringing, the thrumming ceased. In the cylinder, the figures had receded, leaving nothing behind but cold blackness.

When Sid looked back at his brother, Zeb was staring straight at him, his eyes now curiously flat, a scimitar smile stretching his lips. Seeing such a strange, alien expression on his own brother's face sent an agonizing chill creeping through Sid's body.

If Zeb was still in there, he wasn't as strong as whatever had stepped inside him.

CHAPTER FORTY-EIGHT

Leona and the rest of the figures' instructions to the reanimated boy were clear. Kill the other one. They didn't want the sallow boy; he was weak. The new boy was stronger, and the old evil baked into this piece of Georgia swamp had buoyed him up, elevating him into a controllable tool that would last far longer than Leona had. As one of them, she could see that now.

As she churned with the others, the boy's eyes communicated his acceptance. He would do as they asked.

They ceased their movements and retreated back into the icy velvet embrace of the darkness to watch.

CHAPTER FORTY-NINE

In the silence, Zeb took a jerky step toward Sid. Zeb had been yanked back from death, but Sid could see the stiffness of rigor mortis still lingered.

In response, Sid pulled himself up, shakily coming to his feet, facing his brother.

As he rose, Sid's nose entered a stagnant layer of air and he realized the room reeked. Rotting fish, human waste, and a deep mustiness mingled and rolled around the room like a wave. Sunlight and humidity continued to pour in through the open doors.

The doors, Sid thought. *If I run for those, I could probably make it out.*

Zeb's continued advance, his pace growing quicker as the stiffness melted away, cut off that option. He was now standing just a few feet away from Sid, blocking the only way out.

Zeb's eyes were black, his gaze inhospitable. There was no spark of recognition, no playful glimmer dancing across his face as he looked at Sid. Zeb continued to walk forward, shuffling toward his brother like a sleepwalker.

"Zeb?" Sid said, his voice breaking like it had so often when he'd gone through puberty. "It's me, Zeb. It's Sid."

Sid didn't observe any change in Zeb; he just kept coming forward. As he neared, his body curled into a predatory crouch. Sid could hear a sick sucking sound coming from Zeb's chest; when he squinted, he thought he could see the wound rapidly scabbing over and—Jesus Christ—was that new skin generating around the edges?

Sid took a deep breath and steeled himself as best he could. "Zeb," he said, his voice stronger. "It's Sid. Your brother. Look at me, Zeb. You know me."

He thought he saw something dart across Zeb's features, which had turned ghoulish over the course of his restoration. Sid felt a trickle of confidence—maybe Zeb wasn't completely lost to him.

Sid took a few steps back, and a memory popped into his head like a flashbulb. The dark forest, the searing fire, the way his father told stories threaded through with terrifying pieces of Russian myth. He also remembered how Zeb had seen those summers in Russia from the exact opposite perspective: light-filled forest; cozy fire; their father's exciting, adventurous tales. Sid put his hands up, as though to calm the animal prowling toward him.

"Remember Russia, Zeb?" Zeb didn't stop, but his pace seemed to slow infinitesimally; Sid wasn't sure if he'd imagined it. "Remember how you and Papa would go hunt rabbits, and then he'd cook them over the campfire? We'd eat the strips of rabbit and not care when all the juice dripped down our chins? You said it was the best meal you'd ever eaten, and made us all promise not to tell Mom you said that."

Sid was sure he was not imagining the hesitation that squirmed its way across Zeb's face now. "There was that one story—what was it? It was your favorite. It was the one about the half-girl, half-bird creatures. They were like Sirens, but that's not the right word..." Zeb had come to a halt, staring at Sid with an openmouthed expression Sid couldn't decipher. "Sirins! That's what those things were called! The story scared the shit out of me, but you loved it. Remember, Zeb?"

Zeb's features jostled around as though they were fighting each other, and Sid had the distinct impression the real Zeb was battling with whatever had crawled inside of him.

Outside, a crow let out a squawking scream.

Whatever was inside the cylindrical tank woke up at the sound, the pale shapes darting furiously. Zeb's neck turned with a bone-cracking twist, and his eyes locked on the tank. The low thrumming started up again, vibrating maddeningly in Sid's eardrums, but he couldn't make out the words this time.

Sid held his breath. He could only see Zeb's profile, but it appeared the real Zeb, fighting for control, had been quashed by the renewed messages the tank-creatures were sending along the reeking airwaves. The side of Zeb's face Sid could see had recovered the emotionless affect that reopened a slipstream of terror in Sid's heart.

I need more, Sid thought. *How can I reach him?*

Zeb turned back to face his brother. If the real Zeb were a prisoner inside this body, it didn't show. He restarted his horrible sleepwalking shuffle toward Sid.

"Wait!" Sid yelped, instantly annoyed at the helplessness broadcasting itself through his voice. He took a deep breath. "Zeb," he tried, more calmly this time. "Remember Mel's?"

Nothing.

Sid kept trying. "Come on, you remember! That horrible little place that called itself a wildlife park. It was over by Hiawassee, and we stopped at that little diner to ask for directions. We parked next to a Gremlin, and you thought it was so cool. Then we went into the café with all those old people, and there was that cute waitress behind the counter—you were flirting with her! What was her name again?" Sid tapped his index finger against his chin, feigning nonchalance, as though he and Zeb were reminiscing over beers at a cozy bar instead of locked in some sort of duel in this nightmarish place. "Oh, right! How could I forget? Annie May!"

Sid saw the flicker in Zeb's eyes again, and he trudged on with renewed hope. "So, we managed to find the place, and there was basically nothing left. Except for that awful aquarium." Sid paused, looking around. "Didn't feel that different from where we are now, actually."

A rough sound crackled out of Zeb's throat, and at first Sid thought he was growling, or maybe choking. When the sound came again, Sid realized

Zeb was laughing.

Now he knew: the real Zeb was still in there, and Sid was going to get him out. *Big brothers take care of little brothers.*

"Yeah! We had to walk way into the woods to find it, and when we got there, it was this long hallway with this big dark room at the end, and all we had was a flashlight. There were all these moldy tanks set into the walls, and wait—wasn't there like a porno mag or something sitting on a table? Am I remembering that right? Well—"

A colossal, ripping scream from the crow snatched the words out of Sid's throat and sent the pale creatures in the tank into a panic. The thrumming became louder, and the figures started frothing around each other in apoplectic fits with such force they looked like a tornado in a bottle—one of Zeb's favorite childhood toys.

Zeb's face constricted into a grimace, and sweat popped out on his forehead as the real Zeb struggled against the forces shoving him back down, out of the way.

Sid had to yell to make himself heard over the combined cacophony of the crow and the thunderous thrum coming from the tank. "Remember, Zeb? It was so dark in there, and we were filming, doing a pano, and then I dropped my flashlight? It rolled all the way across the floor, landing just perfectly so we got this grand reveal of that...that preserved shark."

Zeb's eyes were twitching; the one that had regenerated took on a popcorn-yellow hue.

"I thought it was so fucking creepy, but you loved it, and you named it Annie May after that waitress in Hiawassee. Then we told the Georgia Aquarium about it, and we had that huge ceremony..." Sid trailed off, looking at Zeb questioningly.

"Zeb?" he said.

Zeb's yellow eyeball had started to swell, bulging out of the blood-rimmed socket. The thrumming from the tank rose to a deafening roar, and Sid considered clapping his hands over his ears; he refrained, not wanting to look weak yet again in the face of those tormentors, whatever they were.

Zeb's head started to snap back and forth, half-looking at Sid, half-looking at the tank. Sid imagined Zeb suddenly ripping apart down the middle, as easily as a sheet of paper. The thought made him feel sick.

"Fuck!" Sid yelled, anger finally outweighing his fear. "Zeb, you fucking come out of there right fucking now! I want to go fucking home!"

Zeb's head started twisting with so much force Sid thought it would spin clean off his neck, *Exorcist*-style. Zeb's yellow eyeball continued to bulge, and the figures in the tank were growing so violent Sid thought they might break the tank.

Break the tank! The thought hit him like a blow to the solar plexus. The way out was suddenly so obvious: break the tank, take away their power. He wasn't sure where this thought had come from, but he knew it was right.

To his left, a spiky metal chair lay on its side in a drift of dead leaves.

In a few quick movements, Sid reached the chair, picked it up, and started advancing toward the tank.

The roar became a howl, the words '*Kill him*' caterwauling around the room. Sid knew he needed to act fast; Zeb wouldn't be able to hold out against that siren command for much longer.

Sid heaved the chair over his head, bending his knees to build up the maximum amount of force. Just as he was about to slam his body forward and smash the chair against the glass, he felt Zeb's meaty hand grab one of the chair's legs, yanking it down. Sid had to arch his back, performing a strange gymnastic movement to get himself out from under the chair, which had become an object of tug-o-war. He whipped around to face his brother, and saw that while Zeb was still shaking, it was more of a twitch. His left eyeball had bulged out so hugely it looked like an overfilled water balloon.

It was now or never. "I'm so sorry, Zeb," he said, and, twisting, rammed the chair upward, sending one of the legs right through Zeb's corpulent eye. The eyeball erupted in a spray of pus and ocular liquid, a disgusting cocktail of bodily fluids. Pus dripped down the back of the chair and started trickling toward Sid's fingers, gripped firmly around the chair's legs.

Zeb howled, which sent a dagger of guilt straight to Sid's heart, but the plan had worked. Zeb jerked his hands away from the chair and clapped them to his eye, which he'd had to lose twice in less than twenty-four hours.

Sid didn't waste any more time. Fear, anger, and desperation combined to give him a strength he normally wouldn't have possessed. He reared back and swept the chair up and over his head, sending it crashing into the glass of the tank with a satisfying boom.

The glass splintered out from the point of contact with the chair, cracks spiderwebbing across the tank's surface with unbelievable speed. Dark liquid started seeping through the cracks; the droplets turned to rivulets that turned to jets, until, with a blast, the tank exploded.

All hell broke loose.

CHAPTER FIFTY

The tank's catastrophic blowout happened so quickly Sid didn't have time to consider what might come rushing out. Zeb clearly didn't, either. His hands were clapped to his ruptured eyeball, cloudy fluid leaking out between his fingers.

Later, when Sid reviewed the crazy chain of events in his mind, he didn't know what he'd thought would happen—but he definitely hadn't expected the bodies.

When the tank finally broke in an explosion of green-smeared glass and foul black water, the bodies came spilling out.

They were remarkably well-preserved. Sid recognized their faces from the pictures in the news stories he'd studied back in his dorm room. There was Katrina Ryen, then came George Bigby, Gina Choate, and Patrick Fenwick, the park's last security officer.

A small girl, her body so old nobody living remembered her name, tumbled out on a black wave. Her hand slapped the cement floor. She was missing all five fingernails.

Leona Franks was last, her body painfully thin and even paler than the rest.

There were more—a full inventory of the tank's inhabitants would have put to rest nearly a dozen missing persons cases, Sid felt sure. But that was not to be.

As Sid watched, with Zeb still nursing his collapsed eyeball, the drift of bodies on the floor began to dissolve, melting into goo. Steam rose like smoke from the gelatinous piles, and the scent of rotting meat permeated the air. Bits of old skin, pale and shriveled, collected in puddles on the concrete. An ear, its lobe perforated by several piercings, floated in a small lake of liquified tissue, until it broke apart and sank like the Titanic.

Beside him, Zeb dropped his hands from his face, staring at the spectacle with his good eye. Neither of them said anything as the sea of viscous human remains mixed with the black water from the tank and seeped through a large drain set in the concrete floor, until nothing was left but sharp chunks of glass and small islands of algae.

*　　*　　*

The deluge of bodies wasn't the only consequence of the tank's eruption. With the collapse of the tank, cell service flooded back into the park. Sid's phone pinged in his pocket, but it was the last thing he was thinking about. As the brothers stood in the aquarium, where ghostly noises and the snarls of impossible creatures still echoed, a low vibration traveled through the earth, traversed the concrete, and came to rest in the brothers' bones, like the harbinger of an earthquake. A splintering sound then shot through the atmosphere and assaulted Sid's eardrums before a massive, tiered set of booms made the first sounds feel like child's play. Sid glanced at his brother, but a thousand-yard stare was plastered on Zeb's face.

Layered into the gradually softening booms were the frantic caws of that damned crow. When the last boom came, the crow's final squawk cut off, blanketing the park in an abrupt silence.

Somehow, Sid willed his legs to work. He crossed over to his brother and laid a tentative hand on his shoulder, simultaneously searching his face for any sign of recognition or awareness. What he saw didn't comfort him— Zeb's face was still blank, his eyelid mercifully shut over the wreck of his exploded eyeball. His shirt was so stained with gore, Sid couldn't bear to examine his chest wound any more closely.

"Let's go, Zeb," Sid said quietly, applying gentle pressure to Zeb's shoulder, trying to turn him to face the flat yellow light streaming through the metal doors. Sid had an uncomfortable feeling those doors wouldn't stay open for long.

Under Sid's guiding arm, Zeb shuffled clumsily toward the exit. Behind them, Sid could hear something coming up through the drain—it sounded like singing.

"Come on," Sid said, more loudly. He channeled extra force into the arm guiding Zeb, urging him to walk faster. Zeb complied, his movements robotic and awkward. After a few tense seconds, during which Sid could swear the singing was growing louder and the doors were starting to shake, he and Zeb emerged into the sharp light. The sun was blazing in the sky, and waves of humidity crashed onto their bodies. The remains of Zeb's shattered eyeball wept pink fluid from under his lashes.

A single objective pulsed in Sid's mind as he hurried Zeb past the crumbling dolphin show amphitheater, the alligator pit (where Sid thought he heard a faint thrashing sound), and between midway stalls.

We have to get out.

His focus wavered when they rounded a corner and came face-to-face with destruction. Clarity washed over Sid; the booms and crashes they'd heard had been the Gullywasher roller coaster's dramatic death rattle. In front of them, sharp splinters of wooden struts thrust up into the air. The old coaster's cars were tangled among the mess, coming to rest like a huge beaded necklace on the piles of broken wood. Bits of metal from the rails clung precariously to the pieces of track that were still intact.

Dust rose steadily up into the air, and Sid coughed, a harsh, hacking noise. He hunched over, still hacking, hands gripping his thighs, waiting for the fit to pass. When he stood back up, Zeb's good eye was trained on him.

Are you in there, Zeb? he thought.

He moved his hand, wanting to put his arm back on his brother's shoulder; instead, Sid's fingers traced the hard edge of something rectangular in his pocket.

"My phone!" he shouted. Sid pulled his phone out, pressed the home button… and saw one weak bar in the upper left corner of his screen. "Zeb! We have service!" Sid was nearly sobbing with relief.

His brother's face didn't change; he still gazed at Sid with a kind of glaring scrutiny Sid didn't understand. But he didn't care about that now; he had his phone, he had service, and he was going to call the police, the fire department, an ambulance, his mom…

He was going to call everybody.

*　*　*

The phone barely rang once before an operator came on the line.

"Nine-one-one operator, what is your emergency?"

The line was staticky, and Sid struggled to get the words out. "I need help!"

The operator clearly hadn't heard him and he repeated, "Hello, nine-one-one operator, what is your emergency?"

Sid tried again, shouting this time. "Hello? Hello? Can you hear me? My name is Sidney Barkov, and I'm at Gullywasher's of Georgia. My brother is hurt and we need an ambulance."

"Alright, Sidney. My name is Bruno. Are you or your brother in immediate danger?"

"I…" Sid's voice trailed off. Were they in danger? In a place like this, probably. "I don't know."

"Alright, that's fine, Sidney. Can you get to a safe place?"

"We can try to get to the parking lot."

"That's good. Now did you say you're at Gullywasher's of Georgia? The old theme park?" The operator sounded incredulous. Sid couldn't blame him.

"Yes! Some woman tried to kill us, and then the roller coaster collapsed, and we need to get out!" Anxiety rose in his voice, making it crack like a china plate dropped on the floor.

Sid could hear Bruno clicking away at a keyboard. "It's alright, Sidney. Don't hang up. I've got police and an ambulance on their way. We can talk until help arrives. You said a woman tried to kill you. Is she still in the area?"

For once, Sid could say something for certain. "No, she's gone."

"Were there any weapons involved?"

"Not...not exactly." How could he even begin to explain what truly happened?

"Okay, Sidney, that's helpful, thank you," Bruno said.

"How long?" Sid asked, pleading.

"Emergency personnel should arrive within half an hour."

"Will they be able to find us?" Half an hour sounded like a very long time.

"I can direct them to you—can you tell me where you are exactly?"

"We're between the big roller coaster and some of the midway tents, but we're walking toward the entrance. My brother is hurt. He's not moving very fast."

"What is the extent of your brother's injuries?"

"I..." again, Sid faltered. "He had a chest wound and something's wrong with his eye." He hoped Bruno wouldn't dig too much into his use of the past tense. Sid wasn't sure if—or how badly—Zeb's chest was still injured.

"Alright, Sidney. Are you hurt at all?"

"No," Sid said. "At least, I don't think so."

"I'll relay this information to the emergency personnel. Just stay on the phone with me until they arrive. Can you do that, Sidney?"

"Just Sid."

"What was that?"

"You can just call me Sid."

"Alright, Sid, thank you. Can you tell me how your brother got hurt?"

Sid felt sure calm, logical Bruno wouldn't believe that piece, but he had to at least try to explain. "Well... a piece of the roller coaster fell down and hit him. Then he wasn't breathing, but...but he's breathing again now."

"Well, just be sure to take it easy," Bruno said, but Sid could detect a hint of irritation under that calmness. Maybe Bruno thought Sid was stupid and reckless for venturing off into someplace dangerous like Gullywasher's. If so, he was right.

Sid tried to urge Zeb to move faster; the effort exhausted him, leaving him panting.

"Are you alright, Sid?" Bruno asked.

"Yeah, I'm just trying to get us out of here fast."

"Sid, is there anything else the emergency personnel should know before entering the area?"

Sid's mouth turned down into a scowl. Here was his chance to say the one thing that really needed to be said. "Yeah. Tell them this place is fucking evil and needs to destroyed."

*　　*　　*

As Sid spoke, his words warbling into the phone's speaker, he pulled Zeb along by the arm. He really didn't know how to answer all of the dispatcher's questions. How could he explain what had happened back in that aquarium without sounding like a lunatic? Not to mention the way Zeb had died, had legitimately fucking died, but somehow he was breathing again, walking next to him. Then there was the way his chest wound had healed over, new skin blooming across the raw meat like a fungus. Sid couldn't be sure if it was completely or just partially healed; there was still so much dried blood covering Zeb's chest. And the eye thing, of course; the crow had plucked out Zeb's original eyeball while he was lying dead in the midway, then somehow it had grown back, only to pop again when Sid pierced it with that chair.

Sid thought that was a little much to share over the phone with a stranger.

They were passing between the still-groaning ruins of the Gullywasher and the flapping, mossy tents of the midway. Sid tried to look ahead and ignore his surroundings; he didn't want to see anything else that might further endanger his sanity.

They passed the gruesome carousel with its deformed animals and the half-collapsed bumper car ring where Sid had seen the tiny bloodied hand. He kept his eyes trained firmly ahead of him, focusing on putting one foot in front of the other and forcing Zeb to do the same. Finally, they rounded the edge of the bumper car ring and turned left toward the First Aid building. From there, Sid could see the log over the lazy river was still in place. He narrated his experience through the phone—"I'm passing the midway, now the carousel, we're moving along, yes"— while walking along the gravel at a speed that didn't seem fast enough.

"Crossing the lazy river now," he said. He wedged the phone between his ear and his shoulder and used both hands to herd Zeb onto the log, following him only when Zeb was safely on the other side.

"Now we're coming to the ticket booth," he said. They passed the rotting building and started down the path bordered by heavy, dank foliage. "We just passed the ticket booth. We're heading toward the parking lot."

"Alright, Sid. Emergency personnel should be almost there," Bruno said.

Sid and Zeb emerged from the leafy tunnel onto the cracked asphalt and stopped short.

Their car was gone.

"Oh God," Sid breathed into the phone.

"What? What is it, Sid?"

"Our car is gone," Sid said, shrugging, even though Bruno couldn't see his gesture.

"Did you see anybody else in the park? Do you know who could have taken it?"

"God," Sid moaned, more loudly. "There was that woman, but she's… gone," he caught himself before he said 'dead.' He didn't want the dispatcher thinking Sid had killed somebody, even if it looked like self-defense. "I didn't see anybody else."

"Alright, Sid. Why don't you and your brother just stay right where you are in the parking lot. Emergency personnel should be there in less than two minutes."

"I—" Sid started, but his phone beeped twice and then died, out of battery.

* * *

Sid stuffed his useless phone back in his pocket. His fingers brushed against something crispy and plastic, and he pulled out a peppermint. Aching for distraction, he unwrapped it and popped the candy into his mouth, which still tasted of bile and stale Doritos.

Zeb, or, maybe more accurately, whatever looked like his brother, was standing motionless about five feet away on the cracked asphalt, staring over the parking lot with a blank expression.

Smacking sounds filled the air as Sid sucked on the peppermint, savoring the sharp flavor that bit through the nasty tastes that had set up shop on his tongue. The sensation soothed him, melting away some of the panic he'd endured dragging Zeb through the park as quickly as possible.

"Zeb?" Sid said, taking a step toward him. "I don't know if you heard me, but I called 911. The dispatcher said the police and an ambulance will be here in less than two minutes."

Zeb didn't respond, but Sid thought he may have shrugged his shoulders slightly.

"I was supposed to stay on the phone with the guy, but my battery died. I'm guessing you don't still have your phone, huh?"

The question was a long shot—Zeb had been largely unresponsive since the tank exploded. So, Sid was pleasantly surprised when Zeb turned to face him, one corner of his mouth curled up. His hands crept over his pockets, trying to feel for that piece of technology so essential to modern life. Finding nothing, he raised his hands in a placating gesture, shrugged his shoulders, and shook his head once, hard.

"Ah," Sid said, disappointed, but comforted at the same time by his brother's attempt to interact. "I figured as much."

Zeb turned back around to stare at the parking lot, then swiveled to face the gravelly path that led down to the guardhouse. Without saying anything, he turned and began walking in halting, uneven strides across the asphalt toward the guardhouse.

"Zeb," Sid said. When his brother didn't slow or even acknowledge Sid, he cupped his hands around his mouth and yelled "Zeb! Hey!"

Zeb didn't change his pace, nor did he look back. Sid galloped forward to catch him.

"Zeb. The dispatcher told me we should just stay here."

Zeb continued to walk, Sid now keeping pace at his side.

"Zeb. Seriously. We should really stay here."

No response.

Sid tried a different tactic. "Where are you going, Zeb?"

Without breaking his stride, Zeb lifted one arm with visible effort and curled his fist, leaving one index finger pointing in the direction of the guardhouse.

"Alright," Sid said. "You think we're going to walk out of here? I don't think that's a good idea."

Nothing from Zeb.

Sid switched maneuvers again. "What are you looking for?"

Zeb raised his arm halfway, his finger still pointing.

Sid considered putting a hand on Zeb's shoulder, forcing him to slow down, but a new, eager gleam in Zeb's eye made him wary. Any sign Zeb was possibly coming back to himself was good, and Sid shouldn't interfere. He didn't know what negative repercussions that might have, like waking a sleepwalker and setting them off on a violent rampage. Ignoring his desire to follow Bruno's instructions, Sid fell into step with Zeb.

After a few moments of silence, the guardhouse came into view, their Civic abandoned in front.

"What the fuck…?" Sid said, staring at the car. "How?"

Zeb ignored the car, his attention fully captured by the graffiti-covered cement-block building. Excited grunting noises burst from between his lips. Sid hoped that was a good sign, but he no longer knew what to think. He wasn't sure he'd be able to reckon with what had happened back in the aquarium, not for a long time. He'd probably need years of therapy to make everything okay again, or at least as okay as possible.

Zeb's grunts grew louder, and Sid thought he could make out one word: "There! There!" He couldn't be sure it wasn't just wishful thinking. His eyes burned with unshed tears.

He desperately wanted his brother back.

Without warning, Zeb surged forward into a shambling half-jog, half-scuttle toward the guardhouse, skirting around their car. Sid followed, shouting, "Zeb! Hold up! Zeb!"

Zeb either didn't hear him or deliberately ignored him; either one would have been typical Zeb.

Zeb rounded the corner of the guardhouse with Sid at his heels, still trying to get him to slow down. Strange noises came from the guardhouse, sending gusts of fear through Sid's body and breaking his skin out in goosebumps. Before Sid could stop him, Zeb slapped a palm on the handle of the guardhouse door and yanked so hard Sid was sure he had dislocated his shoulder.

A few seconds of straining was all it took to pop the door open and send Zeb flying backward. Sid was about to turn and help his brother up off the ground when movement from inside the guardhouse caught his eye.

On the dirty, leaf-littered floor, a pretty woman and a grizzled man were lifting their heads toward the light streaming in through the open door. Across from them lay a pallid, rigid form.

"Help," the woman breathed, struggling to pull herself to her feet.

Sid stooped to grab her outstretched hand and give her a boost to stand, but Zeb cut in between them before Sid could make contact. Grunting like a madman, Zeb crouched next to the lump on the floor.

"He's dead," the grizzled man said tonelessly as he stood. The woman rose slowly to her feet.

"Who—" Sid started, unsure where to go from there. He had so many questions knocking around in his skull, and they all tangled together, leaving him tongue-tied.

Zeb filled the silence, groaning like an outraged bear awoken in the midst of hibernation. As Sid watched, his face a mask of horror and unease, Zeb placed one meaty hand on each side of the dead man's face. He started to squeeze, and Sid was about to lunge forward and stop him from whatever gruesome thing he was about to do, when the dead man's eyes sprang open and he drew in a long, shuddering breath.

CHAPTER FIFTY-ONE

Coming quickly to herself, Sam sprang into action, jumping toward Gruber. She grabbed his wrist and felt for a pulse, all the while murmuring comforting platitudes like "It's alright, Dr. Gruber," and "You're going to be just fine, just fine."

Gruber's eyes were rolling wildly in their sockets, as if he were trying to take in everything around him at once. He opened his mouth, trying to speak, but nothing came out.

"Hey now," Sam said. "Don't try to talk, it's okay." The two boys had moved off to the side and were observing the scene with opposite expressions; the boy who'd inexplicably resurrected Gruber was beaming, while the skinny one looked ready to pass out. Lucas was somewhere behind her, being unhelpful as usual.

Gruber pulled in another quaking breath, inflating his lungs to their full capacity. Sam didn't want to think about his chances of avoiding brain damage, much less how exactly he'd appeared dead as a doornail, even starting to reek of decomposition, but must have been clinging to life. She and Lucas were both clinically trained—how had they made such a glaring error?

Unless, a sinister voice whispered in her head, *you didn't miss it. Maybe Gruber really was dead.*

That wasn't an option in Sam's world, and it wouldn't be suitable as an official explanation to the CDC, either.

Sam continued to murmur into Gruber's ear as the rogue epidemiologist caught his breath. In the relative quiet, she could hear her own heart pounding.

She'd nearly forgotten about the boys when the skinny one spoke.

"Who are you?"

Sam looked up, studying both brothers properly for the first time. A sense of familiarity, of unexpected recognition, twisted through her thoughts.

"Commander Samantha Clements," she said, clearing her throat. "That's Dr. Theodore Lucas, and the man on the ground is Dr. Archibald Gruber. We're all from the CDC."

"Woah," the skinny kid said.

"Who are you?" she asked.

The kid shook his head, as if to clear it. "I'm Sid. This is Zeb."

That's when it clicked—Sam had seen those faces before, heard those voices on countless YouTube videos. A feeling of unreality washed over her. She was there in the same room with the Barkov brothers, her favorite urban explorers.

Sid fidgeted nervously when he saw her face light up. "No way," she croaked. "You're Sid and Zeb Barkov, right?"

The nervousness cleared, and Sid nodded incredulously. "Do we know each other?"

"No, no," Sam said, waving her good hand through the air. "I, um... I watch your YouTube videos."

"You're into urban exploring?" Sid said, as though unsure he'd heard her correctly.

"Are you surprised?" she retorted.

Sid paused, considering. "You know what? Given the shit I've seen, I'd say that doesn't even make my top ten list of surprises."

Sam was silent a moment, considering the brothers. The fact of Zeb's injured eye finally pierced her consciousness. "Oh, Jesus," she said to Zeb. "What happened to you? Can I take a look at that?"

Zeb smiled wanly but stayed silent.

"He's in shock, I think," Sid said evasively. "He got hurt and lost his eye."

"Can I look?" Sam asked again.

"I guess?" Sid said, glancing at his brother. "If he'll let you."

Sam stepped gingerly forward, moving away from Gruber, who was taking deep, heaving breaths.

The room was small, and it only took a few steps for Sam to reach Zeb.

"Mind if we step outside so I can see it in the light?"

Zeb said nothing, but obliged, moving out into the fresh air.

Sam placed her hand gently on the base of his skull and asked him to tilt his head. She raised his eyelid with one thumb.

A red, ragged hole stared back at her, and she stifled the urge to recoil.

Instead, she inhaled sharply, then let it out in a long, low whistle. "That certainly doesn't look too good," she said. She glanced down at his torso, registering for the first time that his shirt was stiff with dried blood. "And what happened to your chest?"

She turned to face Sid when she got no reaction from Zeb. Sid shifted uncomfortably. "Um…he had an accident. He got hit with a piece of wood that fell off the roller coaster."

Sam stooped to examine Zeb's chest more closely, pushing aside the pieces of bloody fabric. Aside from several scratches and a few bruises, she couldn't find much evidence of the wound that had clearly caused so much blood loss. "I'm not really seeing much here," she said, directing her comments to Sid. "But for both wounds, the most important thing will be to make sure they don't get infected."

Sid's face brightened, as though remembering something. "There's an ambulance on the way," he said.

"What?" Sam said, more of an exclamation than a question. "How did you—what—"

"Cell service came back, so I called 911, but then my phone died. They said they're sending police and an ambulance."

"Thank fuck," Sam said. "Excuse my language."

"No fucking problem," Sid said, a ghostly grin stretching across his face.

In the distance, they could hear the long, low wail of a siren.

"Thank fuck," came a gravelly voice. When they turned around to see who had spoken, Zeb was staring back at them and smiling.

CHAPTER FIFTY-TWO

The ambulance barreled down the narrow road toward the motley crew of ragged people standing next to the guardhouse. Sid and the other doctor from the CDC, Lucas, had managed to prop Dr. Gruber between them. He sagged, supported only by their linked arms at his back. Dr. Gruber's broken leg stuck out at an odd angle.

Lights flashing and siren blaring, the ambulance pulled to a stop, nearly hitting the nose of the Barkovs' rundown Civic. The EMT crew stilled the siren and lights and hopped out of the ambulance, a police car hot on their tail.

One of the EMTs walked over to the survivors' little cluster, while the other opened up the back doors and started pulling out a stretcher.

The EMT looked them up and down, taking in the blood, sweat, and other bodily fluids covering each of them. He said, "Okay—it's probably simpler for me to ask, which one of you *doesn't* need an ambulance?"

Lucas raised his hand, as did Sid.

"Alright, ma'am, sirs," the EMT said, nodding at Commander Clements, Dr. Gruber, and Zeb. "Can you walk on your own?"

"He sure can't," Commander Clements said, shrugging her shoulder to indicate Dr. Gruber.

"Lars! We'll need at least one stretcher!" the EMT, whose name tag read 'Boris,' called over his shoulder.

"And the two of you?" he asked.

"I can walk," Commander Clements said.

Zeb only nodded.

"Alright, then," Boris said. "Let's get you folks to a hospital."

As Boris and Lars loaded Dr. Gruber onto a stretcher and helped Commander Clements and Zeb into the back of the ambulance, two uniformed officers sidled up to Sid and Lucas.

"Gentlemen," said the portly, balding one. "I'm Officer Katz, and this is Officer DuBois." DuBois, a lanky string bean of a man with a scraggly beard and watery eyes, waved weakly.

"Dr. Theodore Lucas, CDC," Lucas said.

"Sidney Barkov," Sid said.

"Can you tell us what happened?" Katz asked.

Sid and Lucas exchanged a look. "I can try," Lucas said.

"The emergency dispatcher relayed the information to us that there is a dangerous woman on the premises?" DuBois offered. Katz shot him a look that clearly said *Get back in line, rookie.*

"There was," Sid said. "She's gone now."

"Can you be sure about that?" Katz asked.

Sid shrugged. "Sure enough."

"Okay," Katz said. "Well, we've got a backup unit on the way, and we'll canvas the area. We'll also get a tow truck to bring that car in. I'm assuming it belongs to one of you?"

Sid nodded, and Katz continued, saying the only words Sid wanted to hear. "In the meantime, let's get you both out of here."

CHAPTER FIFTY-THREE

Once she'd had a chance to recharge her phone, Sam had been bombarded with a barrage of emails. Ignoring them all, she fired off a quick note to the EIS officer in charge of the Savannah outbreak investigation.

Kurt—Get your team over to Gullywasher's of Georgia. It's an abandoned amusement park outside of Savannah, and we have good information a drug dealer set up shop there to sell black tar heroin. We've connected that back to at least Patricia Dalco. Take samples.

Sam was sure Kurt Finney would have a ton of questions, but she didn't even know how she would begin to answer most of them. She wasn't ready to reckon with what she'd seen, what had happened—much less explain it to another rational mind at the CDC. Luckily, Kurt responded quickly in the affirmative, and on Friday, his team of EIS officers crossed under the yellow caution tape set up by Katz's colleagues and set off to collect samples. Kurt reported it didn't take long for them to find the stacks of heroin in the aquarium, which they confiscated for analysis.

She'd also heard Lucas and Sid had each done their best to tell the police their piece of the story. Sam was sure they'd been a bit sparing with the facts, but she planned to do the same when she was eventually questioned. The way she saw it, there was no use telling people things they weren't ready to hear and wouldn't understand, especially when the exact events that had taken place at Gullywasher's were impossible to prove now.

Apparently, the officers had listened to Lucas' and Sid's watered-down reports, taking a few notes and offering coffee and slices of pizza. Lucas' version was mostly accurate. He told the police that, taking a short break from the official duties that had brought them to Savannah, he and Sam had set off for a park they thought was still open. Upon arriving and finding it shuttered, they decided to explore anyway. Then some disturbed woman had attacked them, so they'd come back out to look for help. They'd found Gruber shortly before the ambulance arrived.

She wasn't sure what Sid's version had been, but it must have been as straightforward and selectively truthful as Lucas', since he wasn't detained or charged.

Sam and Zeb had been released from the hospital the day before; Sam's arm had been disinfected and wrapped. Luckily, the wounds hadn't been as deep as she'd feared. Sid reported to her that Zeb's chest wound was no more than a mosaic of scratches, which had also been cleaned and bandaged. His empty eye socket had been disinfected in an agonizing procedure that seemed to take forever and packed with cotton before his lid was taped shut. Doctors had scheduled him a follow-up appointment with a premier ocular surgeon and ophthalmologist back at Emory. According to Sid, Zeb still hadn't said much, but at least he was losing the blank expression that had been plastered on his face since they left the park behind.

Gruber was a different story. He was still in the hospital, being treated for bacterial infections and his broken leg, and also awaiting blood tests. When he'd gotten to the hospital, he'd suddenly become animated, words scrambling to get out of his mouth in front of each other.

"The sample! The sample! My pocket! Antitoxin!" he kept repeating. When a nurse checked his pockets, they were all empty. When he didn't stop raving, the nurse had to sedate him, and when he awoke several hours later, he was able to more calmly explain that he was quite sure he needed botulinum antitoxin, and the EIS team needed to take samples from that goddamn alligator pit right now. Gruber repeated as much when Sam went to visit him in the hospital after she had been released.

Now, four days since she'd left Gullywasher's in an ambulance, Sam was cruising back to Atlanta in a rented car. She was happy to be away from Lucas, whom she'd left at the hotel bar, mostly sloshed. Apparently, he'd been told that the CDC human resources department was reviewing his behavior toward his female colleagues, several of whom had come forward with complaints over the past few months. It wasn't much, but it was a start—and luckily for her, the controversy masked any official questions about the trip to Savannah. The CDC would eventually expunge its own monsters, Sam felt sure of it.

The landscape flew by in a green blur, and the sky was a bright blue overhead. She was no longer clutching her arm in pain, and her lab results had come back, revealing no abnormalities detected in her blood. A smile lit up her face as she looked out the windshield at the highway opening up before her. The past few days had been full of terror, pain, and grief, but she was still alive.

More than alive, she felt liberated.

CHAPTER FIFTY-FOUR

Gruber, on his fifth day of observation at Candler Hospital in Savannah, received objectively good news when his lab results came in, but his bafflement at the negative botulism results outweighed any relief he might have felt.

For the most part, Gruber was back to his old self. He couldn't remember anything after he'd crawled out of the pit, and he considered that a mercy. Pieces of dark imagery—snapping jaws, sharp glass, splintered wood, a wormy but life-saving power emanating from a pair of beefy hands—flitted through his mind as he slept, not distinct enough to even be called nightmares. He woke up rubbing the pale circle on his wrist where his watch should have been. The entire adventure had deflated his ego; he was humiliated, humbled, and grudgingly grateful to Clements for cleaning up his mess and spinning a tale that kept him from getting fired. He felt small and disgusting, reduced to a liability when he should have been basking in triumph. *Why did I think I could do it all on my own?*

He felt somewhat vindicated when he received news from Clements herself: the CDC lab had tested both the heroin and the mud from the alligator pit. There was nothing special about the heroin, besides its absurdly high purity.

The mud was a different story.

Environmental samples, especially dirt, are expected to have millions of bacteria, viruses, fungi, protozoa—a menagerie of microorganisms. The microorganisms work together symbiotically to support the overall health of the soil.

However, the sample from Gullywasher's had only a single strain of microorganism, which grew in a small, fire-red colony on a special agar plate. Preliminary genetic testing using established RNA-sequencing protocols had found no matches in the database to any other discovered organism.

On behalf of the CDC, Clements had ordered the entire area of Gullywasher's declared a biohazard and cordoned off until further studies could be done on the new microorganism. In honor of its founder, the bacterium became known as *Lacertus gruberensis.*

Gruber smiled stiffly, working out the lingering rigidity in his facial muscles. Clements had a hand in the naming, he was sure. The Commander was a good person, Gruber knew. If he'd been open with her from the beginning, things could have turned out very differently—maybe he wouldn't be recovering alone in a hospital bed, feeling disgraced. On the other hand, the EIS team would never have found anything if he hadn't shown them the way. At least he had that.

He shifted on the thin hospital mattress and studied the sunlight streaming through the window. He'd been given another chance at life, and he wasn't going to waste it.

Tomorrow was a new day.

EPILOGUE

Snow falls like puffs of cotton over the ruins of Gullywasher's. A high metal fence has been erected around the property and plastered with orange 'Biohazard' signs. The turnoff to the park has been blocked off at the entrance with additional fencing and more tangerine-colored placards.

The way the ash-white snow falls over the spiked biohazard symbols gives the entire park an eerie nuclear-fallout feel, as though the ground itself is emanating something deadly and insidious and will kill anybody who dares to step on it, slowly and painfully.

In the alligator pit, Tarantula rusts into obscurity, his leathery scales falling away in thick strips, leaving behind nothing more than metal framework and creaking hinges.

To any casual bystander, even though there are none here in the toxic wasteland of Gullywasher's, Tarantula looks beyond repair.

How little most people comprehend of the white-hot power of buried evil.

With unseen forces sending energy up through the pit muck, now frozen into a hard crust, Tarantula is far from gone.

Even though it is a cold night for alligators, his tail twitches.

* * *

ACKNOWLEDGMENTS

I first started writing this book while I was stuck in a corporate job that absolutely sucked the life out of me. To combat my anxiety, I would write snatches of this novel in emails to myself during lunches, breaks, and after hours. I pushed so hard to write this novel both because I wanted a creative outlet and because I needed an escape.

Around the time I finished writing this book, the work stress had become unbearable. Both my mom and my husband encouraged me to quit my corporate job and dive fully into writing. At first, I couldn't imagine leaving behind a steady paycheck, but the more I thought about it, the more I realized that was the only viable way forward. I quit my job, started my own healthcare copywriting business, and gave more attention to my novel. Four years later, I've written four novels (this one is the first to be published), grown my copywriting business successfully, and let go of the anxiety that was crippling me.

That's a rather long-winded way to say thank you to both my mom and husband, who supported me while I took a serious leap of faith. My mom also is my forever beta reader, always giving me thoughtful comments and telling me the absolute truth.

I also want to thank my dad, whose excellent proofreading skills made this manuscript so much better.

Thank you also to my many amazing friends and family, who always cheer me on, whether I'm starting a podcast, sending out monthly newsletters, or self-publishing my first book: KC Hampton, Grant Hampton, Nikole Hampton, Eric Hampton, Joanna Hampton, Kayla Devine, Thomas Devine, and all of my wonderful nieces and nephews; all of my cousins, aunts and uncles, and extended family; my incredible friends Camille Holiner and Katherine Vantosh, who have both regularly guested on my podcast and listened to me vent about books, publishing, and writing for many years.

Of course, a big thanks to you, as well—I wouldn't be where I am without readers like you.

VIGGY PARR HAMPTON

MPH is an epidemiologist, content marketing strategist, and the host of the podcast "Horror Humor Hunger." She is a graduate of Georgetown University and Emory University's Rollins School of Public Health. A Cold Night for Alligators was inspired by her graduate research on botulism at the CDC and her lifelong fascination with horror stories.

Connect with her at her website, www.viggyhampton.com or on Instagram or TikTok @viggyparrhampton